# MY WIFE'S STALKER

## Written by Spencer Guerrero

Copyright © 2024 by Spencer Guerrero.

All rights reserved.

No part of this publication may be copied, reproduced in any format, by any means, electronic or otherwise, without prior consent from the copyright owner.

This is a work of fiction. All characters, names, places, and events are the product of the author's imagination or used fictitiously.

# Contents

| | |
|---|---|
| TRIGGER WARNING | V |
| ENJOY THE SHOW... | VI |
| 1. PROLOGUE | 1 |
| 2. CHAPTER 1 | 3 |
| 3. CHAPTER 2 | 31 |
| 4. CHAPTER 3 | 53 |
| 5. CHAPTER 4 | 64 |
| 6. CHAPTER 5 | 75 |
| 7. CHAPTER 6 | 96 |
| 8. CHAPTER 7 | 103 |
| 9. CHAPTER 8 | 124 |
| 10. CHAPTER 9 | 134 |
| 11. CHAPTER 10 | 156 |
| 12. CHAPTER 11 | 179 |
| 13. CHAPTER 12 | 196 |
| 14. CHAPTER 13 | 203 |

| | | |
|---|---|---|
| 15. | CHAPTER 14 | 217 |
| 16. | CHAPTER 15 | 230 |
| 17. | CHAPTER 16 | 237 |
| 18. | CHAPTER 17 | 248 |
| 19. | CHAPTER 18 | 256 |
| 20. | CHAPTER 19 | 270 |
| 21. | EPILOGUE | 281 |
| 22. | THE END. | 288 |
| 23. | THANK YOU READER! | 289 |
| 24. | PLEASE REVIEW! | 290 |
| 25. | MORE BOOKS AVAILABLE! | 291 |
| 26. | ACKNOWLEDGEMENTS | 292 |
| 27. | ABOUT THE AUTHOR | 294 |

# TRIGGER WARNING

## POTENTIAL SPOILERS BELOW

*This book includes murder, death, sexual harassment, a brief non-graphic scene of sexual assault, abuse and some graphic scenes of violence.*
*Reader discretion is advised.*

# ENJOY THE SHOW...

*"Before you embark on a journey of revenge, dig two graves."*
*- Confucius.*

# PROLOGUE

She lived in Rainfall. A small, coastal town with the glimmering view of the deep blue sea among the many fishing boats that traversed the ocean. The entire coast was viewable from towering hilltops. A secret sanctuary with a tranquil atmosphere. The rugged terrain was blanketed with vibrant wildflowers and hardy vegetation.

She wished she was there. She wished she was gazing down at the rich landscape. She adored the panoramic view it offered. Scarlett del Toro was being stalked in the middle of the night. By the time she realized this, it was too late. Scarlett's mind was adrift, as it often was when she went out for her run. She never jogged that late at night, but that night was different. She had an explosive argument with her husband. She needed to get out of the house to blow off steam. It turned out to be the biggest mistake of her life.

She was only a few blocks away from home, but the streetlights had gone out and Scarlett found herself engulfed in total darkness. When she made the crucial decision to turn back, it was at that moment that her stalker stood before her. Before she could act or say anything, her head was violently smashed. She was knocked to the ground and hastily dragged into the Darkpond Woods against her will. She desperately attempted to grab onto tree roots, bushes, logs, and anything else she could feel in the pitch black nightmare she found herself in.

No one heard her screams or cries for help in the deep, unforgiving wilderness. She was aggressively propped up against a tree. That's when her stalker ferociously ripped off all of her clothing. She was sadistically violated in the worse way possible. The stalker kept a hand over Scarlett's mouth until the horrible act was done.

She was violently thrown to the ground as she sobbed and whimpered in pain. As her fate hung in the balance, she thought about all the moments she had with Damian. The ups and downs. The highs and the lows. The joy and sadness she experienced with him throughout the years. She would miss it all. She would've done anything to survive. Absolutely anything. But life was cruel to Scarlett. It told her that her time was up. The cruel scythe of death had arrived.

Despite Scarlett's silent pleas to be left alive, she was not given a single chance. The stalker was forced to end it quickly. Someone was near, a potential witness. The stalker brutally shot her in the chest. Scarlett's body became drenched in a pool of dark blood and mangled guts. She had been gruesomely obliterated by two shotgun pellets. It left her body a horrifying mess of shattered skin, crushed bones, and mashed flesh. The stalker used a sharp knife to carefully carve out her shocked face. Something to add to the collection.

She was then left there to rot and to become a part of the blood-soaked ground.

# CHAPTER 1

The last thing I saw was Scarlett's face, twisting into a warm smile. It was the last image I had of her. The last one I remembered. The day my wife died was the same day my life ended. She was raped and murdered at the hands of her stalker. I knew that this was the truth. I vowed to find him and to make the evil savage pay for what he had done. I wanted my vengeance at any cost, even if it caused my own destruction.

I saw that monster at the scene of her murder. He was too far away to identify, but I knew it was him. I saw the hint of a cruel, ice-cold smile through the darkness of the night. I never forgot it. I promised myself that I'd give him a slow, vicious death.

I was willing to rip out his teeth one by one with a pair of pliers until I got the tragic truth. I wanted to know everything. I wanted to know why my life ended. I wanted to know why the love of my life was mercilessly violated and murdered. After that, I wanted to butcher him. That's how he had left my beautiful wife. A wet, gruesome pile of guts, brains, and shattered limbs, drenched in a dark pool of blood. It incensed me and caused my heart to swell with a burgeoning, fiery rage that I had never felt before.

When I lost my wife, I realized that everyone paid a price for the things they've done. A harsh lesson I learned in my life. No one went unscathed to the tombstone.

## *BEFORE (2018)*

I lived in a coastal town named after its frequent rain and thunderstorms. I called Rainfall my home. It was a picturesque locale situated along a shoreline. There was an idyllic charm you experienced when you stood on a faraway hill, watching the powerful waves crash against the rocky cliffs near the sandy beach. There were a few bustling harbors filled with fishing boats and the shouty fishermen who sailed the ocean.

I breathed in the refreshing salty breeze that wafted through me. I could've stood there all night long. The rhythmic lull of the waves created the perfect atmosphere to fall asleep. All I needed was a soft bed of grass to lie in. I'd stare up at the starry night sky in my own personal oasis. But life wasn't that simple. I had to work for a living, just like everyone else.

I was jolted back to reality when a blood-red sports car behind me impatiently honked their horn. The light was green, and I was in my own fantasy land. It was a Friday night. People were rushing home from work. Some would go to the club or to some other entertainment venue. I was a personal driver. I worked for a high-end client. It paid fairly well but I knew I was a servant to the rich and mighty. That never sat right with me, but it allowed me to take care of myself and my wife, Scarlett. That's the one thing I always came back to whenever I had a shitty day.

*At least I get to go home to my favorite woman every night,* I often thought.

The man I drove for was Abel Armoni. The biggest prick in Rainfall. He lived in some flowery mansion with an above-ground pool, a vegetable garden and a dozen maids who catered to his every whim. If he asked them to inspect the inside of his ass cheeks, they'd do it without question. I wouldn't. That conversation would end with his eyes spilling a dark red liquid. I'd have his pale ass on my bedroom wall. It sounded harsh, but you didn't know him like I did.

I was driving him to his regular destination, the *Armoni* nightclub. He owned it. Well, he actually *inherited* it. He didn't know what it meant to work hard. I used to shed tears and spill blood. All he did was gamble and sleep with hookers. He was a degenerate, but he paid my bills. I swallowed my pride and did what I had to do to survive. I tried to drown out the obnoxious click-clacking of Abel's fingers with the radio music, but he told me to keep it down. He was the type of man who didn't pay attention to his surroundings. He was so rich and powerful; he didn't need to. He had his nose glued to his phone almost every minute of every day. He marched forward and people stepped out of his way. He snapped a finger and whatever he requested was a done deal. No questions asked. It churned my stomach. I secretly wanted to see him fall. He didn't deserve any of it. He was garbage.

"Detective Albert Gamble has no updates on the missing persons cases of Jade Gamble and Lisandra Pierce. Two women from the town of Rainfall who were reportedly abducted by someone called the *Rainfall Abductor*. What a clever name. Geniuses, huh? I wonder how they came up with that. Who gives a shit? Why do they still report this? It's been years. They're dead. They should stop reporting it. It's depressing and it annoys me. I know Albert and Jade, but come on. Let it fucking go. They're long gone," Abel whined.

"What do you think happened to them?"

"Oh, I don't really give a shit. The past is the past. Can you drive faster? I want to get there already."

"Yes sir, right away."

"Keep it down. I need to make an important phone call."

I accelerated as I gritted my teeth. I longed for the day when I could tell him to *fuck off*. He was being a complete dick. Lisandra Pierce was my best friend's wife. She disappeared a long time ago. Many people believe she was abducted that night. I didn't doubt it. She had gone alone to the beach. She wanted to take pictures. She never came home that night. She was never seen or heard from again. It turned out to be the biggest mistake of her life. Jade's story was similar.

It was really tough seeing Ivan after that. He was crumbling, and I was trying my best to keep him from falling apart. He had every reason in the world to end it all, but he didn't. He searched for her for two years. He used to work for a private investigator so he had some skills and instincts that should've proven helpful. Unfortunately, he found nothing. The few leads he pursued went cold. Around the same time, Jade Gamble went missing as well. The police believed the disappearances were connected. I did too.

I reached the private parking garage where Abel had me park and nodded at the security guard at the entrance gate. He lifted the barrier pole, and I zoomed inside. It was a concrete, multi-level structure designed to optimize space with ramps, multiple levels, and wide parking spaces for high-end cars. I drove Abel around in a luxurious black car: The Phantom. He wouldn't dare have me park at the nightclub.

*Those fucking animals will break in and smash up my car. If that were to happen...I'd smash up you, Damian.* Abel had warned me.

He had 24-hour surveillance cameras pointed at nearly every corner of that club. I didn't understand his concern. He was a neurotic guy. He called his car a "collectible." I never understood him. He had money to buy three more and then some. It was a pride thing with him. Abel's head was so far up his own ass, he couldn't see what was in front of him. He couldn't see that nobody gave a shit about his cars. They were friends with him because of his status and his money. The money he would give away at the end of every night. The money he gave away to the girls in his *Crimson Lounge.*

He didn't know about the things that really mattered. People like Scarlett. She had shiny dark hair, tan skin and big brown eyes that were so intense they peered into my very soul. She really saw me for who I was. She was an artist who loved to paint. A dream that I gladly helped finance. Her stepdad never gave her a dime. He was as greedy as they came.

She wasn't perfect, but she was nearly there. She was stubborn and we butted heads over stupid issues. I wasn't much of a talker later into our marriage. She got frustrated over that. I used to get so irritated when she scolded me for not putting away my gym shorts or washing my dishes. But the truth was I secretly appreciated that. It let me know that she still cared about me. She still gave me attention. To me, love was attention. I just loved being near her. We didn't need to talk or do anything. Being next to her was enough.

I parked and escorted the princess out of the garage. He worriedly looked over his shoulder multiple times. Abel didn't like the blackness of the night as he put it. He owned a nightclub but didn't like the night. How ironic. He was a tall, bony man with pale skin, a receding hairline, and small grey eyes. He was 50-something and stalked around like he owned the land he was walking on. He was the son of an internet tycoon named Thomas Armoni. Thomas created a dating website that arranged cheating and affairs. He was a piece of shit, but a rich one, to put it bluntly. When it came to Abel, the apple didn't fall far from the tree.

"I bet you that those idiots are dickin' around. They're never where they're supposed to be."

"I got you, boss."

*Quit your whining,* I thought.

We heard the booming electro-pop-funk music as we approached the club. It was a sleek, two-story building with large windows and vibrant lighting. Bouncers were posted at the entrance. They checked IDs and controlled the flow of people entering. I saw one man in the distance who caught my eye. He had shoulder-length, curly brown hair with dark eyebrows and a fully grown beard. He had a strange appearance. He glanced at me for a few seconds then quickly averted his eyes. I felt like I knew him. I didn't get a good look at his face because it was dark out. He dashed inside before I could look at him further.

That happened to me a lot. I saw a lot of familiar faces. People I knew from high school and odd jobs. I always suspected that one of those random men were stalking Scarlett. I just didn't know which one. A raggedy homeless man wandered towards us. Abel slowed down and eyed him suspiciously.

"Keep an eye on this asshole," Abel whispered.

"I got it."

"Hello. I'm so sorry to bother you, but I'm really hungry. Do you have any change you can spare?"

"Hey buddy, fuck off! If you touch me, you're *fucking* dead!" Abel shouted.

I cringed as his hands shot up in the air. He quickly retreated.

"I'm sorry. I didn't mean to bother you," he pleaded.

I pulled out a $20 bill and handed it to him.

"It's alright man. We got spooked. It's dark out. Have a good one."

"Thank you sir, thank you. Thank you so much." The homeless man bowed then darted down the street.

"Damian! Why the hell did you do that?" Abel scolded.

"I had money to spare, boss."

"He got himself in that situation to begin with. He could be a drug addict or a murderer. You could be funding an addiction!"

"Or he's just a man who fell on hard times."

"You can't be nice to people like that. They're below you. You have to remember that you're above them," Abel jabbed his finger into his temple. He motioned for me to use my head.

"I get it, boss."

*Jackass,* I thought.

As we walked to the entrance, there was a rowdy line shouting at us.

*Hey! Get in line!*

*How come they get to skip?!*

*That's such bullshit! We've been here for hours!*

"I'm the owner of this club. I'm *the* Abel Armoni. You can all relax! Fucking animals," Abel commanded.

He didn't use the back entrance of the club because he wanted people to see him enter. He wanted people to know who he was. He didn't realize that most people didn't care. That included me.

"Welcome home Mr. Armoni," Ringo stepped aside.

He was a towering, tattooed bouncer with a crew cut and a square jaw. He looked like he could punch a hole through a brick wall. That's how thick his hands were. We weren't too dissimilar in appearance. You had to have a few pounds of muscle to work for the *prestigious* Armoni family.

"You're finally doing your job, Ringo. How nice of you. You knew I was coming, didn't you?"

"I didn't," Ringo swore.

"Whatever! I don't believe you. Remember, ladies get in free but only one free drink. If I find out that I'm being fucked with, I will fuck that person. I will fuck them *hard*."

"Are you changing the rules?" I asked.

Abel leaned over to me and said:

"I don't want these whores free loading. I actually work for a living."

That wasn't true. Abel barely lifted a finger. He had his managers and club staff do most of the work. That was called being filthy rich. A young man in a black pinstripe suit approached Abel. He immediately looked annoyed.

"Hey Mr. Armoni! I'm a huge fan! My name is Ricky Cole."

"Hey kid, back off. I'm not gonna sign your girlfriend's ass."

"That's not what I want actually."

"Excuse me?" Abel snapped.

"I'm Ricky Cole and I want you dead." In the blink of an eye, Ricky pulled out a knife and lunged at Abel. The people in the line screamed as Abel hopped backwards and fell to the floor. Ringo grabbed Ricky by his collar but he managed to slip out. He jumped on top of Abel and was about to thrust his knife deep into Abel's chest. I quickly yanked him back by his shirt and put him in a headlock. I chopped down at his arm causing him to drop the knife. Ringo swiped it up and pocketed it.

"What the hell do you think you're doing, kid?" I asked.

"Let go of me! Let go of me! He's a fucking piece of shit! The allegations! They're all true! He's a monster! He's a rapist! He's a fucking rapist! He raped my sister! Victoria Cole! I'll fucking butcher that motherfucker!"

"Kill that son of a bitch! Kill him now! Choke him to death! Slash his neck if you have to! End his life!" Abel shrieked.

Ringo called the other security guards outside. They came in like a SWAT team. I shoved Ricky towards them and they gladly lifted him up. It didn't matter that he was kicking and screaming. He was gonna get thrashed...*hard*. That's how they did it at *Armoni*. Anyone who caused any sort of trouble got beat senselessly to a pulp. First, they allowed everyone in the line to enter the venue. Abel didn't want anyone to record the assaults that took place. They carried him a few blocks away to give him a violent beatdown he'd never forget. He tried to murder Abel so I assumed they'd leave him half-dead for the police to take care of. I helped Abel up as he dusted off his jacket.

"Jesus fuck! That little shit wanted to stab me! What the fuck was that about?!" Abel complained.

"He mentioned allegations. He called you a *rapist*."

"What allegations? A rapist? That's insanity."

"Allegations against you, I guess. He mentioned his sister. Victoria Cole."

"I have no idea who that is. You can't believe anything the media says about me. It's all sensational garbage. They'll do anything to get clicks and views. It's called clickbait, Damian. When you're as successful as I am, that's what happens. You get a lot of unwanted attention and a lot of slutty girls claiming things that aren't true for a quick payday."

He never missed an opportunity to mention how successful he was or how girls were *sluts*. A true gentleman.

"Good thing I was here. That could've been bad."

"Yeah, well, that's your job. You're here to protect me. If you weren't good at your job, we wouldn't be speaking right now."

"That's a bit harsh."

"I'm just telling you the truth. I know I'm Scarlett's stepdad but that doesn't really mean anything to me." Abel strolled inside while he texted on his phone. He never gave me a chance to answer his bullshit statements. Not like I'd give him a piece of my mind anyway. I couldn't afford to get fired. I had to bite the bullet. I saved the man's life and I couldn't even get a simple *thanks*. It boiled my blood, but I was being stupid. Why would I expect that from him?

"*Code Green*. We're all good," Ringo patted me on the back.

"Good work, Captain. Stupid kid huh? He has no idea," I sighed.

"He does now. He's got an eyeball popping out of his head," Ringo replied.

"Christ," I grimaced.

*Code Green* meant that Abel was safe and secure. It was a term his security team used. I utilized it as well since I was his personal driver.

"You look like you can use a drink," Ringo smirked.

"I need several."

"Come on in."

"He'll throw a hissy fit if he sees me."

"He's in the *Crimson Lounge* tonight. He won't be out until morning. He has six girls in there."

"Six girls? How do you know?"

"I picked them out myself."

"You're an animal."

"I follow the boss's orders. That's all. Just like you."

That was Ringo's way of telling me to get off my high horse.

"All of his orders?"

"Not this again. I'm not having a philosophical debate. It's too late for this."

"Fine. I'll get a drink. If he sees me…I'll pop out *your* eyeball."

I flipped him off and he returned the favor. That's how I was with my closest friends and my brother. It was our twisted way of showing our love for one another. We cursed at each other, called each other names and professed our deep desire for the other friend to jump off a building. It was all in good spirit. As strange as that sounded. Ringo wasn't that close to me but he was a decent coworker. One of the only guys I talked to.

When I entered the club I was met with a sea of drunks, dancing girls and cigarette-puffing businessmen who were actively cheating on their wives. It was an electric, pulse-pounding atmosphere. I almost tilted over because of the sheer volume of people there. Everyone in Rainfall went to *Armoni*. It was the only nightclub worth going to in our small town. There was a DJ at a central stage while bars lined up the sides of the building. LED panels and funky artwork adorned the textured walls. There was a diverse array of dynamic, neon lights illuminating the dance floor. Many club goers desperately wanted an escape every night.

I spotted my favorite bar and squeezed through a group of college-aged frat boys clinking glasses and taking shots. I took a seat on a stool and nodded at the bartender, Johnny. He pointed at me. That meant he knew what I wanted and the goods would be delivered to me shortly. My usual was a rum and coke. I kept it simple.

I felt a heavy presence next to me. I already knew who it was. I sighed and glanced to my right. There he was, giving me a shit-eating grin. It was Sebastian Gunner. A hulking, brutish bodybuilder with curly blonde hair and bloodshot green eyes.

"What the fuck are you doing here, old man?"

"I'm not that much older than you."

"Answer the question."

"I'm obviously having a drink," I chuckled.

"You're still a little pussy faggot, huh?"

*Jesus Christ,* I thought.

"Are we really gonna do this now? Stop instigating."

"Sounds good to me," Sebastian downed his drink and stood up.

"Still injecting huh?"

"Hey! That's not fucking true!" Sebastian growled.

He slammed his hand against the chair. People around us started to stare. I dryly laughed, trying to diffuse the situation. I didn't want the attention. Sebastian was starting to seriously piss me off. My patience was running thin.

"Relax Gunner. Save your 'roid rage for whatever girl you're currently dating."

"It should've been me. Scarlett should be with *me*!"

"You're very drunk."

"I'm fine."

"You used to hit her. Do you remember that? I do. I remember that very well. You're an *abuser*," I said with anger bubbling in my throat.

"I...I'm past that. I don't do that shit anymore."

"I doubt that."

Sebastian charged at me and grabbed me by my collar with both hands. I wrapped my hands around his as he stared at me with darkened eyes. I kept calm and slightly squeezed. I knew what to do in these types of situations. I had worked security in the past. Confrontations were common.

"Go on, keep fucking with me. Go on! Got anything else to say, dick face?!"

I saw Ringo rushing towards us with four security guards. He bumped and squeezed through the crowd to reach us before something bad happened. It wasn't for my sake. It was for Sebastian's.

"If you try anything, I'll break your hands," I warned.

"Hey, break it up! You're both out of here. Now," Ringo commanded as he got in between and pushed us both aside.

"Don't fucking touch me. I'll go on my own," Sebastian shrugged off the guards who placed their hands on him.

"Thanks Ringo. I'll go."

"I'm not done with you, Damian. I am not done," Sebastian threatened, pointing at me.

I held my hand up at Ringo to ease him and approached Sebastian.

"The next time I see you, it won't end well for you. That's a promise," I whispered.

"Oh, I'm gonna kill you. You piece of shit. You motherfucker. You *never* threaten me! Who the fuck do you think you are?!" Sebastian yelled as Ringo and the guards held him back.

I walked through the crowd that had formed and smirked at them. He was the crazy one, not me. I kept things cool. I had to in my profession. I dealt with a lot of hotheads and psychos. Sebastian Gunner was a prime example. An unhinged drug addict who loved to provoke violence. Life wasn't kind to people like him.

---

When I left the club, Dani Shepherd approached me. My heart fluttered, but only because I was caught off-guard. I sincerely loved my wife, but almost everyone was subject to temptation sometimes. I never acted on it or attempted to. I wasn't that type of man. Did I have thoughts from time to time? Sure, but that's what they were, thoughts. Thoughts that were buried in the back of my mind, thoughts I seldom remembered because of my head injury.

Truth was, I just happened to talk with her a lot. I worked with her because she was Abel's assistant and she was a good person. She was a short, tan-skinned woman with long dark hair, a bright smile and warm brown eyes that were genuinely friendly and inviting. She had many romantic admirers. It was easy to observe that, Scarlett was the same. That's why she had a stalker. Scarlett and Dani were the type of women who had to be careful around men, through no fault of their own. Some men were entitled pigs, I would know.

"Hey," Dani smiled.

"Hey."

"I wanted to tell you that Abel caught wind of what happened."

"Oh shit. Of course he did. Does he wanna talk to me?"

"I spun the story for you. You're fine. I told him that Sebastian Gunner is known for being a drugged-up lunatic and that you did what you had to, to protect yourself."

"Thank you, Dani. I really appreciate that. I'm just glad I didn't have to break his hands...or his jaw."

"You should've."

We warmly laughed. Dani had dated Sebastian in the past. She didn't know any better. He was a tall, good-looking guy with green eyes. He had some charm back then too. It was easy to fall for that type of man when you were young.

"He definitely deserves it."

"He does and you can definitely kick his ass," Dani winked.

I smiled. She was just being nice. Any other psycho would've taken that as an invitation to take her to bed. Especially at my age. I was in my late 20s, but I looked older. I was a fit, olive-skinned man with a thick, partial goatee. I had dark brown eyes and black hair cut to a medium length. I kept my body in good shape and had decent biceps for someone who didn't work out anymore. Dani saw me for who I was though, and more importantly…Scarlett did too.

One time, I had to scare away a couple of guys who had cornered Dani in a bathroom hallway. We were at a business event with Abel. He got angry with me for pulling out my gun on them, but Dani needed help. I didn't care that Abel had screamed at me.

"Do you need a ride home? I heard you didn't have your car with you."

"Yeah, I was just gonna get an Uber. Abel's staying the night. I can't take the Phantom."

"I'll take you."

"Are you sure?"

"Damian, I got you. I'm not gonna leave you stranded, dude."

I knew my wife wouldn't care. She knew Dani already. We had fought about her before when she thought I was cheating on her with Dani. I'd never. I was deeply upset that she thought I would, but I understood her. Dani was an attractive woman and we worked together a lot. It was easy to think I'd give in to temptation.

When I climbed into Dani's silver sedan, a sweet fruity aroma filled my nostrils. It reminded me of home. Scarlett was home. When we hit the road, I stared out the window. I gazed at the rows of streetlights. My mind drifted to Scarlett's stalker, as it often did. It made my stomach broil with absolute rage. A depraved man was out there sending disturbing messages and packages to *my* wife. There was nothing I had been able to do about it, which frustrated me even more. I wanted to wrap my hands around his throat. I wanted to crush him until he exploded.

"What are you thinking about?" Dani asked.

"Hm? Oh, sorry. I'm sleepy."

"You're quiet but usually not this quiet."

"I'm always thinking the same thing, Dani."

"Your wife's stalker."

"The nightmare never ends."

I curled my hand into a fist and shook my head. Our society judges a man on how able he is to protect his family, which obviously included his wife. In that aspect, I felt like an abject failure.

"The police still haven't done anything?"

"He disables the security cameras I install. I'm pretty sure he has broken in, but they never find any DNA. What the hell are they gonna do at this point?" I scoffed.

"I'm really sorry, Damian."

"It's just...my wife is being terrorized by a man I can't see...a man I don't know...and there's nothing I've been able to do about it."

Dani opened her mouth but no words came out. She stayed quiet. I didn't blame her. What was she supposed to say? It would get better? That would've been a complete lie. It was getting worse. It was mental torture. That stalker knew how to drill himself into the part of me that enraged me to my core.

"So...how's your dating life?" I had to change the subject.

"It's alright, I guess," Dani laughed.

"I don't wanna talk about my wife's stalker."

"That's fair. Umm…I don't know. It's going good. He works at the club actually. He's part time for now."

"Oh. What's his name?"

"John Santoro. He's nice. I like him."

"That's his real name?"

"Yeah, he has Hispanic roots."

"That's interesting. Scarlett's maiden name is Santoro."

"That's a funny coincidence. Maybe they're cousins."

I gritted my teeth. Scarlett wasn't related to some random idiot named John Santoro. Scarlett's family meant nothing to her. They had turned their backs on her. They saw a pathetic, struggling artist with a pipe dream and told her just that. I considered them lower than dirt.

"I doubt it. What does he do at the club?"

"He's a busser."

"You can do better, Dani."

"At this point, I don't care what guys do for a living, Damian. I just want a guy who's…nice. A man who's actually kind. It's hard to come by nowadays. Most men wanna send me pictures of their semen splattered on themselves. It's pathetic. It makes me scream."

"I'm assuming John Santoro hasn't done this yet?"

"Nope. He's a gentleman. A rare commodity. Or at least he has the brain to hide it until we get serious."

I scoffed. Dani defiantly raised her brow at me.

"You're going to get serious with this guy? Is that a good idea?"

"I am a grown woman who can do what she wants. You're not my daddy, Damian."

"I wouldn't want to be."

"Oh, fuck you."

I chuckled as she scowled at me.

"Jesus, it was a joke, Dani. I care about you. That's all. I want the best for you."

Dani's scowl softened into a sweet grin. She affectionately rubbed my arm.

"Don't worry, I can take care of myself. I promise. If I need anything…I'll let you know. Like always." She gave me a friendly wink.

"Well, I'm happy for you then. I hope it works out."

"Thank you. Stalker aside…how are things with your wife?"

"They're good. We argue and stuff, but to this day she's been the only person who understands me. We're both lonely people who like being together. She's the only person I've ever wanted a future with."

"That's so sweet, Damian. I want that some day."

"Maybe it'll be with John Santoro."

---

I lived in a small one-story house near the foggy Darkpond Woods. It was old but comfortable. I resided in an idyllic, isolated area that was about 15 minutes away from the nearest shopping plaza. We didn't have many neighbors. Most of the houses near us were either decrepit or vacant. The few neighbors we did have were elderly and harmless. The most memorable one was Elsa Dietrich. A German woman. She was the only person in our cul-de-sac who didn't require a caregiver. I had heard strange rumors regarding her family. Something about sacrificial killings and being an ex-Nazi. I didn't pay much attention to it. It sounded outlandish. People liked to make shit up about foreigners.

Scarlett wasn't sure about it, but I convinced her otherwise. I needed to be away from people. I badly needed to protect Scarlett after the things that had happened in my life. I needed peace for once. I told her that the location would serve as great inspiration for her paintings and portraits.

After Dani dropped me off, I quietly entered my house. My footsteps creaked on our wooden flooring which ruined my plan. Thankfully she was still awake. We lived in a cabin-esque structure with exposed wooden beams and stone walls furnished with woven textiles. That was courtesy of Scarlett's beautiful, artistic mind.

I found her in the living room. She was seated on her stool, drawing on her painting easel near the lit fireplace. The easel was a self-supporting wooden frame for painting and drawing. We had curated that area as her own personal art studio. She liked to call it her own organized chaos. There was an array of brushes, paints, canvases, oils, pastels and other tools she regularly used. She had a sketchbook with multiple drawings and artistic clippings from lifestyle magazines. She was very experimental and open-minded when it came to her artwork.

When I approached her, I gently wrapped my arms around her and planted a kiss on the side of her head. She smelled like honey. She was sketching a portrait of us. We were embracing in the Darkpond Woods. We were surrounded by what looked like dark spirits. Scarlett loved her metaphors.

"You're up late," I commented.

"I got inspired."

"By us?"

"I was thinking about how lucky I was to find you. Any other guy would've left me after all the shit we've been through. But you didn't and you never will."

"I'm the lucky one."

"You never let me compliment you."

I sat beside her and affectionately rubbed her back.

"Is this a metaphor for something?"

"Yes. The dark figures represent all the assholes we've had to fend off to keep our relationship strong and in tact."

Most of those assholes were Scarlett's "admirers." I liked to call them perverted pieces of shit. It was mainly a high school problem.

"I still have one to fend off. When I find him…"

Scarlett massaged my neck and looked at me.

"Don't worry about that. It's okay. He'll get tired eventually. It's not your problem."

"Of course it's my problem, honey."

"It's not."

Scarlett couldn't convince me that it wasn't my responsibility to hunt down her stalker and erase him from existence. She deserved nothing less. I was her husband. My job was not only to love her but to protect her. She didn't have anyone else, but me. I was it. I didn't shy away from that. I didn't want to.

"How did it go tonight?" Scarlett asked.

"It went fine. I guess. Your stepfather still behaves like a donkey."

"What happened?"

"There was a man who tried to kill him. He attacked him with a knife. I stopped him. He wasn't very grateful."

"God, are you okay?" Scarlett pulled away to search my eyes.

"C'mon, you know who I am," I smirked.

"Still, that sounded really dangerous."

"I need the job."

"I know, I know. I'm not saying otherwise," she sighed.

"It is what it is, for now. You keep doing your art thing and you'll go viral. After that, we'll be loaded."

"It's not only about money, Damian. Art is beauty. It lights a fire in my soul. It's one of the few things that keeps me alive and happy," Scarlett smiled.

"Other than me."

"Other than you."

We kissed and it still felt like it was the first time I had ever kissed her. I belonged with her and she belonged with me. It sounded corny, but that's how our love was. When I woke up everyday, I was reminded of her existence. She was the first person to enter my mind.

It filled my heart with warmth and a feeling that things would be alright as long as she was with me.

"I have to tell you something," Scarlett said shakily.

I was immediately filled with dread.

"What's wrong?"

"He sent me something."

"The stalker."

*The stalker.*

The mere mention of that word boiled my blood. I wanted to throw my fist into the nearest wall. Better yet, I wanted to drive it into her stalker's chest and yank out his heart. I wanted to act out my deepest, most violent urges on that man. I wanted to eviscerate him with a chainsaw until there was nothing left, but shreds.

"Yeah. It's him again. I don't know what to do anymore. He'll never stop changing phone numbers and social media accounts. He's beyond obsessed."

I had compiled several of his phone numbers into a notes document on my phone. They never seemed to be associated with anyone, but I always kept them. You can find the truth in the most unexpected places. Something Ivan liked to say.

*904-111-1110*

*904-221-0807*

*904-417-0226*

*786-025-1007*

*786-250-1105*

*786-052-1021*

"What did he send you this time?"

"*I want you, red. I need you, red. I'll fuck you in his bed...until he's dead.*"

"Nice rhyme. That sick son of a bitch. If I ever find him..." I curled my hand into a fist and dug my fingernails into my palm. I was beyond agitated. That man was harassing my wife and there was nothing I had been able to do about it. Scarlett grabbed my hand and gently uncurled my fist. She touched the bloodied marks on my palm.

"Don't get angry again. There's no point. We can't let him ruin our lives."

"Our lives are already being ruined."

"Hey, stop that. Stop saying things like that. Forget about him."

"If you wanted me to forget about him, then why did you mention it?"

Scarlett stood up and stormed away to the kitchen.

"You told me you wanted to know. Don't blame me for this. You think I want this asshole messaging me this garbage? I'm the one he's stalking. Not you."

I followed her.

"I know, but it hurts me just as much. You're my wife. You're not alone in this. Even if I have to feel the dread you're feeling...so be it. I'm *with* you."

"Okay."

"Did he send you anything this time?"

"This time, no. He didn't."

"I'm sorry about this."

"It's fine. I've been dealing with creepy men almost my whole life. At least now I have the best person to lean on."

I nodded. Scarlett took my hand and led me to our darkened bedroom. She plopped down on the bed and reached out her arms. I softly climbed on top of her and allowed her to pull off my shirt. She brought me in closer and deeply inhaled my chest.

"I don't think I smell that great right now, honey," I gently chuckled.

"You smell like an evergreen tree and...man musk. I like it."

"Man musk? Well...I am a manly man."

"Right...that's enough talking."

I buried my face in her neck and planted deep kisses as she ruffled the hair on the back of my head. Scarlett smelled like sweet vanilla mixed in with an aroma of earthy honey. I basked in her scent as I pulled off her shirt and tried to forget about the world around us. A world where a stalker was terrorizing my wife.

We were in bed with our arms wrapped around each other. I was still breathing heavily from the various rounds we went at each other. On the other hand she was fine and seemed fit to go longer. I set aside the messy curls that were covering her eyes and caressed her cheek.

"I don't know about you, but I'm satisfied."

Scarlett turned and looked at me dead in the eye.

"I'm not." She pulled her arms off of me and gave me her back.

I gaped and sighed. She laughed.

"Oh thank god. You were joking right?"

"I was. I'm sweaty enough."

"I am too."

"I wouldn't mind getting sweatier," Scarlett teased.

"Me neither," I blurted out.

We both let out a hearty laugh. I scooted closer to her and embraced her.

"Do you still think about Sam?"

My heart dropped.

"Well...I don't usually think about my dead brother after sex."

"That's not what I meant." She hit me with a pillow.

"Do *you* think about my dead brother after sex?" My eyes popped out.

"You're insufferable. Of course not."

"I'm just trying to get to the bottom of this odd question."

"I was just wondering if you missed him. That's all."

"I do miss him. I think about him everyday. There isn't a thing in this world that doesn't remind me of him. He was a sweet guy. He had his issues, but who doesn't?"

"Your parents were never the same after that. Do you think they'll ever move back?"

*Not only them. I was never the same after that. I loved my brother. He was one of my best friends. He was the person who was always supposed to be there.*

"I don't think so. They needed to get away from here when he died. St. Devil isn't exactly heaven on earth, but it works for them."

"Aren't there serial killers out there? I've read horrible stories. There was one named Kilhouser and some other businessman. I think his last name was Snow. He has an insane story."

"They'd rather live in a place called St. Devil than be in the place where Sam died. That tells you how painful it was for all of us."

"Why didn't you leave?"

"I didn't go because I had you. You stitched me back together after I broke apart."

Scarlett turned to face me and put her hand on my cheek. She lightly kissed me.

"That's very sweet."

"I learned from you."

"You were always sweet. I just brought it out of you."

"You did. You and Ivan."

"Oh Ivan. The stuff he's been through…he's like another brother to you."

"He is. He's the only brother I have left."

Ivan Pierce was a good man. The type of man who did right by you. It didn't take long for a person to realize that he had been raised right. I was lucky to know him, but I didn't like the secrets he kept from me. It had been about Scarlett. He had betrayed me.

# CHAPTER 2
## 2015

There was a disturbing package sent to our door. It was a wrinkled, black shoebox with an ungodly amount of tape draped all around it. It wasn't marked with anything. It was as anonymous as they come. They always arrived like that. Scarlett's stalker always managed to disable or destroy our security camera. It drove me up the wall. He always managed to do it whenever I wasn't home. He was careful and patient. I knew that much about him.

I carefully brought it inside and placed it on my kitchen counter. Scarlett came over and stared at it. She was frustrated. I could tell by her creased forehead and downcast eyes. I took out my boxcutter and cut away the tape. I slowly took off the lid and tossed it aside. When I peeked inside I saw three objects. It was always three. A red bra, a red pair of panties and red fishnet stockings. Scarlett looked and gasped.

"They belong to you. Don't they?"

She slowly nodded, hand over her gaping mouth. I seized the box and rocketed it into the ground.

"Fuck!"

Scarlett tried to reach out but I held up a hand. My temper was flaring and I wanted no one near me. That bastard had been inside my house. *My fucking house.*

"He was in here, Scarlett. Whoever it is…they were in this house."

"He's an obsessive freak. I don't…I don't know what to say. I don't know who it could be."

"We don't know. The fucking useless police don't know. What the hell? What the hell is going on, Scarlett? Are we losing our minds? This is fucking madness."

"Whoever it was…also stole my bracelet. The silver one that had my name on it."

"Are you serious? They…they stole it? *Fuck. Fuck*!" I slapped the counter, hurting my hand.

"Baby, relax. Please relax. This is why I didn't want to tell you." Scarlett rubbed my shoulders.

"Jesus, Scarlett. What the hell are we supposed to do? This is…this is driving me *insane*." I was on the verge of breaking down. It felt like a cold metal hand was crushing my chest, sucking away all of my oxygen. It was like trying to chase down your own shadow. The man was invisible.

I didn't tell her but I was absolutely terrified. I felt like such a chickenshit admitting that to myself but it was the pathetic truth. There was a man who had managed to break inside my home, undetected. Not only that, he had stolen my wife's private underwear and jewelry. That told me that he was sexually motivated. He wanted to do something to my wife. That thought alone was enough to set me off again. I was very close to becoming a raging lunatic.

"Why don't we call Ivan?" Scarlett asked.

"Ivan? Why?"

"Maybe he can help. I would like to talk to someone else about this. I feel like we're driving each other nuts."

"He used to work for a private investigator. It can't hurt. I'll call him."

When Ivan arrived, he was in his usual cheery attitude. That quickly changed when he saw our grim faces. He was your everyday man with a light complexion and light brown eyes. He had dark hair that draped over his ears and had a lean-muscular body composition. He took a seat on top of the couch and listened to what we had to say.

"Well, holy shit. I knew you were having problems with some stalker dude but I didn't think it was this serious. I thought it was some online weirdo or something. You know, like those Indian dudes who comment *super sexy feet* and *delicious mommy boobs* on Instagram," Ivan chuckled.

"I know what you're talking about. This isn't that."

"This has been going on for months. Sometimes it's frequent and sometimes he stays quiet for a few weeks," Scarlett explained.

"Sounds like a real problem, guys. Were there any signs of forced entry?"

"One of the windows in the back was busted, pried open. Cops came and took a look around. We haven't heard anything back. We probably never will. They don't take this shit seriously. They don't give a shit," I muttered angrily.

"Yeah, I get that. It's frustrating. I'm sorry you're dealing with this," Ivan offered.

"Thank you. We're trying our best to stay sane," Scarlett sighed.

"Do you have any idea who it could be? Clearly, we're at our wits end," I said.

"Man, I don't know. Maybe it's someone we knew from high school? Scarlett had a few admirers back then," Ivan suggested.

"You're right, but I don't know anyone who stayed here. Most people moved out of state for college."

"I know someone, Damian. I got a guy who works for me now. It could be nothing but his name is Luke Prescott. Remember him?"

"I do. He had a reputation of being very strange. I think he used to like me. I don't know. It was a long time ago," Scarlett said.

"I knew I remembered that correctly. The guy was a freak. Now that you guys have told me all of this stuff...my head's spinning a little bit." Ivan rubbed his forehead.

"What do you mean?" I looked up and crossed my arms.

"He seemed interested in you, Damian. I thought it was just because you went to the same high school as him. He was interested in Scarlett too. He asked a lot of questions. I thought it was general curiosity, but now I'm not so sure."

"What kind of questions?" Scarlett stepped forward, concern etched on her face.

"What you did after high school. What I thought of you. Your boyfriend history."

"What the fuck?"

Anger strangled my throat as I remembered Luke Prescott. He was rumored to be a complete pervert who took pictures of girls when they weren't looking. He was a freak.

"What did you tell him?" Scarlett asked.

"I told him the truth. I said you were great people and great friends. I didn't answer him on the boyfriend history."

"Is there anything else he asked?"

"Not really. He knows where you live though. The general area, not the exact house."

"*What?*" Scarlett shuddered.

"Ivan, when the hell were you planning on telling me this? This is serious. This could be her fucking stalker. He knows where we *live*?"

"You know what, man? He was really casual and normal about all this. It didn't even cross my mind that he was a freak."

"What do you think now?" I asked.

"Let's go talk to this fucking guy, Damian. You and me. Something's not right," Ivan urged.

"Wait, what are you two planning?" Scarlett asked, eyebrows raised.

"We're just gonna talk to Luke," I said casually.

"I don't think that's a good idea."

"Scarlett, do you want me to find your stalker or not? We need to put an end to this."

"Do you plan on intimidating him?"

"Rest assured, we're not gangsters, Scarlett. We're not gonna strap him to a chair and put car plugs on him," Ivan commented.

"We should," I remarked.

"Damian, you're not that type of man. Don't even joke about that."

Scarlett had grown up poor where there was violence at every corner. It was the only thing she had known and the one thing she had wanted to forget.

"Don't worry, miss. I won't let him. I use my words," Ivan promised.

"I don't," I said.

Scarlett stormed towards me and grabbed my face. She tilted it downward and stared at me with her dark, intense eyes. The eyes I had fallen in love with.

"If you're not sure it's him, I don't want you to lay a finger on him," Scarlett warned.

I glanced at Ivan who visibly gulped. I smirked and wrapped my hands around my wife's. I softly pried her off of my face and kissed her forehead.

"Okay honey."

Ivan was the owner of a private security company that operated in Rainfall. It was called *Pierce Security.* The headquarters were in a warehouse located in the construction district. A bustling area that included construction sites, heavy machinery and various building materials. All of those projects belonged to the Armoni family.

The warehouse was a large storage facility with inventory management systems, surveillance cameras and alarms to safeguard valuable items. It protected physical and digital assets that belonged to a myriad of tech businesses. Aside from that, Ivan had private security personnel available for dispatch for any type of high-risk events. Events I used to work with him before things went south one deadly night.

Ivan and I headed to a concrete box of a room that was located near the entrance of the warehouse. It was the break room. It had a long, wooden desk with swivel chairs, a flat-screen TV and a mini-fridge. It was a decent room, all things considered. Ivan wanted his employees to have a comfortable place to unwind. We had both worked in restaurants where the only space to sit was an empty water bucket outside, near the dumpsters.

"Where is he?" I asked.

"He's already inside. He's drinking a beer."

"To him, we're all just watching the basketball game right?"

"Exactly."

When we entered, Luke was there. He was drinking a beer and calmly watching the game on the TV. He turned and nodded to us. He was a moderately-sized man with short blonde hair and mellow green eyes. It took me some time to recall his face from high school. It had aged but it was him.

"Hey man. How's the game?" Ivan plopped down next to him. I quietly sat down at the foot of the table and observed Luke. Ivan was a talker. I was mainly an observer.

"It's going good. We're winning," Luke said dryly.

"Do you remember Damian? We all went to the same high school."

"You mentioned that, Ivan. I remember Damian."

"I remember you too, sort of," I said.

"We were both quiet, but you had more friends than me...and girlfriends," Luke chuckled.

*Interesting.*

"We both had a few. We were ladies men," Ivan laughed.

"Now you're both tied down. Ivan and Lisandra. Damian and Scarlett. Lovely couples," Luke smirked.

"How did you know we were married? I never told you that," Ivan said.

Luke shifted up and glanced at us. He saw our smiles but definitely sensed the hostility behind them. Luke seemed like a smart guy. He wasn't an idiot. He sensed our suspicions. Why else would we invite him to a random basketball game at work in the middle of the week? If we were friendly, we would've gone to a bar. We were at a place with no witnesses.

"Online, Ivan. Everyone posts everything online. It makes things easier. It's how I found this job opening after all."

"Easier? What do you mean?"

Luke shot up his arms. My guard went up and my hand went to my holster.

"Nice shot, Butler! Wow. What a three. He's been hitting tough shots this season."

I took my hand off and breathed. I was on edge. I needed to chill. I almost blew Luke's face off for cheering at the TV.

"What did you mean, Luke?" Ivan repeated.

"Oh, sorry. I meant that it was easier to catch up with everyone. I haven't seen you guys in years but I know a lot about your lives. I know that you're both married to your high school sweethearts. I know that you owned a security company, Ivan. That's why I reached out. I know that Damian is a personal driver for Abel Armoni. A rich and powerful man in this town. Scarlett's stepfather. He seems like a decent man."

"He isn't," I strongly stated.

"I'm sorry?"

"He's not a decent man, Luke. He's entitled garbage."

"Why do you work for him then?" Luke asked.

"I need to make a good living."

"The irony of life, huh?" Luke mused.

"Yep, that's life."

I drank my beer and eyed Luke. Something was off. That much was clear.

"Did you move away from Rainfall after high school?" Ivan asked.

"I did."

"Where to?" I chimed in.

"A nearby town for work. I didn't go to college or anything."

"Why you'd come back?" Ivan asked.

"I was working at a factory an hour away. *Gaumont Scientific*. I built training dolls for nursing students there. I didn't want to be there anymore. The commute was tedious. It was time for me to come back."

"Did you meet someone?" I stood up and got closer.

"Uhh...well, no. Technically, I haven't met anyone. I haven't been romantically involved with anyone."

"Shit, man. I'm sorry to hear that," Ivan patted him on the back.

"What do you do to satisfy yourself?" I turned the volume down on the TV with the remote.

"What?" Luke stuttered.

"You heard him," Ivan added.

"This is getting a little bit weird, guys," Luke chuckled.

"Sorry man. We didn't mean anything weird. We're just guys talking shit, you know?" Ivan fist bumped him.

"Yes. We're just talking," Luke smiled.

I turned and went back to my seat.

"You've never had sex with a girl, *ever*?" Ivan asked.

Luke's watch beeped. He promptly stood and bolted towards the door.

"I'm so sorry about this. I have to go guys. I have an important errand to run. This was fun. Let's do it again next week." Luke exited before either of us had the chance to say anything.

"What the hell? Should we let him go?"

"He seems harmless, Damian. Just let him leave."

"Harmless? You've gotta be shitting me. That guy behaves like a sociopath."

"You barely know him now. We can't make assumptions like that."

"What if he heads to my house?"

"You have a plan for that already."

"I do, but—" I trailed.

"We'll talk to him again soon. Don't worry, we'll do everything we can to rule him out."

"I don't think he's innocent. That's all I'm saying."

"Let's hope he doesn't kill himself," Ivan turned the volume back up on the TV and grabbed another drink from the mini-fridge.

"If he's the stalker, I hope he does."

"Jesus, man. You should value human life more."

"You should value it less."

We glanced at each other and laughed. It was late and we were drinking. We typically said moronic shit to each other.

"You're a monster, Damian."

"Listen Ivan, I don't hate people. I hate the things they're capable of."

Later that week, it was a foggy morning. I wiped the mist off the Phantom's car windows with a microfiber towel. A gift from Abel. He didn't want me using normal towels. *Only savages used normal towels.* Abel lived in his own little bubble, devoid of normal interactions with everyday people. He felt he stood tall above everyone else and it showed. I got in and zoomed down the street adjacent to the deep, dark forest. I often thought about Scarlett's stalker living in those woods. I imagined him as a homeless, half-naked savage of a man. I didn't know what I would've done if I saw such a man coming out of the woods. Would I stop and question him? Would I run him over? Would I tear him limb from limb, if I knew what he was?

I drove past a crime scene near the Darkpond Woods. There were five police cars surrounding a cliff that veered off-road into a beach down below. A dangerous area that had been there for years called *White Abyss Beach*. All the locals knew they had to be careful. I figured it was some tragic accident. It had happened before. Another tourist probably tried his luck and must've slipped down below.

A few officers were setting up yellow tape. One cop was signaling for cars to continue forward. It looked like they had been there for hours. I slowed down and tried to get a better look, but a cop shouted at me to *keep it moving*. I wasn't about to argue with him so I went on my way.

*What the hell is that about?*

I soon made it home. My wife was where she usually was in the living room. She was painting a black figure chasing a deer on a blank, white canvas. It was a work in progress, but it was coming out beautifully. Scarlett was a natural talent. Something that was gifted to her after everything she had been through. She deserved it. I gently gripped her arm and kissed her on the cheek. She softly shoved me away. I held up my arms.

"What?"

"I'm trying to concentrate. I can't have any distractions."

"Honey, are you serious?"

"I am."

"I saw some cops near *White Abyss*. I wonder what that's about. It looks like a serious accident," I mentioned.

"Yeah," Scarlett muttered.

I shrugged and sat down near the kitchen. I drummed my fingers on the marble counter and stared at her. Eventually she glanced at me and widened her eyes.

"What?" Scarlett snapped.

"Are you mad at me about something?"

"No."

"You usually allow your husband to kiss you while you're painting...among other things."

"Don't try to be funny right now."

"Scarlett, what's wrong?"

"You never told me how your interrogation with Luke Prescott went."

"I did tell you. It went fine. It wasn't an interrogation. We were catching up. Nothing happened."

"You never told me how it *really* went."

"Scarlett, if there's even a sliver of a chance that someone is your stalker…I'm going to do my due diligence and ask questions. I'm doing this for you."

"That's interesting."

"Can you stop acting weird?"

She got up and took out her phone. She showed me a developing news article from the *Rainfall Page*. I read the headline:

## LOCAL MAN REPORTEDLY MURDERED IN THE WHITE ABYSS.

My heart thumped hard in my chest as I continued to read. The alleged victim was a blonde man with a medium build. He had green eyes. The body had not been recovered. What was believed to be Luke's clothing was caked in blood. It sat at the edge of the beach where the ocean met sand. It was drenched in sea water.

"This is why those cops were there. Holy shit," I whispered.

It looked like a murder. They found his wallet tossed aside a few feet from the bloodied clothes. Luke's license was inside. If he had any cash and credit cards, they were stolen. The dead body was believed to have been washed out to sea. An extensive search was being carried out to find it.

The whole thing was bizarre. The clothes had been left there but there wasn't a body? It almost sounded staged, but the article reported that the blood was heavily believed to belong to Luke Prescott.

*Luke Prescott is dead? I spoke with him a few days ago. This is insane.*

"Luke...Luke is dead. What the hell? What the hell happened?"

"You read the article, Damian. They think he was murdered. Why? I don't know."

"Wait a second. You don't think I had something to do with this, do you?"

"Of course not but...what are the odds that you talk to him and then this happens? Seriously, what the hell happened? Did you threaten him?"

"We did not threaten him in any way. I promise you, Scarlett."

She began to tear up and hid her watery eyes with her hand.

"This is very upsetting," Scarlett sobbed.

I walked over to her and held her in my arms.

"It's alright, honey. It's okay. We're gonna be fine."

"Why was he killed?" Scarlett whispered.

"I don't know. Maybe he got involved with the wrong people. Luke was a strange guy, honey. Who knows what he could've done."

Why was Luke murdered mere days after we talked with him? What happened to him in between? Did we have something to do with his death? Did he piss someone off?

I called Ivan to meet me near an old wooden picnic table in Darkpond Park near the crime scene. It had an abandoned playground with rusted swings creaking in the wind, eroded slides covered in graffiti and overgrown weeds crawling up the play area platforms. It didn't always look like that. It had been built anew more than a decade prior. It was one of my regular hangouts with Ivan and Sam. Sam would smoke pot while he joked around with Ivan. He used to egg him on about Lisandra. He told him he'd get married to her eventually. Ivan used to tell him to knock it off, but Sam had been right. Ivan married Lisandra. I married Scarlett. Sam married no one. It was for the best.

We sat and watched from afar as several news vans piled onto the scene. The cops weren't having it and were forcing them to keep their distance. Ivan shook his head and sighed.

"Fuck man. I figured something was up. He didn't show up to work after we blasted him with questions. He never answered his phone either."

"Because he was dead," I muttered.

"Are we responsible for this? What the hell did we do, man?" Ivan said shakily.

It was an interesting question, but no. That didn't make any sense to me. Just because we talked to him didn't mean we were guilty. It looked suspicious but we had done nothing. There wasn't even a body that had been recovered. I knew something was amiss, but I didn't know what. What I did know was that Ivan and I were not responsible for Luke's death.

"We're not, Ivan. We all have our choices. He probably did something stupid and got himself killed. That's not our problem."

It sounded heartless but it was true. We did nothing to him.

"I'm losing my mind, man. This is messed up. What if the cops start asking questions? What if they know we talked to him?"

"Talking to someone isn't a crime," I gripped his shoulder.

"I know but..."

"Listen to me, Ivan. We didn't know him that well and we don't know what happened to him."

"Right. We don't know what happened to him."

"Do you...do you think he was Scarlett's stalker? Do you think he was murdered because he was guilty? Maybe...maybe this is karma."

"You think so? I mean, it's not that crazy of a theory. Stranger things have happened." Ivan scratched his head.

"How else would you explain something so strange and sudden? I think it was him. I think Luke has been watching us for a long time, Ivan. That motherfucker got what he deserved."

I finally felt relief for the first time in a long time. I felt ill for being happy. A person was dead after all. It was horrible. There wasn't anything nice about it. Still, I was glad that it was over. It had to be. It had been a torturous nightmare. One that needed to end. I wanted to believe it was him and I did. I believed it with all of my heart.

"He knew us, Damian. He really knew us. He was a fucking weirdo too. All the ingredients of a psycho and a stalker."

I visited Scarlett in our beautiful backyard. It was tranquil with a garden of vibrant marigold flowers, lush greenery and a blooming tree that provided shade for her to paint on her easel. I made sure to keep my distance. She was still angry with me. It didn't take long for her to notice I was there. She gave me a dry smile. That meant she was easing up on me.

"What are you working on?"

"The same thing."

"I see. It looks like it's gonna rain soon."

"We do live in Rainfall," Scarlett smirked.

"I know you're upset at Luke's death."

"Luke's death happened a few days after you interrogated him with Ivan. I'm sorry. I just find it upsetting."

"Do you really think I had something to do with that? Scarlett, please. Do you not trust your husband?"

"I know who you are, Damian. Like you said, you're my husband. I know how angry you can be. I know how obsessive you become. It's in your nature."

It was not. I just did what I had to, to protect my wife.

"I talked to him for you. I didn't want you to suffer anymore."

Scarlett put down her brush and reached out her arm. I went towards her and embraced her while kissing her hand.

"I know, honey."

"Trust in me."

Scarlett lightly grasped my face. She was teary-eyed. A lot of conflicting emotions seemed to be raging inside her intense eyes.

"I don't want you to be a killer. Please Damian. Not that."

"Never, Scarlett. I'll never be a killer."

"You believe that Luke was my stalker?"

"Yes I do."

"Okay. I trust you. I hope it's all over then."

"I do too."

I lied to Scarlett that day. I was willing to be a killer for her. I'd break that promise to defend her and to get rid of the people who stood in the way of our love.

---

The next two weeks were blissful. There was no more looking over our shoulders. No more replacing busted security cameras. No more sleeping with one eye open. No more changing the locks of our front door every month. It was over. Scarlett wasn't upset at me anymore. My job had few mishaps and Abel was still an asshole, but I tolerated it. Dani helped me in that regard.

I met up for drinks with Ivan at the bar and it was like the glory days with my brother, Sam. We drank, goofed off and watched the game. When we Ubered home, we were shocked at the fact that our wives hadn't called or texted. We took it as a silent victory. I knew that my wife wanted me to relax and unwind after that tumultuous time in our life. That piece of shit stalker robbed days and nights from us. It took a serious toll on our minds.

"Lisandra hasn't called because she's happy like me," Ivan giggled.

"Why?"

"We're finally trying for a baby. We finished renovating the guest room and it is now baby-ready."

"That's awesome, man. I can't wait to meet the little one. You're gonna be a great dad."

"I hope so. I'm scared. I might shit myself when my kid is born. I'm just letting you know."

"I didn't need to know that."

We both doubled over and laughed. I saw the driver roll his eyes but he was smiling. We were very giggly when we were hammered.

"How about you and Scarlett? Baby time? Raw dog time?" Ivan asked.

"Christ, keep your voice down."

"*Sorrrryyyyy,*" he slurred.

"We're not trying yet, but soon. We're waiting until Scarlett's art career takes off."

"That's really nice of you, man. You always supported her with that stuff. You're not a dickhead after all."

"I love her. I'll always support her."

*Hell. I'd kill for her.*

"Not a lot of husbands would do that. They'd probably tell her to get a real job. You're a good man."

"I'm not like other husbands."

Once the driver dropped off Ivan, it quickly became silent. He was my best friend. We became even closer after my brother's death. That was one of the hardest times in my entire life. My parents weren't any help. They were divorced and they hated each other. The constant bickering and arguing was enough to ignite me. I always wanted to go nuclear on them but I kept my cool. I kept it in. After Sam died, they never spoke with me again. I was completely shut out. It was like they wanted nothing to do with their remaining child. I told myself that I didn't care, but it shattered me. That was a reason to band together and to support each other. Instead, it became radio silence forever.

That was one of the main reasons why I loved and supported Scarlett so much. My father was trash. He never supported my mother in any of her art-related ventures. She also painted, drew and even did pottery. She was a beautiful soul that was squandered by my father's oppressive belittling. I saw it tragically unfold over many years. The slow, painful erosion of my mother's dreams.

I refused to see it again with Scarlett. If I was a different type of person, I would've taken revenge against my father. I would've made him pay. I would've made him regret every single little fucking thing he did that ruined my mother's life. Sometimes, I regretted not doing so.

When I got home, I didn't notice the package near the front door. It was a black shoebox. I tripped over it and almost stumbled to the ground. I placed my palm against the wall to keep my balance. My heart sank and an overwhelming sense of dread coursed through every vein in my body. I barely moved for the first two minutes. I crouched down and ripped the shoebox open in a violent frenzy. It was unmarked. There were three polaroids and a folded piece of paper. One took place in the grocery store. One took place in Scarlett's car. One of them was in our own backyard. Scarlett was in all of them.

I sobered up instantly and angrily ripped up the pictures. I opened the note and read it. *"Dear Scarlett...I wanted to let you know that I've been following you closely. You haven't heard from me but I'm always here and I always will be. Do you know how far people go...for the people they love? If there's one thing...just one thing in this world that rings true, it's that. People go far beyond what they thought they were capable of...for love. Well...I love you Scarlett and one day...you'll be mine for the taking."*

I crumpled the note and hurled it at the blackened sky. I fell to my knees and placed my palms on the ground. I saw the tiny droplets of water streaming down to the ground from my eyes. It wasn't over. It wasn't done. Scarlett's stalker was still out there. It wasn't Luke Prescott. I was beyond shocked. I was destroyed.

"Who...who the *fuck* are you?" I whispered to myself.

# CHAPTER 3
## PRESENT DAY
## (2018)

There was a huge argument that day. One I wished I had been able to take back. It was nasty, ugly and I regretted everything that was said. As much as I wished it had never happened, it was inevitable. There wasn't a way around it. For most men it came from a primal place of jealousy and possession. I knew that Scarlett wasn't my possession nor did I want her to be. But what she did was not smart given the circumstances. The circumstances had everything to do with how it all went down.

It was drizzling outside, but I didn't care. I was impatiently waiting for Scarlett to get home. I was irate. I held the pictures in my hand as I crossed my arms. When she pulled up and got out, I made a big show. I waved the pictures in front of her perplexed face as she rushed to the front door to avoid the rain.

"What is it, Damian? What the hell are you showing me?"

"Take a look yourself."

I shoved it into her hands. She took one glance at each photo and cringed. She quickly handed it back to me. She looked at me in disgust.

"Why would you show me that?"

"Because I needed to know."

"What?"

"Why would you show yourself like that?"

They were three photos of Scarlett. She was nude. It was at the beach at night.

"I wanted to fucking feel free for once. That fucking guy…I don't know. I don't care."

"You don't care? He took these photos of you, Scarlett. What the hell were you thinking? Going alone, naked, to the beach at night? Are you serious? Did you really think that was a good idea? You're way smarter than that."

"I'm so tired of walking on eggshells, Damian. I did it because…because I'm exhausted. I did it to defy him. I did it to feel free. I wanted to show him I didn't care."

"So, you were counting on him taking pictures of you?"

"No, of course not. I'm as shocked as you."

"He could've killed you, or worse."

"You're being dramatic."

"*Dramatic*? This man is clearly not stable. He also sent over three photos of his own genitalia. Do you want to see what he was doing?"

"No, you sicko. What the hell is wrong with you?"

"What the hell is wrong with *you*?"

"Maybe we should move. We should've moved a long time ago. We're being stupid. I don't know why we've stayed in this hellhole for this long."

"No! No we're not. This is our dream home. We're not gonna let this piece of shit dictate our lives."

"That was my point! I wanted to show him I didn't care!"

"That was a dumb way to do that, Scarlett."

"I used to do it all the time. You know that. No one ever goes there. That's why we love this place."

"Given the circumstances, you should've never even thought of doing that."

"Dream home, huh? Yeah right. This is a nightmare," Scarlett scoffed.

"This was so stupid, Scarlett. You were so vulnerable. He could've done something to you. I'm serious." I urged.

"You're being insufferable. Nothing happened. It's my stalker. I'll deal with it."

"I'm just trying to keep you safe."

"Whatever. I'm sick and tired of this." Scarlett stormed off.

"Where the hell are you going?"

"I need to clear my head! Leave me the hell alone."

"Fine then! Fuck off," I mumbled.

I went inside and slammed the door shut. I yanked a beer out of the fridge and plopped down on the couch. I turned on the TV and tried to forget about what had happened.

*Yeah, let me go to the beach at night, naked. That's not dangerous or stupid. No one's gonna sneak up behind me and bash my head in with a rock. I'm powerful. I'm making a statement. I know everything and my husband is a bumbling, fucking idiot.*

I took a quick swig of my beer and grimaced. I launched it against the wall. The glass bottle shattered and all the liquid spilled out. I took a deep sigh as I stared at the sprinkled shards of broken glass on the floor. It was true. My wife had always gone skinny dipping alone at that beach. Sometimes I went with her, sometimes I didn't. All the times I had gone, no one was there. It was a ghost town. But the circumstances changed as time went on. There was a deranged stalker after her. He took photos of her. He had been there. He took photos of himself…committing depraved sexual acts. It was beyond disturbing. It was the work of a man who had a severe mental illness and obsession with my wife.

I tried to relax and closed my eyes. Next thing I knew, I was fast asleep. I woke up startled to a loud banging at my front door. I jumped up and rubbed my eyes. I sped over and pulled open the door before they busted it down. I saw two police officers standing in front of me. A third man was in the center. He looked different. He looked in charge.

"Are you Damian del Toro?"

He had a weathered face and a deep, gravelly voice. He wore a jet-black suit jacket with leather brown shoes and a policeman cap. He smelled like cigarettes. I never forgot that smell or that man.

"Yes, hi. That's me."

"I'm Detective Albert Gamble with the Rainfall police department. We tried calling first but there was no answer."

"What? What happened? What's going on?"

Detective Gamble cleared his throat and glanced at his fellow cops. I grew nervous.

"Were you married to a Scarlett del Toro?"

"I was. Well, I am. We're still married. What's going on, Detective?"

"I'm so sorry, Damian. She was found dead by some hikers a few hours ago."

"What? No. No, no, no, no. That can't be right. She...she was just here. That doesn't make any sense. You don't know what you're talking about," I blurted out.

"We identified her body, Damian. It is her. It's Scarlett del Toro," Detective Gamble said softly.

Detective Gamble took off his cap and tightly gripped it. He stared at the floor. I began to grow dizzy. My heart was being painfully choked by a sudden hurricane of grief that enveloped me.

It felt like a dozen knives were being plunged into my chest all at once. It was never-ending. I collapsed to the floor and sobbed. My reddened face was twisted with anguish and sorrow. It was an ugly mess of tears, snot and saliva coming out all at once. My shoulders shook uncontrollably. The weight of my misery was thick enough to be felt in the air. I saw Detective Gamble kneeling beside me through my blurred vision. He had one hand resting on my lap and remained silent. He didn't know me and he didn't know my wife. He only did what he could to comfort me. He remained there through my guttural screams and through my unrelenting agony at the news I had just heard.

My wife was gone. My love. My Scarlett. She was supposed to be an accomplished artist. She was supposed to achieve that dream. We were supposed to go to art galleries together. We'd see her artwork there and I would stand proudly beside her. All of our blood, sweat and tears would be worth it. It would be validated. Not anymore. That was done. No dreams and no family. I never got to experience raising children with Scarlett. I never got to see her as a mother. That cut deep inside me with a razor-sharp blade. It ripped out my throbbing guts and spilt them onto the ground for the entire horrible world to see.

All I saw was red, blood and death. Someone was going to pay. I didn't care if it destroyed me. All I knew and wanted from then on was *revenge*.

---

It was a gruesome sight. She had been viciously attacked and dragged into the Darkpond Woods. I was escorted through a squad of police officers, their cruisers and yellow tape. I felt like a ghost floating through the wind. I didn't feel real. None of it felt real. I never thought that someone would ever stalk my wife. I never thought that someone would be vile enough to rape and murder my wife. I learned to stop assuming things that night. Anything could happen to anyone. It didn't matter if you were good or bad. Some of the most evil, depraved people in this world had the power to ruin good souls.

Death had no sympathy and no prejudice. It came for everyone. Sooner or later, everyone paid a price. My wife's murder was mine.

I asked to see my dead wife. I needed to see it for myself. I didn't care how gruesome or horrific it was. I walked through dried leaves and fallen branches to get to the stretcher where she was. Every footstep I took made a harsh, crunching noise due to the forest debris. I imagined it as Scarlett's bones being broken as I got closer and closer to her. I arrived at the crime scene and all of my air was sucked out of my lungs.

Scarlett's body was hidden underneath a tarp. There were a few crime scene marker cones surrounding her. She was on a bed of dried leaves, moss and bramble. Tears quietly flowed out of my eyes. I tried to move forward, but I couldn't. I was paralyzed. The next chapter of my life was unknown. We had it all planned out. The children, the art galleries, the family vacations, growing old together...those plans were gone forever. All of our dreams, goals, ambitions and love...was destroyed. Obliterated. Decimated. I was empty. I wanted to die alongside her, but I knew I couldn't. I needed to be alive, so I could kill the man who did that to her.

Detective Gamble put his hand on my shoulder. I flinched. Any little thing frightened me. I was completely lost in my own torturous thoughts. I needed to snap out of it.

"I'm so sorry. I know how it feels."

I angrily raised my shoulder to shove his hand off. I turned and faced him. My blood was running hot through my veins.

"What do you know about how I feel, Gamble? What the hell could you possibly know?"

Detective Gamble sighed and gave me a sympathetic smile.

"My wife's name is Jade Gamble."

"What?"

"Yeah."

"She's missing," I muttered.

"For a long time now."

I cooled down and gently patted his shoulder.

"Sorry. I...I forgot that was your wife."

"It's alright. I do know how you feel. My wife is dead. A body hasn't been found and may never be found, but she's dead. I know it. I accepted that a long time ago. You're going to want the world to end. It won't get better. Not for a while," Detective Gamble solemnly stated.

I looked at him in surprise. The detective's soulless, gray eyes were unnerving. He was the type of man who simply knew how it was. Whenever he said something, he meant it. There wasn't an ounce of nonsense I felt in him. He was as straight-laced as they came.

"I know it won't get better."

"Listen to me, Damian. Just give it time. Allow yourself to grieve and to feel the weight of your sadness in your chest. It will suffocate you, if you let it. Remember to breathe. It won't get better but it'll be easier with time. When you start to forget her, you will begin to heal. Not all the way, but...you'll have sense of normalcy in a few years."

"A few years?" I choked out.

I couldn't think about forgetting Scarlett. She was the person I wanted to love in life. I wanted no one else. I needed no one else.

"I won't lie to you. It's the hardest thing you'll ever experience in your life."

I trusted him because he didn't tell me anything I *wanted* to hear. He told me everything I *needed* to hear. I hated him so much for telling me all that the night of my wife's brutal murder. Later, I silently thanked him in my own way. He led me out of the forest and we stood adjacent to the closed-off street where all the police cruisers were. He reached into his coat pocket and gave me a flask.

"I don't want any water, but thank you."

"It's not water. Drink it."

I gave him a curious look and took a sip. It was strong. I wasn't sure what alcohol it was but it burned my throat on the way down. I coughed and wiped my mouth. I drank some more until I decided I had enough.

"You drink on the job?" I asked.

"No, not anymore. I have that for victims such as yourself. You need it more than I do."

"Thanks," I nodded.

"I wish you the best of luck, Damian."

"You're not gonna uh...ask me any questions? Police always think the husband did it." I let out a dry laugh.

I was so delirious I didn't care what I was saying. I had half a mind to jump off a cliff. The cliff where Luke Prescott was murdered.

"If you did it, I'll find out. But I don't think you did this. I've been at this for a very long time. I know a guilty man when I see one."

"You must be talented."

"I'm not. I'm traumatized," Detective Gamble squeezed my shoulder and walked to his cruiser.

"Should I call someone?" I called out.

"I already did," Detective Gamble replied.

I turned and saw Ivan jogging towards me. Tears began to well up in my eyes. He was the only one I had left. We tightly embraced each other. I dug my head into his shoulder and cried.

"I'm so sorry, man. I'm so fucking sorry. I can't believe this shit," Ivan said with a pained voice.

"I loved her so much, Ivan. I need her back. I want her back."

"I'm sorry, man. I'm so sorry. This...this is so fucked up."

When I lifted my head, I saw Ivan's sorrowful eyes observing mine. I collapsed to the ground and sat there. My mind was loud and racing with blank thoughts. I was so overcome with dejection that I refused to let any of them register. I just wanted to exist. I didn't want to think of anything and I didn't want to know anything.

*Scarlett is gone. Scarlett is gone. Scarlett is gone. Scarlett is gone. Scarlett is gone. Scarlett is gone.*

I saw a figure in the distance. It was past the flashing lights of red, white and blue. He stood at the end of the road where it curved right. He was staring right at me. I couldn't make out the specific features of his face but I saw his lips. I saw lips that twisted into a cruel smile. A flurry of rage bubbled in my stomach. The person walked away into nothingness. I wasn't sure if I had actually seen someone that night. What I did know was that I was being taunted. Scarlett's stalker had been taunting me for years.

It was time to finally hunt him down and to make him pay. I had nothing to lose and nothing to hold me back. Death was coming for that worthless son of a bitch.

# CHAPTER 4

There was a typed note delivered to my house shortly after my wife's death. It had been wedged in the door. It read, *"I'm so sorry this happened, Damian. I loved Scarlett as much as you did. I loved her so much. I am devastated and distraught. I am forced to find a new object of affection for my obsession. A tall order. Take care, Damian,"* I immediately trashed it. I knew it was from her stalker. A mentally ill maniac who I wanted to strangle. The man I needed to kill.

When I found the person responsible for destroying my life, I promised to give them the same courtesy. I knew that only then, I'd find peace. I had to talk with someone about what I was going through. I met with Ivan at a spot we called the *Bridge*. It was a quaint, small bridge near a field of lush greenery, cypress trees and hedges adorned with historical plaques relating to the founding of Rainfall. It was near Darkpond Park.

The *Bridge* spanned a narrow stream and was built out of weathered wood. As we stepped across, the wooden planks creaked beneath my feet. It reminded me of all the conversations and crazy fun I had back then. That quickly dissipated once I heard the consistent hum of the flowing water. It had a knack for causing dread to wash over me. It reminded me of Sam. It reminded me of death.

Ivan and I leaned forward on the wooden railings. We gazed across the river.

"Remember Sam?" I asked, the slightest hint of a smile formed on my face.

"Of course I do. How could I not? Your brother was a riot, man. I loved that guy."

"He died on this bridge."

"I know. I still remember the day. It's funny…the pain I felt on the day he died was more powerful than all of the joyful memories I had with him."

"That means you loved him as much as I did."

"I believe that."

"We have to right?" I wondered aloud.

"It's the type of thing that happens in life that you don't think will ever happen. Just like my wife. Lisandra vanishing? That never crossed my mind once. Then it happened."

"It's the horrible stuff that you read about in newspapers. It ended up happening to us."

We remained silent. I reminisced about Sam and what he meant to me. I wished he was still alive. I wished I could hug him. If anyone could help me get through my wife's death, it was him. I was lucky enough to have Scarlett when Sam died. I wasn't sure what I would've done without her.

Ivan was around, but Scarlett was a force. She didn't allow me to wallow in self-pity for too long. She forced me to get on up and continue living. She made me realize that I needed to go on for Sam. If I allowed myself to be eaten up by the tragedy of Sam's death, it would've been a betrayal of his memory. That's what Scarlett did. She was rough and real with me when she needed to be. She got me to keep on living. She taught me to breathe after my brother's death. The man who murdered her had no idea what he was in for.

"I'm gonna find the man who did it and I'm gonna kill him," I said coldly.

"Damian…no. You can't."

"Don't try to talk me out of it, Ivan. I don't want to do it. I need to do it. My wife deserves it. Do you know what he did to her after he murdered her? He carved out her face. Her face! A monster did this, Ivan. I'm going to make sure he never does anything like that again."

I couldn't even look at Scarlett's face one last time. The monster who murdered her had carved out her face. He mutilated her like she was his toy. I wanted to eviscerate that sick bastard until there was nothing left.

"As much as it pains me to say it, Scarlett's gone. She has no say in this. This is about you and your revenge."

I shrugged. It was true. I wanted revenge, but I also needed the truth. Detective Gamble told me they were actively investigating the case but I needed to do it myself. Scarlett was my wife. I would do things and go to places the police wouldn't. I wasn't afraid of anything at that point.

"I need to know the truth, Ivan. I need to see the man who did this to my wife. I want to see him face to face. I want to ask him why. Why did you do it? I deserve an answer."

"I don't think he'd tell you."

I slammed my hand against the railing.

"I don't care. I'll force him to. My entire life and future was cruelly taken from me. In the blink of an eye. Just like that."

"You're going to destroy yourself, Damian. You don't know the things you might find out in your search. Things you wished you never knew."

"He brutalized her entire being. He fucking *raped* her. What kind of monster rapes a woman and then *murders* them? This guy is a complete fucking sociopath. This town will thank me when I get rid of him."

"I understand why you're hellbent on this."

"I could use your help, Ivan. I'm not going to obligate you. That isn't fair. If you don't want to do this with me, you can walk away right now. I won't hate you. I promise."

Ivan put his arm around my shoulder.

"Shut up man. You're my brother. I have to make sure you don't lose yourself."

"I won't."

"I hope so. When Lisandra went missing, I searched two long years for her. I nearly lost everything."

"I remember. I was there."

"I still don't know what happened to her. No body, no trace...nothing but dead ends. She vanished one night and never came back. I've moved on. I'm better now. I'm gonna help you move on too."

"Who knows? Maybe this is all connected. Jade, Lisandra and Scarlett. My wife, your wife and the detective's wife. Maybe we'll find the *Rainfall Abductor*."

"Don't get my hopes up. It'll crush me all over again."

---

The funeral home was a simple, white building. When I entered the lounge area, Scarlett's mother was speaking with one of Abel's business associates. Soraya Armoni-Santoro, a woman who loathed me with all her heart. I made sure to ignore her. Some of Scarlett's acquaintances from the art world were there too. They were whispering amongst each other. I wasn't close with any of them but I knew who they were. I recognized one face that didn't belong. She was a thin woman with a long blonde ponytail peeking out of a baseball cap. She had a light complexion with blue eyes and a moon-shaped birthmark on her right cheek. The agitation was palpable on her face. I didn't think she was there to pay her respects, but I was in mourning. I didn't care enough to inquire.

It was an open floor plan with black leather couches, phosphorous white walls and dim lighting that hummed overhead. Some people were picking out snacks at the vending machine. They squeezed themselves inside a closet-sized kitchen that was located in a corner of the building. An art gallery owner named Simon expressed his condolences first. Scarlett's nameless acquaintances were next. The woman with the moon-shaped birthmark remained silent and scowled at me. The rest were a blur. I got through everyone as fast as possible and made sure to say *"thank you for coming."* That was all. I wasn't interested in having a conversation about her. I would've broken down.

I spotted Abel near the chapel doors. He was on the phone. He was being loud and obnoxious. I barreled towards him, fully prepared to give him a piece of my mind. I entertained the idea of shoving the phone down his throat. He was her stepfather. What the hell was he doing? Before I reached him, Dani intercepted me. She hugged me. I was caught off-guard but I embraced her back. She looked up at me with watery eyes.

"I'm really sorry, Damian. I know you loved her a lot."

"I did. I miss her so much."

"Don't pay attention to Abel. He's an asshole. Nothing new there."

"Horrible stepdad. At least he paid for the funeral. That's about the only thing he paid for."

"Don't worry. People like him always get their karma."

"I wouldn't mind hand-delivering it to him myself."

The chapel doors were opened and everyone was allowed inside. Abel immediately rushed in, still on the phone.

"I'm gonna head inside. You?" Dani asked.

"I'll be there in a second. I'll find you." I spotted Ivan across the lounge, in the kitchen. He was mixing cream in a cup of black coffee. He glanced at me and nodded.

"How are you, man?"

"As good as you'd expect."

"Careful, Damian," he pointed at the chapel.

"What?"

"Dani Shepherd, is it?"

"Jesus, Ivan," I scoffed.

Ivan took a sip. He motioned the cup at me.

"You want?"

"I'm good, thanks."

We started walking towards the chapel.

"Girls like Dani take advantage of vulnerable men."

"How do you know that?"

"I've heard rumors."

"Oh, fuck the rumors. I know her. She's a sweet person."

"How well do you really know her?"

"Well enough. I work with her. You don't." I crossed my arms.

I had known Dani for a few years now. She was a good person with no ulterior motives. Maybe that's why Ivan found her so suspicious.

"I'm just trying to look out. This is gonna be a tough time for you. You don't need anyone taking advantage."

"No one takes advantage of me."

I saw a flicker of movement from the corner of my left eye. When I turned, Scarlett's ex-boyfriend was already in front of us. He completely shocked us as we both took a cautious step back.

"What did you do to her?" He growled.

Sebastian's white dress shirt was disheveled and his eyes were bloodshot. He gave me a good whiff of his breath. It reeked of alcohol. It was Scarlett's funeral and I was fully prepared to break his teeth, but I promised myself I wouldn't cause a scene. I didn't want to fight Scarlett's ex-boyfriend at her own funeral. I didn't want to disrespect her and it would've been classless. I wasn't like Sebastian. He was an uncivilized savage.

"Have you been drinking?" I asked.

"*Answer the damn question.*"

"Hey, hey, hey. This isn't the place for this." Ivan put up his arm and Sebastian violently swatted it away. Ivan held up his arms in surrender.

"*Fuck off.*"

"I'm not gonna cause a scene, man. Cool it, Gunner," Ivan said, irritation in his voice.

"I didn't do anything to her. I loved her. She was my wife. You idiot."

"She was a good woman. This is my fault. I shouldn't have left her. I shouldn't have fucking left her with you."

"You didn't leave her. She broke up with you." I corrected.

"I don't believe you. Nah. I don't believe you. You're a liar." Sebastian vigorously shook his head.

Ivan and I exchanged worried looks.

*What the fuck is this guy on?*

"Are you okay?" Ivan asked.

Sebastian suddenly pointed his finger in my face, then stomped away. He busted right through the front door and marched down the street. I stared at him until he disappeared from view.

"What the hell is his problem?" Ivan asked.

"I wish I knew."

"Scarlett's ex-boyfriend huh?"

"That's him. High IQ and all. He also dated Dani briefly. They quickly found out he was a massive douchebag."

"He's bigger than I remember," Ivan scoffed.

"He's a real piece of work."

"Be careful with that gear head."

"I'll keep an eye on him. I have a feeling he's going to try something stupid."

Ivan entered the chapel. I was following him in when I staggered backwards. I thought I saw him. The man I had seen before at the club. He had shoulder-length, curly brown hair with dark eyebrows and a beard. When I looked again, he was gone. I was losing it. Scarlett's death had taken a toll on me. I saw and heard things that weren't there. I heard Scarlett's screams when I woke up most mornings. I was living a nightmare.

"You okay?"

I gathered myself and took a deep breath. I gave a half smile to the worried onlookers inside the chapel. I softly shook my head.

"I can't go in. I'm not ready yet," I whispered.

"All good, man. Do you wanna get out of here?"

"No, I shouldn't. It's a bad look. Scarlett would be pissed off at me. I'll hang outside for a little while. You pay your respects, my friend."

"If you need me, I'm here," Ivan nodded.

He was the only person I had left. The only person I could talk to and not feel judged or out of place. Dani was close, but Ivan had been there for many years. He knew me before and after Sam's death. He knew me before and after Scarlett's death too. I spotted Elsa Dietrich, my German neighbor, sitting on one of the couches. She stared out the window and appeared to be lost in thought. I needed to greet her. I hadn't seen her before.

"Hey Elsa. Thank you for coming."

"My work is done, Damian. I had no reason not to come. I'm so sorry about Scarlett. She was a lovely woman," Elsa said in her thick German accent. She stood up and warmly grasped my hands. She was a large, square-shouldered woman with a tightly wound ponytail and beady green eyes. She had thick, calloused hands and was an oddball.

"She was," I whispered.

"I've lost loved ones too. Notably, Angela. My daughter."

"I didn't know that. I'm sorry, Elsa."

"It's alright. A lot of time has passed. It was long ago."

I always assumed Elsa had been alone all her life. She often went to the Darkpond Woods to fish and hunt game. It was related to her career. She was a taxidermist.

"How's the hunting going?"

"Good, fine. Damian, I wanted to inform you. I was in the Darkpond Woods that day. The day your Scarlett was murdered."

"You were?"

"Yes. I was fishing and scouting ducks to shoot. This was during the afternoon. Your wife was still alive. I go very deep when I hunt game. Federal laws and all that. On the long trek back to my house, I saw her. She was taking groceries out of her car. A man was watching. I found it peculiar, but I minded myself. I wished I hadn't, but he disappeared as I got closer to him. I didn't get a good look at him."

That was a few hours before our explosive argument. How I desperately wished things panned out differently.

"I think I saw that man too. At the crime scene. A man who was watching. He was smiling." My stomach was in knots. It was him. It was that man. Whoever it was, he had something to do with Scarlett's murder.

"I...I think it was him, Damian. The man we both saw. I think that man raped and murdered your wife," Elsa said gravely.

I needed to find him.

# CHAPTER 5

I was asked to meet with him at a bar called *Milton's*. That's what the half-burnt, purple neon sign said outside. I carefully walked into a gritty, run-down place with flickering lights and worn furnishings. I passed by cracked barstools and chipped tables. I spotted cat-like scratches and stains on the bar counter. It was a regular spot I used to frequent with my brother before he died.

I crinkled my nose when the musty smell wafted over me, and my eyes watered as I sped through a haze of cigarette smoke to get to him. I saw grizzled bums holding their drinks to their chests like newborns. It disgusted me. They looked shameful and I was sure they felt it too. I didn't want to end up like that after Scarlett's death, that's why I needed closure. I needed to know what happened.

I sat down across from him in a booth. He stuck out his hand. I shook it. I respected Detective Gamble. He was a man who knew what he was doing. Unfortunately, he had limited resources in a town as small as Rainfall.

"How have you coped?" Detective Gamble asked.

"I've been alright."

"Drinking a lot?"

"Some days I do, other days I have work to distract me."

"I remember when Jade disappeared. I felt a gaping void. I used to feel her next to me when I slept. I'd wake up and remember what happened. I was losing my shit in those days."

"I'm losing my shit now."

"You're doing a good job of hiding it."

"I'm keeping my anger internal."

I nodded and drummed my fingers on the table. I was hoping he'd give me information regarding Scarlett's murder. I knew that these types of investigations were strictly kept under wraps, but I had a coincidental connection with Gamble. We both had lost our wives. We each felt something that not a lot of other people understood. We had that in common.

"What happened that day, Damian? I know what you're thinking, but I have to ask."

"I didn't kill her, Gamble."

"I know, but I would still like my question answered."

I thought about it. It played like a crystal-clear video in my head. It was the last time I saw her alive. I wished I could go back. I wanted to tell her that everything was going to be alright and that I was sorry. That's what I would've said if she came back.

"I'll be honest. We had an argument earlier that day."

"What about?"

"She was keeping a secret from me. Scarlett's stalker had messaged her nude photos of himself."

"An anonymous phone number?"

"Yeah. They're all anonymous. I called the police about it more than few times, but there was nothing you guys could do. I never found out who her stalker was."

"Is there anything this alleged stalker did to Scarlett that was of a similar nature?"

"He also left behind obscene messages. He had fantasies about sexually assaulting my wife. He wanted to tie her up and impregnate her. He wanted to *breed* her. I wanted to rip his spine out through the phone."

"I'm sorry to hear that. This guy sounds sick."

"He also left behind shoeboxes at my front door. Some had sets of Scarlett's underwear and her bras. There was also polaroids of Scarlett running errands in different places. He had broken into my house too. Police came by and never followed up."

"I'm sorry about that, Damian. I'm sure they tried their best."

"I tried too. He always found and blocked my cameras. He'd destroy them too. I almost caught him a couple times after a while. I'd hear a noise at the door and take off running. By the time I reached it, he would be long gone. The camera would be on the ground and smashed into a million pieces."

"That sounds terrifying."

"It was."

I didn't consider myself a good man. I couldn't protect my own wife. She often asked me why I'd get so angry or obsessive over who her stalker was. It was because of that reason. I couldn't keep her safe.

What kind of husband was I? I asked myself that everyday after she was murdered.

"What happened after your argument?"

"Well, she was pissed off and stormed out of the house. I decided to stay put. That's when I fell asleep. You woke me up."

"You didn't go anywhere else?"

"Nope. Can't go anywhere if you're asleep."

"Good point."

I proceeded to tell him about that day, about a week after it had happened. It broke me inside, having to recount the final moments until my wife's brutal murder. I often wondered if she thought of me in her final breath. I wondered if she hated me for not being there. I knew I hated myself. There wasn't a single ounce of doubt about that.

---

Detective Gamble couldn't reveal anything to me because it was an ongoing investigation, so I sat at home and drank. I drove for Abel when he needed me. Dani was sweet and checked up on me. She brought me a gift basket and tried to convince me not to drink. I couldn't promise her anything. I ran my fingers through my hair, to the back of my head. I carefully felt the small indentation where my stitches had been. It had taken a toll on me. I couldn't remember things sometimes and I saw things that weren't there. I was worried that the man I had been seeing...didn't exist.

My head had been beat in by a rich man. I shouldn't have done what I did to him, but I felt he had deserved it. I was a man who believed in vengeance. I exacted payback on those who wronged me and the ones I loved. It felt right to me.

I went over to my laptop and pried it open. I typed in *Rainfall Jogger Murdered*. I swallowed down the thick lump in my throat. The house still smelled like her. Scarlett's scent was comprised of honey mixed in with sweet vanilla. That's what she liked to tell me anyway with a finger pointed in my face.

*Don't you forget it. I am a divine woman who smells divine.* She'd joke. I used to pull her into my arms and we'd laugh together. She'd fight tooth and nail to be let go but she didn't want to be. I didn't want to let go either. We'd crash into a wall and slide down. We'd catch our breath and just lie there for a good while. I'd give her a warm kiss on her rosy cheek while she'd massage my arm.

I wiped away a few tears that had dropped onto my trackpad. I found an article from the *Rainfall Page* titled *Rainfall Jogger Murder Case: Suspect Arrested...Michael Madden*. Michael Madden. I didn't know who that was until we found him. I meticulously read through it. Apparently he was seen near the crime scene that same night. They questioned him, but they had to let him go as there was no evidence that he had done anything in relation to Scarlett's murder. They questioned the hikers who found her too, but it had been an elderly couple. They didn't even fully understand what they had discovered.

I got up and pressed my knuckle to the wall as hard as I could. I did it until it hurt and until it turned blood red. I released and put my head against the wall. I shut my eyes and tried to focus on the throbbing pain in the back of my head. I took deep breaths and tried to relax. I needed to talk to someone. I texted Dani. She replied within a few minutes and a half hour later there was a knock at the door. I sped over and opened it. She smiled at me. I managed to grin back. I stepped aside and let her in.

"Would you like anything to drink? Water or something?"

"I'm okay. Thank you." She plopped her purse down on the decorative wooden table between the TV and the couch. She sat down and clasped her hands together. I sat on the further end of the couch.

"Why are you so far away?"

"It's easier to talk this way. I can see you better."

She made a slight nod.

"So, how's it going?"

"I'm sorry I called you over here. I didn't wanna bother you but…"

"It's okay. Abel doesn't need me for a couple of hours."

I noticed the concern that was etched on her face. What was I doing? I didn't want to burden anyone with my problems. That's how I always was. I dealt with heavy shit on my own or with Scarlett. Sometimes, I didn't even involve her. When she died, that left a black hole in my heart. I suppose I was looking for anyone who was close enough to me to fill that hole. But suddenly, it felt disrespectful to Scarlett. I was being selfish.

"I...I don't wanna bother you," I stood up.

"Damian, it's okay. You can talk to me."

"Dani, you must have stuff to do. I'm sorry for making you drive over here. I'll pay for your gas. I'll buy you dinner. I'm really sorry."

"Listen, Damian. Lately I feel like someone has been following me. It's been creeping me out. I could use the company. Trust me. I don't like feeling alone."

"Who's following you? What are you talking about? Are you okay?"

"I...I don't know. Maybe it's just me. I never actually see anyone. I'm just being paranoid. You know how this town is. It rains a lot and there's that *Rainfall Abductor* freak out there."

"I know what you mean. The town doesn't feel safe anymore."

"I'm glad I'm not the only one."

"Dani, I want you to let me know if you ever see anyone sketchy. Better safe than sorry. I'll take care of it," I promised.

"I know you will."

"Do you want me to escort you home?"

"I'm not letting you do any of that, Damian. You're not getting rid of me. Tell me what you wanted to talk about," Dani commanded.

I sighed and slowly sat back down. I was a mess. My whole head was a tornado of fragmented thoughts rushing in and out. One came after the other and they were all jumbled together. It felt like static and white noise were blaring in my mind.

"My head hurts."

"What?"

"My head injury. Remember?"

"Bruno McCoy. The rich art guy."

"You remember the story."

Dani shook her head and pursed her lips.

"That wasn't good."

"I know."

"It was pretty foolish but it was noble. You did it for your wife. You're a good guy."

"Thanks."

Bruno should've been my cautionary tale, but I was hard-headed. I didn't like letting things go. He had left Rainfall a long time ago. He was in Greece the week Scarlett died. He was hosting some art festival for rich people. Bruno's trips were well-documented. He traveled the world and splashed that information all over his social media. The thought had brushed my mind once…what if Bruno was the stalker? I erased the idea. He had a thousand women at his disposal. It was a terrible thing to say but it was true. What reason would he have to stalk her?

"Can I get a water?" Dani asked.

"Of course," I shot up and went to the fridge. I set aside the collection of half-full beer bottles I had. I out-stretched my arm to the back to get a water bottle. I shut the door in disgust. I was seriously a hot mess. I went back to Dani and opened it for her. I gently set it beside her and sat closer to her.

"How's Scarlett's mother? Soraya, right?"

"Yeah that's her. She hates me. She blames me for it. She rattled off like a hundred messages to me."

"Oh my god. What did they say?"

"She uh...she told me I should've been the one. The world would've been better off. It's fine. She's in a lot of pain and she's angry. We're in the same boat."

Dani gripped my arm.

"Why would she say that? You were a great husband."

"Maybe I could've been better. If I had found her stalker...this wouldn't have happened."

"You don't know that for sure. Don't do that to yourself."

"It's been hard, Dani. No Sam. No mom and dad. I feel alone. I sound so pathetic," I sighed.

Dani suddenly wrapped her arms around me and hugged me tight. I softly put my hands on her back. My chest warmed and I felt genuine comfort in her embrace.

*I love you Scarlett. It's not what you think.*

When she let go, she cupped my face in her hands. I stared back at her in shock.

"You are *not* a pathetic man. I work for one. I would know," Dani said strongly.

"Okay," I said softly.

She gave me a playful slap on the cheek and leaned back into her spot on the couch.

"You'll get through this, Damian. Just hang in there."

I nodded. She was right. I needed to.

"Will you do me a favor?"

"Sure."

I pulled out my phone and opened the internet app. The page I needed popped up. I handed it to her. She cautiously took it.

"What's this?"

"It's a transcript of the press conference the police department had regarding Scarlett's murder."

"Oh wow. What did they say? Did you read it?"

"Some of it. Except the part where they mentioned how she died. The details are gruesome. I was hoping you could tell me the gist of it without the extra…stuff. If you're alright with that."

"I'll do it." Dani started scanning over my phone. I saw her eyes widen after a couple of seconds. She had found it.

"What does it say? How did that monster kill her?"

"She…this is heavy, Damian. Are you sure you want to know?"

"I do."

"Okay. It seems that she was violently knocked down…then she was sexually assaulted."

"My god."

"Are you sure you want to hear this? This is devastating."

"I want to know." Dani took a deep breath and continued.

"Due to how her body was injured, it's believed she was shot in the stomach with a shotgun. The empty shell casings are missing from the scene. The killer most likely took them."

I nodded and rubbed my eyebrows. A tight knot formed in my stomach. It felt like I had been gut-punched twenty times in a row. I had the sudden urge to grab my TV. I wanted to smash it against the counter until it was nothing but shards of glass and plastic. I restrained myself. I wouldn't do that with Dani there. She didn't deserve to see me behave like a feral beast.

"Is there anything else?"

"No."

"How did they know she was raped?"

"You've heard enough Damian."

"Dani, tell me."

"Damian, stop."

"How graphic is it?"

She sighed and looked away from me.

"There was...some serious vaginal tearing and bleeding. That's all." She tossed the phone back. I caught it and placed it facedown on my lap.

"Thank you. I'm not trying to be a sicko. I just...I needed to know."

"That's fine."

"She suffered. She suffered so much," I whispered.

"I'm so sorry," Dani offered.

*If you did this Michael Madden...I'll find you and I'll be the last person you'll ever see.*

I met Ivan at the *Rainfall Rip-It* gun range, a place he visited once a week. It was important to him. He needed to prove to himself that he was able to handle a gun and control it. He always used the same one. It was symbolic for Ivan. It demonstrated that he had conquered that part of himself he was most ashamed of.

We wore earplugs and safety goggles with impact-resistant lenses. The range was divided into 6 individual shooting bays, separated by solid partitions. When you entered one, there was an electronic target system with paper targets in your direct line of sight. The targets moved closer and farther towards you depending on your desired difficulty.

Ivan and I liked to have it far away. We appreciated a challenge. That was the only way we improved our accuracy when we worked security together. You never knew when you'd need to use a gun. The muffled sharp crackle of gunfire echoed throughout the range. I shot my target several times with an M9 handgun. I imagined it as the monster who killed my wife. I imagined the blurred man I saw at the crime scene.

Ivan signaled me that he was done. We headed backwards, towards the gun wall to return the weapons. We exited the range and marched over to Ivan's truck. We leaned against it as we took in the fresh, airy night breeze. There was a dingy motel across the street called *Frank's Motel*: a shabby building with a burned-out neon sign and a craggy parking lot. The crappy red paint on the walls was faded and rust had accumulated on an old service truck that had been there before Christ was born.

I smiled to myself for a split second. Scarlett and I had stayed there for a few nights. The room had dull lighting, peeling furniture and was roach-infested. The bed felt like a pile of jagged rocks. The paper-thin walls allowed screaming to penetrate in from our shouty neighbors. Despite all that, we found a way to enjoy ourselves. Scarlett found a way to make it work. She usually did. I remembered one night that we were in that horribly uncomfortable bed. We were snuggling with each other because the heater wasn't working. Shocker.

*Let's just forget about the noise and the roaches,* Scarlett muttered.

*It's hard to forget when I see a tiny family of them speeding across the floor.*

*That is revolting,* Scarlett shuddered.

*Shall I commit genocide on them?*

*No, Damian. Don't be like that,* Scarlett laughed.

*I'm so sorry the landlord kicked us out. I hope the security gigs pick back up.*

*It's fine. We're surviving. We're looking towards the future.*

*And what does that look like?* I smiled.

*I'm a successful artist and I'm providing for the both of us.*

*While I get to play and watch basketball all day,* I added.

*You'd eventually coach our kid's sports teams.*

*Kids huh?*

*Don't you want to be parents?* Scarlett asked innocently.

*Of course I do. I can't wait, baby. I'll do anything with you. I'm all in with you.* I had promised.

*Even though times aren't the best right now...I love you, Damian.*

I grabbed her arms and gently brought her closer. Our noses touched.

*You smell,* Scarlett snickered.

*Not as bad as you.* I cupped her face and kissed her deeply.

"Damian?" Ivan waved his hand in my face.

I had been daydreaming. I longed for another day with Scarlett. Just one more night in that horribly shitty motel. We'd talk about our dreams while we'd hold each other as tight as possible. I missed her so much. I didn't want to let her go.

"Yeah? Sorry. Got a lot on my mind."

"I know buddy. Me too. I worry about you."

"So, you know this Michael Madden guy huh?"

Ivan sucked in his teeth and looked off into the cloudy sky. I could tell that he was carefully formulating his answer. He knew what I was after and would try to dissuade me from going through with it.

"Yeah. I uh...I worked at a restaurant with him back then. He was a dishwasher. He was alright. I didn't talk to him much. It was a brief thing."

"Got an address for him?"

"Jesus, man. What do you wanna do?"

"I wanna ask a few questions."

"You wanna knock his front teeth out," Ivan guessed.

"Not a bad idea."

"Promise me you won't do that shit and we'll go."

"I promise. Where is he staying?"

"He's over by Snell Lane. He lives near the drug store. I took him home a few times."

"Let's hit it."

We arrived at a mostly empty neighborhood. Half of the houses were under construction and the others were either rundown or vacant. They had dilapidated roofs, boarded up windows and filthy walls. The street and the sidewalks were littered with potholes and cracked pavement. The front yards were unkept and overgrown with weeds.

We reached the house number *0905* and parked in a parallel spot across the street. Ivan knocked.

"Hey man! It's me, Ivan Pierce. We used to work together. I was wondering if you wanted to catch up. I was in the neighborhood," Ivan called through the door. We waited for a reply.

After a few minutes, I banged on the door like a lunatic.

"Open the door, Michael!"

"Damian, calm down. If you scare him he'll never answer."

"Are you sure he's in there?"

"There's a car parked."

That was all I needed to hear. I started kicking the door. I aimed for the spot just below the knob. I continued until the cheap door gave way. When we broke inside, Ivan quickly shut it. The first thing I noticed was the pungent odor. It smelled like a mix of soiled underwear and marijuana smoke. Michael Madden lived like a pig. The living room was a mess of dirty laundry, storage boxes and empty food containers.

We found him on his torn couch. He was smoking out of a bong. He was a husky guy with an uncombed mullet and a thick mustache. He was blowing out smoke and leaning back when we broke in. He slowly turned his head towards me. He shrunk in fear when he saw my enraged face as I charged towards him. He squeaked out a pathetic yelp as I gripped his shirt with both of my hands. I brought his face close to mine. If Michael Madden was my wife's rapist and murderer...I wanted to see his face before I ended his life.

"*Was it you?*" I asked aggressively.

"What? Who are you? Why the fuck are you guys in my place?!" Michael blubbered.

"*Did you rape and murder Scarlett del Toro?!*" I shouted.

"Damian, no! We're not doing that!" Ivan commanded.

"What?" Michael squeaked.

"*Did you rape and murder my wife?! Answer the fucking question! You were arrested! Why were you let go?! I want the truth,*" I snarled.

I was beyond logic and reasoning. I wanted someone to pay. I wanted to smash his teeth in and break his skull in half. Ivan yanked me back and struggled to keep me at bay. He boxed me out and used all his weight to prevent me from punching a hole in Michael's face.

"Let me go, Ivan!"

"Stop! We need to talk to him first! For fuck's sake, Damian. Calm down!"

"Are you the man Elsa saw?!"

"Damian!"

"It's him. It has to be him."

"Why don't we find out first before you get arrested for attempted murder?"

"It wouldn't be for *attempted*," I stated plainly.

I stopped trying to force myself through him. He stepped back and held a hand up.

"Are you cool?"

"I am. For now."

All he had to do was admit it. Once he admitted it, Michael Madden was as good as dead.

"Hey Michael."

"Hi."

He was absolutely terrified. He was holding himself and I was certain that he had soiled his pants. I felt a tinge of guilt but swallowed it away. There wasn't any room for that.

"I'm sorry for coming in like this," Ivan said.

"I'm not," I added.

"We used to work at the restaurant together, remember? I'm Ivan Pierce. You knew my wife too. Lisandra." Ivan swallowed.

"Shit, yeah. It's been a while, Ivan. I remember you. You were a pretty chill guy. Why are you here? What's that other guy's problem? I didn't do anything. I swear." Michael's voice trembled.

"My name is Damian del Toro."

"Oh," Michael muttered.

"Why were you arrested?" I asked as I got closer, never breaking eye contact.

"I um...they thought I killed that lady. I didn't."

"What lady?"

"Scarlett...something. Is that your wife?"

"She was my wife, yes."

"I swear it to you. I didn't kill her. I don't kill people. Please believe me."

"Explain to us why you were arrested then," Ivan said.

Michael seemed to be quickly sobering up. He put the bong on the floor and held his knees. He looked like he was about to vomit. Beads of sweat rolled down his forehead and his armpits were drenched. I didn't think that was innocent behavior. All I was reading was *guilty*.

"I was in the area. I uh...I was drunk. I was drinking with friends. I went to the Darkpond to pee. When I came back to where my friends were, I saw that they had left me," Michael slowly explained.

"Then what? Go on," I said impatiently.

"The police found me alone. I had been waiting for a ride home. They saw that I was drunk and took me in. Since I was the only person there, they thought I had something to do with that lady's murder."

"She's not just a lady. She was my wife. You will respect her, you piece of shit," I threatened.

"Damian! Calm down. He's explaining it man. We can't jump to conclusions."

I nodded abruptly and looked away in anger. I knew that Ivan was being calm and reasonable. I respected him for it, but I wasn't in the headspace for staying calm. I wanted blood to be spilled.

"I'm sorry, I'm sorry. Look, I didn't kill Scarlett. I'm sure she was a lovely woman. I'm sorry she's dead, but I had nothing to do with that. They took me in, asked me questions and then I was let go. They...they just did it for show. They don't have suspects, I think. That's what I read online. *Rainfall Abductor* conspiracy theories, you know?" Michael rubbed his head.

*This guy is bottom of the barrel,* I thought.

"So you did nothing," I mumbled.

"I swear to you sir. I did nothing. I smoke pot and I drink with my buddies. I didn't even know your wife. Scarlett is someone I knew nothing of."

"Why would he kill her then?" Ivan asked me.

"He didn't," I sighed and rubbed my face.

"We're sorry about the door man. It's been a tough time," Ivan offered.

"I get it. It's cool. Is it...broken?"

"It was a crappy door. You needed a new one," I said.

"What he meant was, we'll get a new one and fix it."

Ivan shot me an irritated look. I gave Michael a brief thumbs up. He hesitantly gave one back. When we left, Ivan hoped Michael wouldn't call the police. I remembered that he had been smoking out of a bong that had marijuana. I knew we were gonna be fine, but Ivan tended to worry about those types of things. I'd get annoyed with him in the past over that nagging, worrisome quality that he had. At that point I knew that I needed it more than anything. I needed someone to pull me back out of the fire. I was at risk of charging full speed ahead into my own simmering pool of unbridled rage.

"I'm not fixing that door."

"Please don't assault suspects like that."

"I apologize. I thought it was him."

"You need to stay cool if we're gonna continue to do this. We can't get into deep shit with the police. We're done if we do," Ivan warned.

"You're right, but when the time comes, I'm doing it."

"Doing what?"

"What I have to. To avenge Scarlett."

"We'll see about that, bud. Let's just focus on finding the actual scumbag who did it."

"Nothing can prepare that sorry bastard when I find him. Nothing."

I knew that at the end of it, it would be a battle between Ivan and I. He wanted to stop me from committing that cruel, cold-hearted act of murdering another human being. No matter the circumstance nor the justifications...murder was murder. It was cruel. It was senseless. It ate at your soul. It devoured a piece of it and gave it to whatever god or devil you believed in. It haunted you for all time. Ivan didn't want me to lose myself, like he almost did. He didn't know I didn't care about that. I was willing to pay any price to avenge my wife.

I owed it to her.

As we walked across the street, we spotted something wrong on Ivan's black Jeep. We glanced at each other then quickly jogged towards it.

"You're joking," Ivan said angrily.

I circled the car. All four tires were slashed and had lost all air. That wasn't the worst part. *Murderer* had been spray painted on the front windshield in red.

"Who could've done this shit?" Ivan asked.

"Someone who thinks that we're murderers."

I obviously knew that I had nothing to do with my wife's murder but my mind wandered for a split second. Ivan. It couldn't have been. He was my best friend. I loved him like a brother. He was the only person I had left. It couldn't have been him. He had no reason to. Ivan's wife had also gone missing and was most likely dead.

*Did he have something to do with that?*

I scolded myself. I was being insane. I was being fed the untrusting poison that resided in the darkest corners of my mind. The part of my mind that thought *what if?* It was dangerous and highly venomous. Ivan was a good man and he had been a good husband. I observed him as he called a mutual friend who was a mechanic. I heard the restrained anger in Ivan's voice. That's what he sounded like when he was about to go off the rails. He was an expert at hiding it. Was he an expert at hiding other secrets too?

# CHAPTER 6

As they towed Ivan's SUV to a garage, we ordered a car to take us to our next destination. It was raining, as it often did. I watched the droplets squiggling down the window as I blankly stared outside. The leather seats were comfortable but the smell of cheap cologne violently permeated my nose. It reminded me of Scarlett, and how she used to say she'd kill me if I ever smelled like that. I believed her. I always made it a mission to get the very best for her. She never asked for much.

"You really think she'll want to talk to us?" Ivan asked.

"Michael Madden was a dud and I don't know where else to go. I think she knows more. It can't hurt."

Our driver dropped us off at the front yard of Elsa Dietrich's house. It was a grey, antiquated home with large rectangular windows, white columns, and a concrete staircase that led up to the heavy wooden door. It looked like a sized down version of one of those old, horrible plantation homes from the pre-civil war era. I hoped Elsa's home didn't have a similar history.

The front lawn was well-tended and uniform, albeit bare. There were two miniature fir trees that stood parallel to each other near the entrance. We carefully approached it as we took in the eerily quiet atmosphere that surrounded her home.

"Do you sense that?" Ivan asked.

"I do. It feels...depressing. It feels like something tragic happened here. Maybe many years ago."

"What do you know about this lady?"

"I know she lives alone and she likes the woods. She was married and she had a daughter once, Angela. She hunts and fishes. She's a bit strange."

"She strikes me as an old wise woman who knows many little dark secrets about this town. She's like something out of a folktale," Ivan mused.

"I hope she knows something. Every minute counts."

I knocked on the heavyset door. The deep, booming noise reverberated and echoed throughout the whole yard. Elsa opened in under a minute. She suspiciously peeked at both of us through a small crevice. She kept the door slightly ajar.

"Hello there. May I help you?"

"I'm sorry to bother you, Elsa. I was hoping to ask you a few questions if you weren't busy. I'm with a good friend, Ivan Pierce."

"Nice to formally meet you, Ms. Dietrich."

"Likewise, Ivan. No, I don't mind. Not at all! Come in please." Elsa opened the door and led us inside.

I examined her living room as she motioned for us to sit down on brown, antique chairs she had near a front window. The interior of Elsa's house was wrapped in catriona wallpaper. She had taxidermy mounts of deer on top of her rustic fireplace. It was laid with mahogany bricks.

Above the front door was a glass encasement housing a hunting rifle. Porcelain figurines, framed pictures and vases were placed inside an integrated wooden cabinet near heavy silk curtains. The hardwood floor was polished and squeaky clean. It creaked as we walked across it. The French brass chandelier attached to the ceiling shook and chimed as we sat down.

I thought it felt like a haunted house, but I also lived in isolation like Elsa. My house didn't feel that way. I wasn't sure why Elsa's home felt so creepy. Maybe it had something to do with her deceased family.

"Do you two want anything to drink? I have water, wine, soda and beer." Elsa asked as she plopped down across from us on a comfy recliner.

"We're good. Thank you Elsa," Ivan grinned.

"I see that you do taxidermy."

"Oh yes! I do it for freelance work and as a hobby. I sell online. Something to keep me busy, you know? I stay cooped up in this shit hole all day and night," Elsa giggled.

"I know how that feels," I admitted.

"We're both alone now, Damian. I'm sorry we share that similarity now. It's a horrid feeling."

"I'm sorry too."

"I'll help in any way I can. I want you to catch the monster who did this. Even if it seems like he doesn't exist. It's like he vanished into thin air," Elsa exclaimed.

"Elsa, I wanted to ask you about the man you saw watching my wife the day she was murdered."

"Yes, Damian. I looked further into that. I was curious. To my eyes, he looked like that man who died three years ago."

I already knew who she was talking about, but men didn't come back from the dead.

"Are you sure?"

"The features were very similar. It could've been a doppelgänger. Maybe a secret twin brother."

*A secret twin brother? That's a little far-fetched. Maybe I should've listened to the rumors.*

"You're talking about Luke Prescott, right? The man who...was murdered," I shuddered.

It still affected me. I often wondered what had really happened. Why was he murdered?

"That's correct. There's a lot of blonde, caucasian men with green eyes in Rainfall. I think it looked like Luke Prescott but it could've been anyone. My late husband looked like that. Like a *Nazi*. He acted like one too," Elsa hissed.

"Right," Ivan awkwardly commented.

We weren't expecting that *word* out of Elsa's mouth.

"There was also a luxury car I saw driving around that same afternoon."

"You mean my car? The Phantom?"

"No, no Phantom. I've seen yours. This was a different one. Who's that rich guy you work for again? Albert?"

"Abel Armoni. He owns the nightclub."

"Ah yes. I've never been to one but my husband Martin always went. He was a good man once. Then he turned into a bad one. Isn't that funny? The day a man gets married they turn into the monster they've been hiding from us. Are you a bad man, Damian?" Elsa pointed at me.

The question took me by surprise. I didn't think I was a bad man, but I had done bad things in my life. Things I regretted. Things that made me hate myself. What was the factor that decided if you were a good man or a bad one? Where was the line drawn? Before I could answer, Ivan interjected. He motioned to a framed photo beside Elsa on a wooden stand.

"Who's that?"

Elsa glanced to her side and briefly smiled. She carefully grasped the photo and closely examined it. She turned it around and showed it to us.

"This is my daughter, Angela."

The photo was grainy but Angela looked very beautiful. She had straight, dark hair with brown eyes and tanned skin. She was on some kind of farm with a red barn house behind her.

"What happened to her, Elsa?" I asked as I leaned forward to see her.

"She died in a fire. It was an accident. That barn house you see? Gone. Dust."

*I had to ask,* I thought.

"I'm so sorry to hear that, Elsa."

"I loved her once and dearly. I miss my family very much. What became of us was…a complete and utter horror." Elsa teared up and quickly wiped her eyes.

"She's at rest now." Ivan comforted.

"No she's not! She was murdered! They say it was an accident, but I know it wasn't! It was bloody murder!" Elsa shouted.

We were both taken aback. Ivan stood up and held his arms out in peace.

"I'm sorry. I didn't mean anything bad by what I said."

"I never got revenge for what happened. The revenge I wanted and deserved. I had been betrayed. I still hear the walls screaming at night." Elsa had a fire in her eyes that burned bright. I had never seen that side to her. There was so much more to Elsa that I had not known.

"What screams?" Ivan asked cautiously.

"The screams of Martin and Angela burning to their deaths," Elsa said quietly.

"Sorry to bother you, Elsa. We'll be on our way," I said.

"Thank you for your help," Ivan added.

The air became charged with too much emotion. It was more than I could handle. We all shared tragedy and it was palpable. My chest became heavy with sorrow.

"I hope you find the man who raped and murdered your wife, Damian. Get the revenge you need. Do what I wasn't able to do," Elsa said sweetly.

*Finally, someone else who understands my need for vengeance.*

I smiled and nodded as I quickly closed her front door behind me. We hurriedly descended the steps and started the trek back to my house.

"Why did we choose to walk again?" Ivan asked.

"Good scenery."

There was a nice, cool breeze. It wafted through the rows of cypress trees that stood on opposite sides of the road. The road that led to my home. A place I didn't enjoy living in anymore.

"That Elsa lady has had some *shit* happen to her, man. How the hell did you not know any of that stuff about her family?"

"She never mentioned it. I didn't ask. I had heard rumors, but they sounded stupid. People talk shit because she's a German woman who has guns and hunts. I guess…I don't know. Maybe she feels like we can relate now."

"That's a fucked up way of looking at it."

"I know, but we both have gone through tragedy now. Well, all three of us."

"She doesn't know about Sam?"

"Not many people do."

My phone chimed. I slid it out my pocket. It was a text message from an anonymous number.

"*I know who raped and murdered Scarlett del Toro,*" I read aloud.

I paused and Ivan followed. We gave each other grave looks.

"Who the hell is that?" Ivan asked.

"I don't know."

# CHAPTER 7
## 2012

I loved working security with Ivan. The job was difficult, dangerous and demanding at times but I knew that I could run straight through a wall with Ivan. He was the type of man you wanted by your side. He was loyal, dependable and he knew what he was doing. He was more restrained than I was. Whenever I'd fly off the rails, he'd be there to make sure I didn't make too much of a mess. He liked to use his words. I liked to use my fists.

I adjusted my bulletproof vest that was apart of our all-black standardized uniform. We each had a heavy duty flashlight, a pocket knife and a baton strapped to our utility belt. We wore caps that said *Pierce Security* along with tactical boots. Some old friends would laugh at Ivan for having us decked out in full gear, but I knew the truth. Ivan cared about the safety of his guys. You never knew what could go down in a job. Sometimes it got real hairy.

We were at a rock concert that night. The band *Skeleton Crew* was playing. It was an indie rock band on the rise. The venue was a mid-sized theater a few miles away from the construction district. It was an old warehouse that had been converted for live music and stage plays. It was a rugged site with brick walls, a hard cement floor and limited capacity. Despite that, it was an electrifying locale. The grand wooden stage had all the lighting rigs, amplifiers and speakers necessary to blow the roof off the place.

Strobe lights with dynamic colors and effects added to the intoxicating atmosphere. Murals and artwork depicting skeletal figures playing guitar and drums were placed behind the band. Acoustic panels were strategically placed throughout to minimize echo. A high-energy crowd of college students were all dressed in black with skull beanies, ripped sweaters, jean shorts, spiked boots, multiple ear piercings and black face paint. There was one guy who had a green mohawk, a tattoo of a colossal spider eating a pigeon on his arm and piercings along his eyebrows with a nose ring. They jumped and screamed along to the powerfully violent music.

We heard guitars being shredded, drums being banged on and the lead singer growling his heart out for his adoring fans. Ivan and I remained in the back with earpieces so we wouldn't go deaf. We hung out near the concession stand.

"How do people listen to this shit?" Ivan said covering one ear.

"Maybe they had a bad childhood."

"In that case, why aren't we fans of this stuff?"

We laughed and shrugged at each other. The band's management team had hired us to make sure there wasn't any illegal drugs being used. They got banned from a previous venue for just that. It wasn't exactly their fault but that was the type of crowd they attracted.

They also had a mosh pit that ended with someone's foot getting broken. We were around to make sure shit didn't go awry. Everything needed to go smoothly for *Skeleton Crew*. As the evening went on all was well. My nerves had calmed and I was comfortable enough to talk freely with Ivan. It felt like it was going to be a calm night. I stared at some graffiti on the wall in front of me. It looked like a dark figure was coming out of a creepy forest. It reminded me of Bruno McCoy, the art gallery douche. He was on the same level of prick as Abel Armoni.

"You remember Bruno? That art dealing scumshit."

"Of course I do. The guy was a real asshole."

"The dumb things we do when we're young and in love, huh?"

"We're still young, man. That was only a year ago."

I threw my head back in awe. It had only been a year. A year since Ivan and I confronted Bruno outside of his art gallery. We did something we shouldn't have and I ultimately paid the price for it. Scarlett did too. That was my biggest regret of all. Ivan held up two fingers at me. Our signal for trouble. I followed his eyes and saw a guy shuffling his hands inside of a suspicious small bag. A young woman was impatiently waiting for him while nervously darting her eyes in every direction.

*"Alright fellas, standby. We have illegal drug gang activities taking place,"* Ivan signaled into our ear mics. I smirked and shook my head at him.

*"Drug gang? Really?"*

I followed Ivan as he approached the suspects. I was about to crack a joke when I heard the sharp crack of several gunshots pierce my eardrums. I immediately ducked down and covered them. My stomach churned as waves of dread quickly filled my insides. The band stopped playing and everything erupted into chaos. The screaming, terror-stricken crowd dispersed and ran in all directions. They desperately tried to escape a shooter I couldn't see. I scanned through everyone while simultaneously avoiding people so I wouldn't get trampled. I stuck myself flat to the wall and spotted a still person who wasn't running. He was holding down a young woman's stomach. I took a closer look and waited for the strobe light to shine on them. When it did, I saw that there was blood everywhere. The man turned his head. It was Ivan. He was screaming into the ear mic. When my head stopped buzzing, I focused and listened.

*"Suspect is heading towards the east exit! Caucasian man with long dark hair wearing a black ski mask! Armed and dangerous! He's our shooter!"*

Without thinking, I ran through the crowd and turned right towards the east exit. There wasn't anyone in the area and for good reason. The shooter just catapulted himself out of that same exit with a gun in hand. I sprinted forward without hesitation. I rushed through the heavy metal door and opened it with my shoulder.

An ice-cold shiver ran down my spine. My gut felt like it was being jabbed with broken shards of glass as I rushed forward. Every ounce of my body was telling me to stop and to turn back. It was telling me that death was imminent, but I couldn't stop. As far as I was concerned I had a job to do. I had to catch him.

I found myself in an alleyway with a lone streetlamp barely lighting the dark, narrow path in front of me. The ground was slippery, slick with rainwater. I heard puddles violently splashing a short distance away. A surge of fear injected itself into my veins. I did my best to ignore it. I squinted my eyes and saw someone running. I went after him, traversing across potholes and around massive garbage dumps.

When the man slowed down, I did as well. I took cover behind a pile of wooden crates.

*This is fucked.*

Gunshots suddenly rang out, ricocheting off walls and balcony railings above. I heard careful, creaking footsteps coming closer and closer. My heart was in my throat as I saw his shadow on the wall creeping in. I held my breath and slowly crouched down. I tried to time it as best I could. I slowly peeked my head out and saw his legs. I lunged forward and grabbed both of them, pulling him up. My muscles ached and burned as I caused him to tumble down. I shot up and thrusted my elbow into his neck.

As he struggled to go free, he stared at me with bewildered eyes. I tried to unveil his ski mask but he swung hard at my face and clocked me with his gun. I staggered off of him and rushed back towards cover before he had a chance to shoot at me. He shot aimlessly through the air. I held my breath as the bullets whizzed by my ears.

I tried to catch my breath as I heard him run off as fast as possible. Ivan approached me, along with the other security guards.

"Damian! Are you okay? Holy shit. You chased that psycho?"

"I did. He got away. I'm sorry."

Ivan grabbed my arm and pulled me up.

"Don't be sorry. You're alive. There's nothing to be sorry about. The police will be on that guy's ass now."

Several police cruisers with their sirens blaring roared in the distance, right on cue.

"What happened with the girl?"

Ivan shook his head and looked down.

"Shit."

"Well, *Skeleton Crew* is pissed off and the rest of their tour is cancelled. We'll be out of a job for a couple of months. Sorry man. I know how much you need this."

"I'll figure it out with Scarlett." I placed my hand on his shoulder.

---

As soon as I entered my house, Scarlett was waiting for me in the living room. She wore a crimson red silk robe and sat on the couch with a singular night lamp on. When I stepped closer to her, I saw that she had a scowl on her face. She tightened the straps of her robe around her torso and stared at me indignantly. I sighed and sat in front of her on a barstool. My head hung low. She was mad at me. That much was clear. I didn't know why yet but I knew I was about to find out.

"Why are you up?" I asked.

"I can't sleep until you're home."

"I know, but you're usually in bed. What's wrong?"

"What happened at the concert is all over the news. I was worried sick, Damian. You wouldn't answer your phone. I was scared." Scarlett sniffled.

"Honey, I'm so sorry. My phone's dead. It was an insane night. It doesn't happen often but it happens. I'm trained for these dangerous scenarios. I know what to expect and I know how to handle it. I don't want you to worry." I reached for Scarlett's hands. She brushed me off.

"Nothing can train you for a man pointing a gun at your face and firing. That's instant death."

"I like to be more optimistic than that."

"I knew you shouldn't have worked security. Even Lisandra told me she didn't like Ivan's business."

"Now you're talking shit with Lisandra? My best friend's wife? Are you serious?"

"She's worried too. She doesn't want Ivan doing it either."

"That's his business. He's not gonna give it up."

"You should find another job before something happens to you."

I angrily stood up and glared at her.

"Why the hell would you even say something like that? I do this job to support us. I don't necessarily *want* to do it but it pays the bills. No one loves their job but they do it because they have to."

*And right now your dreams of being an artist are just that...dreams. Dreams don't pay, therefore the world doesn't care about them.*

I didn't dare say my thoughts out loud. They were purely fueled by the anger I felt in that moment. I didn't mean that. Scarlett's dreams meant everything to her, so in turn, it meant everything to me. It was frustrating how things didn't seem to be going anywhere, but that was the life of an artist. You had to knock on a thousand doors before someone answered.

Scarlett stayed quiet.

"What? That's it? You have nothing else to say? That's shocking," I snapped.

I got closer to her and inspected her face. I saw that her eyes were misty and she was looking down. My heart sank and I immediately dropped to my knees beside her. I softly put my hands on hers. Thankfully she didn't brush me off.

"Sorry," she choked out.

*I'm an asshole.*

"What's wrong?" I asked sincerely.

"My mom called earlier. She heard about what had happened at the concert. She was acting like you were already dead. She was telling me about how I could start another chapter in my life without you. She was so happy at the fact that you could've been dead."

"Jesus Christ. What did you tell her?"

"I told her to fuck off."

I squeezed her hand and smiled.

"That sounds about right."

"The thought of you dying…breaks me into a million tiny little pieces. I don't want you gone. I don't want you to leave me. You need to stay with me until we grow old and die together," Scarlett demanded.

"I want us to grow wrinkly and ugly together," I joked.

"That sounds perfect," Scarlett chuckled.

"I think we're both very stubborn people and we both know what we want. Most of the time that works out, but this time…one of us has to give in."

"Yeah." She croaked.

I got up, gave her a soft kiss on the lips and tightly hugged her. I rubbed her back and truly appreciated having her with me. She had me and I had her. I thought about almost being shot and killed back at the *Skeleton Crew* concert. It had been a moment of absolute terror. One part of me wasn't afraid of death because it would've been swift and final. The other part of me felt immense guilt for Scarlett. I couldn't leave her alone. It wouldn't be fair to her.

"I'll uh…I'll try to find something else. Ivan won't be happy but he'll get over it. He'll understand."

"Wait, really?" Scarlett pulled away with a renewed brightness in her eyes.

"Yes."

"You can work for Abel!"

"Your stepdad?"

"Yeah, he'll hook you up with a job. He needs a personal driver."

"Are you sure that's a good idea?"

"It's the best idea."

"What's your mom gonna think?"

"I don't care what she thinks. She's worse. She just married him for money."

"Do you think he'll like me for the job?"

"It'll be fine. He'll hire you. Trust me."

"Does he even remember me?"

"I'll remind him."

---

I had heard a lot of things about Abel Armoni that year. He was Scarlett's stepdad but I never saw him much. That job was an opportunity to see if it was all true. I met him in the lobby of the *Riverview Hotel*. The lobby area was spacious and impressive. It featured a high ceiling, circular chandeliers, and modular black leather sofas. I sat in a marble chair next to him, near a large table of fine wood. He knocked on it. The professionally-dressed ladies at the concierge desk gave him disapproving looks. He was dressed in a dark blue Armani suit with black dress shoes and a gold watch. I was casually dressed in a polo shirt and a pair of black jeans. I felt like garbage next to him.

"Cheap shit," Abel muttered.

I gazed out the expansive windows that were situated towards the middle of the lobby. It showcased the breathtaking, scenic views of the waterfront where a few boats were docked. I hadn't heard what Abel had said. He obnoxiously snapped his fingers in my face. I focused on his perfectly punchable face and resisted the urge to break his jaw.

"Hello? Hi? Are you here? Do you need this job or not? I've got places to go and people to see."

"Sorry, I'm here."

"Okay and? You're Scarlett's husband huh? Holy Mother of Christ," Abel sighed, exasperated.

"I'm here for the job, sir. I want it."

"Good. You actually sound intelligent. That wasn't so hard, was it?"

"I'm sorry?" I asked through gritted teeth.

"No, I'm sorry. For agreeing to take this stupid fucking meeting. You're lucky Scarlett is my stepdaughter. She's a gorgeous little lady. She can be very convincing. If it wasn't for her, I would've told you to *fuck off* a very long time ago."

"What?"

I was in such disbelief. That's all I was able to squeak out. I couldn't believe he was speaking to me like that.

"Damian, are you on a substance? I'm trying to have a conversation with you. Listen like a normal adult. Were you labeled a *retard* as a kid? Is that it?"

I couldn't believe my ears. Abel was treating me like I was some piece of trash floating in the wind. He treated me like I was nothing to him. Like I was shit at the bottom of his heel.

"I'm having a hard time following. You're speaking too fast."

"Okay, clearly you were. Listen carefully, Damian. I want you to tell me about the concert incident. What the hell happened?"

"I was doing security with one of my closest friends, Ivan. He has a company. There was a gunman. He shot at someone in the crowd. It looks like it was a drug-related incident. I followed him outside. I confronted him but he got away."

"You're finally reminding me why I'm here. You either have brass balls or you're *really* stupid, kid. Why didn't you shoot him?"

"Band didn't want any guns inside. It was the one job where I could've used one."

"I bet you would've blown that asshole to bits."

"I wanted to."

"You're not only going to drive for me, Damian. You're going to protect me as well. If needed. The people who are going to be closest to me, need to know how to kick some ass."

"I understand."

"You seem like you don't really talk much, but I trust you'll do the job well. If you don't, you're gone. Got it?"

"That's crystal clear, Mr. Armoni."

"My assistant will go over the exact details of the job with you. I have a meeting with an important client now," Abel stood up and straightened his jacket.

I followed and firmly shook his hand. I stared into his eyes and held his icy gaze. I wanted to show him that I wasn't some punk off the street. I knew what I was doing.

"Thank you sir."

"Have we met before?"

"A few times yes. They were brief encounters."

"I can't seem to remember. I meet so many people these days. A lot of wealthy businessmen and clients. I tend to keep the most important people at the forefront of my mind."

"That's understandable."

*If anyone deserved a broken nose, it was this motherfucker.*

"Room 417. You'll be meeting Dani Shepherd."

He scampered off as I prepared myself to meet Dani for the first time. It looked like I had earned at least some level of respect from my pseudo father-in-law. Not that I particularly cared about that. It was for Scarlett's sake. That's what I kept telling myself. She didn't love him, but she did appreciate his money. He gave her a small stipend each month to buy food and household products. Nothing more, nothing less. I definitely still needed a job to support us, but Abel would only give me a salary if I worked for him. I was fine with that. I had no issue earning my keep. I didn't expect any handouts.

I saw Abel meet with a blonde woman near the concierge desk. She was thin with long blonde hair. She had a light complexion with blue eyes and a moon-shaped birthmark on her right cheek. It was the first time I had seen Victoria Cole. It wouldn't be the last.

---

I sat in hotel room 417 on an embroidered chair and waited for Dani Shepherd. The room was adorned with lavish furnishings and plush fabrics. Velvet and silk were used for drapes, bedding and upholstery.

Strange pieces of high-end, contemporary art were neatly placed on the wall behind the king-sized bed. In my eyes, the *art* on display resembled chicken scratch more than anything.

The color palette was rich with deep hues of burgundy and gold. It had the makings of an inviting ambiance, but I felt anything but invited. It felt like an elaborate prison cell in disguise. I didn't trust a single thing Abel had his fingerprints on. He tainted and manipulated everything to his own liking. This was the price of giving power to men like him, the type of men who had no reservations or conscience. They did as they pleased and got anything they wanted. The word *no* was deeply insulting to men like Abel.

I thought about the man I had chased. He had shot at me and could've easily killed me. I could've died and I would've made Scarlett a widow. I would've left her alone. A pang of guilt suddenly struck my chest. I clutched it and breathed. The gunshots rattled my ears again causing my head to pound. That was when Dani strode in. I hadn't heard her and by the time I noticed she was there, her hands were on my shoulders.

She gently shook me and peered at me with concerned eyes.

"Hey, are you okay?"

I attempted to shake it off and nodded.

"Yeah, I'm fine. Sorry about that."

"Is everything okay?" She retreated and sat at the edge of the bed. She had on a red button-down shirt with black dress pants and black satin pumps. She styled her hair in a tight bun. She toyed with her necklace which sat on her chest. It had a big silver '*D*' amulet. I never forgot that necklace.

"Yes, everything's fine."

"I know Abel wanted me to tell you about the details of the job but I've had a long day. I'm dirty. I need a shower."

"I see."

"Are you dirty?" Dani began unbuttoning her shirt. My throat ran dry and I swallowed.

*Uhh...what the hell is going on?* I thought.

"No, I showered. I'm clean."

"I noticed. Would you mind if I showered?" Dani unbuttoned the very last button on her shirt which exposed a white undershirt she had on. I breathed a sigh of relief. She got closer to me and ran her fingers up my arm. I anxiously looked up at her. She stared back at me with a glimmer in her bright brown eyes. I softly moved my arm away from her hand and clasped my own hands together.

"Listen, you seem very nice but...I'm married."

"I saw your ring. Are you happily married?"

"I am," I said strongly.

"Not many married men are able to resist temptation. Do you want to touch me?"

My heart started racing and my palms grew sweaty. The collar around my shirt began to tighten and a dry lump was forming in my throat.

"I don't know what's going on here. I just want a job driving for Mr. Armoni. I'm confused." I stood up and turned away from her. I rushed towards the front door and stared at it.

*If any more clothes are off, I'm leaving.*

"I respect that. Does Scarlett treat you well?"

"Very well. She's my wife and I love her. I love her so much, I'd kill for her. We only have each other, you know? Both of our parents weren't the best. We weren't born lucky. We drew the bad cards. When we found each other, we both knew we had drawn a good hand. Does that make sense?"

"I can tell you're a good man."

I slowly turned and saw Dani buttoning up her shirt.

"Thank you. I try."

"It's good you're taking this job. You can keep an eye on Abel." Dani's face became stony.

"What do you mean?"

"He gets obsessive. He loves women. Maybe a little too much. He has no boundaries and no problem quenching his thirst whenever he wants to. That's what happens when you give that much money to people who can't control themselves."

"Why are you telling me this?"

"Most men I test, jump at the chance to sleep with me. I don't actually go through with it. I tell them to go to hell and I report the results to Abel. I don't want anyone weak-minded joining our ranks."

I staggered backwards and darted my eyes around the room. It had been a test. What kind of test was that?

"This was Abel's test?"

"This was *my* test. You passed. You'd be surprised at the amount of married men who fail. It's pathetic. I don't work with perverts or people who can't be trusted."

"I know how men can be. I am one."

"I'm serious about Abel, by the way. If you really love your wife, keep an eye on him. He has a history. Don't tell him I said anything."

"A history of what?"

Before Dani was able to answer, Abel barged in.

"Alrighty! Done with my meeting. Everything good here?"

"Yes sir. How did it go with Victoria Cole?" Dani asked.

"Very well. She's a lovely woman," Abel smiled.

"The rest of your day is freed up, as you requested."

"Atta girl," Abel cooed.

"Did you need anything else from me?" I asked Dani.

"I'll email you your work schedule."

"You may leave now," Abel commanded.

I turned the steel handle and pushed the door open. I turned around and briefly saw Dani's distraught face as Abel sensually rubbed both of her shoulders. The door slammed shut before I was able to see anything more. I pressed my head against the door.

*It's none of my business.*

That was a colossal mistake I regretted in my life. I should've made it my business. I should've asked Dani why Abel was touching her in that manner. But I desperately needed the job and that's why I kept my mouth shut. That's why Dani kept her mouth shut too.

---

I was at the *Bridge* with Sam, my brother. We usually met up on Sunday nights to talk and vent. It was the best way we kept in touch. It was a serene place. We'd watch the ripples in the stream and the swimming ducks that would emerge from the water below.

"Don't you ever fucking scare me like that. Okay? You're a piece of shit. I mean it. You are a piece of garbage," Sam warned.

"Fuck off."

"I'm really happy you're alive, bro. I'm serious," Sam gripped my shoulder.

"It was one of the scariest nights of my life. Even scarier than the night I asked Scarlett to be my girlfriend."

Sam and I chuckled.

"Shut the hell up, Damian. Did you see his face at least? What did you tell the cops?"

"Bro, I...I didn't. I don't remember. I told the cops I didn't know who it was."

"I read online that it was drug-related. That was a crazy ass shooting at a concert. Where people are supposed to have fun and feel safe. Ridiculous man."

"I was there to keep people safe and I failed, miserably. How do you think I feel?"

Sam held my head close to his.

"Don't talk like that. It wasn't your fault. You did all you could. You had the balls to go after the guy in the first place. He had a gun. It is not your fault." Sam rubbed my head and playfully shoved it.

"If only I had a gun," I sighed.

"Guns are nasty. Guns kill people. You don't want to be the man who kills someone. That shit weighs on your mind."

"Have you ever killed someone?"

"Hell no. I don't want to and I don't need to. I don't want that shit on my conscious. That little incident you had with Bruno McCoy...that was terrifying. You wanted him dead."

"I had a good reason. You know what he did to Scarlett," I said angrily.

All the vengeance-fueled emotions and feelings of that day raged through my hot-blooded veins.

"I do know and I know what he did to *you*," he pointed at my head.

"A lesson learned."

Sam took out a cigarette and lit it. I hated his smoking but I tolerated his habit so we'd be able to talk. It reminded me of our father's nasty habits. Instead of taking us to little league or to our basketball games, he'd rather smoke and drink alone. A man I loathed and a man I promised myself I wouldn't become.

"So you're starting a new job huh? Driving for that rich prick, Abel Armoni."

"I'm not happy about it either, but it's a job. Who really loves their job? Look at dad. I'm surprised he hasn't drank himself to death yet."

"That'll be a day of celebration."

"Looks like the rumors about Abel are true. Apparently he loves women very much. Too much."

"Isn't he Scarlett's stepdad now?"

"Officially yes. Soraya married him. I didn't think about it before, but the way he looks at Scarlett…it's not normal. He doesn't look at her as a daughter. He looks at her like she's a piece of cooked steak. I haven't even been out with him much, but I've noticed."

"Trust your instincts, bro. You and I know the type of man Abel is. We grew up with one. We were *raised* by one."

"How many times did dad cheat on mom?"

"Too many to count."

"I'll never end up like him."

"I know you won't. You're a little reckless and overprotective, but you're doing good."

"Overprotective? Have you seen the guys that catcall Scarlett in the street? I have to keep my eyes peeled. I have to be a watchdog."

Sam got up and flicked his cigarette away. He crushed the small orange light it emitted with his shoe.

"You're lucky that you're a decent looking guy."

"Why do you say that?"

"Scarlett might've dumped your ass already if you were ugly."

"Get the fuck out of here."

"What? I'm telling the truth. As your sexier, older, more intelligent brother, I do not tell lies. I tell truths."

"You tell bullshits," I replied.

He shoved me and we laughed.

"You remember Luke Prescott from high school?"

"Of course I do. He was obsessed with women he couldn't get, like Scarlett."

"Now that guy was a freak from hell. Didn't he install a mini-cam inside the girls' volleyball locker room one year?"

"That's what they say. He never got caught, but I believe it."

"I wonder where he is now."

"Probably dead. The guy was a scumbag."

We started walking towards the other side of the bridge. That's where things got hazy for me. That's when the worst thing that could've happened, did happen. It had been an ordinary Sunday night. A usual night for my brother and I. But, that's the night my brother died. It was the night Sam was murdered.

# CHAPTER 8
## 2018

*I know who raped and murdered Scarlett del Toro.* That's what the text message had read. Ivan didn't want to follow the messenger's instructions but I felt compelled to. We had to follow every single lead that came our way. It was obviously some sort of trap but that person had something to say. I intended to hear them out.

The anonymous person wanted us to meet at the ruins of an old, decayed church. It had been known as St. Michael's once. The weathered stone walls had collapsed and were deteriorating. Moss clung to the stone fragments of the eroding structure and softened the harsh edges of what was once a great church. We parked in front as it began to drizzle.

"This is a bad idea," Ivan sighed.

"I know, but we don't have many options."

"We do have one but—" Ivan trailed.

"What?"

"It doesn't matter now."

Ivan climbed out of the car and carefully traversed the ruined stone fragments of the church. I followed and maneuvered around the vines that had snuck their way through crevices in the walls. I sent a message that we had arrived. We prepared for the worst.

"Have they said anything?" Ivan asked, trepidation in his voice.

"Not yet."

"This is dumb man. Why the hell are we here?"

"No stone unturned. Any little clue, any little conversation, any little secret can lead us to the stalker who murdered my wife. The same man who might have something to do with Lisandra's disappearance."

"My wife was never stalked, Damian. She was taken. This is different."

"You don't know that. She could've been followed without anyone knowing."

"Maybe man. No one ever broke into my house either."

"You never know what the truth might reveal, Ivan. Keep an open mind." I urged.

He shrugged. He knew I was right. He had come to terms with the fact that his wife was most likely dead. He didn't want any false hopes. He might've not wanted to know what ended up happening to her.

We heard squeaking footsteps coming from behind a fragmented wall. We both took a few steps back. The tip of a sharp blade slowly came out. We saw the tattooed hand and then the person wielding it. He stood tall and his cheeks were flushed. The man's eyes were red and he looked like he hadn't slept in days. He was firmly grasping a machete.

"Sebastian?" I asked. The irritation was clear in my voice. My face grew warm as I developed the urge to knock his teeth out for putting us through his nonsense.

"Gunner? What the fuck are you doing here, man? You sent the message?" Ivan stepped forward and crossed his arms.

"Yeah, it was me. I knew you guys wouldn't listen to me otherwise. I needed the both of you here. I know you hate me Damian but I have some shit you need to hear. I loved Scarlett too. We have that in common."

"What you and Scarlett had wasn't fucking love!" I rushed forward. Ivan held me back.

"Cool it! Don't start anything."

"You don't know anything about love, Gunner. You beat her. You abusive piece of shit. You belong in the ground."

"Say what you want, but I know the truth. I've seen it. Ivan was seeing your wife. Your own best friend."

"What?" Ivan glanced at us both and furiously shook his head.

I stared at him. Sebastian's face was unmoving. He seemed very sure in his answer. It couldn't be. Ivan was my best friend. I had known him for years. He had known Scarlett for years. He had been there since the inception of my relationship with her. He knew about the ups and downs. He was there when her stalker began terrorizing our lives. We had questioned Luke Prescott together. The man who we thought was guilty. He was there when news broke of Luke's apparent murder. He was there with me then, helping me catch the man responsible for destroying my life.

"You're insane. Ivan would never betray me like that. Why would I trust you?"

Sebastian took out his phone. He quickly scrolled through it and faced the screen towards us. There it was. A clear picture of Ivan and Scarlett having a coffee. They were at the bakery that was smack in the middle of town. I didn't travel there often. Suspicion was rising in my gut as it began to broil.

"Wait a minute, Damian. That's not what it looks like. Please allow me to explain myself."

"*That's not what it looks like.* That's what everyone says when they've done something that, well...is exactly what it looks like," Sebastian smirked.

"Shut up, Gunner! You fucking moron. You're making a big drama out of nothing. We haven't even talked about you fucking with my car. Are we in high school? I'm gonna call the police."

"It's the truth," Sebastian coldly declared.

"Go to hell, Gunner. You slashed my tires for nothing. What are you suggesting? Why were you following us? Worried about something?"

"I wanted to get Damian's attention. I did love Scarlett and when I found out she was murdered..." Sebastian rubbed his watery eyes.

"You're so full of it," Ivan snapped.

"I knew something suspicious was going on with you, Ivan. Where were you that night?" Sebastian asked.

"I was working, as usual. I had an overnight gig."

"That's what you say. Can you confirm that?"

As they went back and forth, my head whirled with many possibilities. I was vulnerable. My emotions were still raw. If there was any chance, anyone killed my wife...I considered it...with extreme prejudice.

"There's a reason the police didn't talk to me. I'm not a person of interest." Ivan answered.

Sebastian threw back his head and laughed. He dismissively waved his machete at Ivan.

"The police only arrested one guy. That drunk dickhead, Michael Madden. There are no persons of interest. It's a crap shoot. No one else was seen near her that night."

"Those hikers were," Ivan said.

"The elderly couple? Oh please."

As much as an idiot Sebastian was, he was speaking the truth. The leads ran colder than the snow that fell in the winter.

"What are you trying to gain here?" I interjected.

"Justice for Scarlett. I have more pictures, Damian. It was a recurring thing."

"I'm going to call Detective Gamble," Ivan threatened.

"Don't call him," I commanded.

"Damian, believe me. It wasn't like that. It wasn't *recurring*. It was a few times. She had reached out to me."

"I believe you, but what were you doing with her? Why didn't you tell me anything? Why was she reaching out to you?"

"You guys were having issues. She just needed to vent. It was because of that stalker asshole. The same guy we're trying to find now.

You guys were really frustrated and fighting a lot. Your head injury had you on edge."

"Of course she said that."

"Bruno McCoy did a number on you. She told me you were getting too obsessive and angry with her."

"He was breaking into our house and stealing things from her. Panties, bras and other private things. He was toying with us. Of course I was obsessive. I was obsessed with keeping her safe and protected. I can't believe you never told me anything. That's a betrayal."

"She made me promise to stay quiet. I'm sorry."

"If Lisandra had reached out to me, I would've told you. It's common courtesy. I thought we didn't have any secrets between us." I looked at him up and down in disgust. I was infuriated.

"I told you so. I knew you were gonna want to hear this," Sebastian commented.

"Why the hell were you even following Scarlett and I? How did you even find us? Maybe it was Gunner. Maybe he's involved. Sounds like some serious stalker activity to me."

"I was in town on business. I just happened to see you many times. I knew the pictures were gonna be useful some day," Sebastian laughed.

"Is there anything else?" I raised my eyebrows at Ivan and tried to keep my burgeoning rage at bay. I couldn't believe it. Ivan had been meeting my wife behind my back. I only saw that and took it as a betrayal. I would've never done that to him.

"There's a secret she told me and she didn't want me to tell you. She threatened me, Damian. I didn't know what to do."

Violent instincts took over as I stomped towards Ivan and strongly dug my elbow into his neck. I pinned him against the wall. He used both his hands to pry my arm a few inches away from him. I kept pushing forward. I was incensed. Sebastian slowly approached us with his machete raised.

"Threatened you how, Ivan?! What are you telling me?!" I shouted.

"Let's do it, D. Let's kill this motherfucker."

"Fuck off Gunner. Are you happy with this? You have no idea what you're talking about. I did nothing. I would never harm Scarlett. *Ever*," Ivan pleaded.

"Did you…did you sleep with her?" I whispered.

Ivan looked at me with pained eyes. He softly shook his head.

"No. No man. I'd never. Are you crazy?"

Maybe I was crazy. I got angry whenever Scarlett had mentioned it, but she was right. The head injury had affected me in a very negative way. I was more irritable and prone to anger. I didn't remember some things. I couldn't recall familiar faces. Some days I felt like I was losing my mind. There I was, listening to that idiot Sebastian Gunner. I was so hellbent on finding the truth, I had been willing to listen to whatever he was saying. I had been far too desperate, but I didn't entirely blame myself. I couldn't. My world had been shattered.

I slowly took my elbow off of him and stepped backwards. I reached out with my hand but promptly brought it back down. I felt immense guilt.

"I'm sorry. I don't know what I was thinking."

"It's fine," Ivan muttered.

"Fuck, Damian. Why do I even try to help you?" Sebastian lunged forward with his machete out. He charged forward to impale Ivan, but I tackled him down through his side. I struggled to grab the weapon, but he was overpowering me. He was dragging our intertwined fists towards my face. The tip of the machete was getting closer and closer. One strong push and I'd lose an eye…or worse.

"Stop this shit!" I yelled.

"He's the one! He raped her and he murdered her! He was jealous!"

A sudden boot kick met Sebastian's temple with great ferocity. It caused him to drop the weapon. I hastily grabbed it and pressed it against his neck. Ivan was gripping my shoulders, preventing me from digging deeper into his vulnerable throat.

"I'm gonna kill him. Let me slit his throat. Let me finally end this. He deserves it."

"No! Don't! Gamble will throw you in prison. Our entire investigation will be fucked. Better if we don't involve the police."

"What the hell are we supposed to do with him?" I asked.

"Why don't you take the stupid thing off my neck before you accidentally puncture me and kill me?" Sebastian groaned.

"You're lucky that Ivan's here," I warned as I lifted the machete.

"Trust me, I don't want him around either. Gunner is the scum of the earth."

Sebastian suddenly threw me off of him and made a mad dash for it. I tried to grab his foot but missed. I wanted to run after him, but Ivan held me back.

"Let him go. You'll kill him and I don't know if I'll be able to stop you. Don't go to that dark place."

"God damn it, Ivan. We could've at least tied him to a tree. What if he keeps hindering our investigation?"

"He's a drug addict. I don't think we'll have to worry about him. He was obviously on something. He brought a machete. He's a lunatic who thought he was going to convince you that I killed your wife."

"Ivan, I need to know. What was the secret? What did my wife tell you?"

He sighed and leaned against a jagged rock. He stared at the ground and took a minute before answering.

"You're not going to like this at all."

"That's obvious," I replied.

"I saw someone touch her. In a way they shouldn't have."

"Jesus. When?"

"I was swinging by your house one day. I saw them on the front porch. You were working. There was a man with Scarlett. I saw his face but I didn't know who he was back then. Scarlett never told me a name. He hugged her and slapped her butt. He then squeezed it. It was very fucked up. She pushed him off and slapped his face, hard. No surprise there."

My chest was bubbling and raging with sheer fury. Why did degenerate men feel like they could have their way with my wife? Just because she was a beautiful woman, didn't give anyone the right to disrespect her in such a vile way. I knew she didn't like it when I would get overprotective, but it was necessary. I was the reason why she died. I would carry that heaving chest of guilt within me for the rest of my life.

My mind began to race on who it could've been. I remembered her stepfather. The man I worked for. The man who was rumored to have his way with women.

"Who was it? It was that spineless shit, wasn't it? Abel Armoni. He's the only man who could've gotten that close to her."

"No."

"What?" My heart dropped.

"It was Michael Madden."

# CHAPTER 9

I weaved in and out of traffic lanes while Ivan hung on for dear life in the passenger seat. I had my hands firmly on the steering wheel with a keen eye on the cars zooming around me. On more than one occasion, Abel had pressured me into getting him to a hotel or a safe house quickly. He usually had important business meetings in hotels. The safe house was another story. Whenever Abel suspected that someone was trying to take out a hit on him, he'd order me to take him to a place only I knew of. For whatever reason, he trusted me. I never aired out my grievances with him out loud and I always obeyed him. I was loyal. It was worth something. He was a man of power and influence, after all. Many cars were on that very road because they were rushing to get to the famed *Armoni* nightclub. Otherwise, it would've been deserted.

"Do you have to drive so fast?" Ivan inquired.

"You should've told me."

"I only recognized him at the apartment. I didn't tell you because I knew you would've killed him. I'm trying to keep you out of jail. You can't fall apart. Not like me."

"While we were wasting time with that fucking moron, we could've been interrogating Michael Madden. The man who assaulted my wife!" I swerved around a honking truck and sped up, narrowly dodging a turning motorcyclist.

"It wasn't a waste of time. We can cross his name off the list of suspects. Despite everything, he apparently loved her. I don't think he killed her or stalked her."

"He's not smart enough for that. He can't even stay sober for more than 12 hours."

I emphatically beeped at a slow-moving van in front of me. An elderly woman stuck out her hand and flicked me off. I maneuvered around and returned the favor.

"Classy," Ivan commented.

"When were you planning on telling me that secret?"

"Right after the church. I swear. I wanted to pursue him just as much as you. I was trying to figure out a way to confront him without cracking his skull."

"Why didn't Scarlett want you to tell me about your meetings with her?"

"She didn't want to worry you. She loved you, man. I could tell when I talked to her. There was nothing but love in her eyes whenever your name was spoken."

"She must've threatened you with something bad for you not to tell me a single thing."

"She said she would've told you that I tried to sleep with her."

"Jesus Christ, Scarlett."

"She *really* wanted me to keep my mouth shut."

"Sounds just like her."

"Madden also gave her something. I saw it. It looked like some sort of paper document. Scarlett kept quiet about that too."

"Document? What the hell is going on?" I asked myself.

We reached Snell Lane and I screeched my car to a halt. I parked down the street and jogged over to house 0905, Madden's place. It was dark out. The streetlights were burnt out. We reached the front porch. I looked in through a crack in the blinds of the front window. It was pitch black.

"I don't think he's home. There's no car."

"Shit. I think he bolted."

"You think we spooked him?" I turned the knob of his front door. It was open.

"I think we might've scared him off." Ivan scanned the street behind us. He made sure no one was looking.

"I hope not. Looks like he never fixed the door."

We cautiously entered. We used the flashlight from our phones to navigate through the giant mess he had left in his wake. Clothes, cardboard boxes and empty cans of food were thrown all over the place. It looked like a tornado had ravaged through his whole house.

"Looks even messier than last time."

"I wanna take a look around. Maybe we'll find something." I began sifting through the couch cushions, underneath piles of clothes, through desks, drawers, cabinets and anything else that could give me more information about him. I needed to know why he was at my house with Scarlett that day and what he gave her. Ivan searched his bedroom.

"He's definitely gone. The closet's empty," he called out.

"Shit. Do you think he left town?"

"It's possible."

"We had him and he slipped right through our fingers."

Ivan came back with a yearbook and some half-torn papers in his hand.

"My bad man. It's my fault."

"It doesn't matter now. What do you have there?"

Ivan opened the yearbook and flipped through the pages. He pointed at Scarlett's high school photo. It was circled.

"Michael had this under his bed. He might've forgotten about it. She's circled. Obviously suspicious, but there's a few other girls circled as well. Victoria Cole is circled too. They all have one thing in common. They're pretty."

"He could've circled them because of that or because…they're targets? Victims?"

"I don't know. We need to find out more about him and I think we have a way." Ivan passed me a half-torn paper. It was a crumpled tax document from *Armoni Ventures LLC*. It had his name on it and his earnings from a few years ago.

"He worked for Abel?"

"That was stuffed in his nightstand at the bottom of a million other random documents. The guy is a mess."

"Abel has so many people on his payroll. I know he doesn't work at the club. He might've done maintenance for his house."

"Maybe he's an errand boy."

The thought struck me like lightning. I nodded. That was a possibility that made sense.

"Abel gave money to Scarlett every month. That thing Michael gave her could've been a check."

"Why a check?"

"Maybe he sent Michael to check up on her. Abel doesn't behave like a normal person. Who knows what his reasons are."

"We should get out of here. How the hell are we gonna find Madden?"

"We ask my boss. I have a job tomorrow."

---

Abel had a rousing speech to give at *Deacon V. Snow University*. It was a sprawling campus with large, stone buildings and a central plaza filled with picnic tables and an indoor gym. The exterior surroundings housed a sandy volleyball court, a yoga square and an outdoor swimming pool. Abel was situated on a makeshift podium near the front gates of the university. Several rows of foldable chairs were perfectly lined up in front of him. Many college students attended and attentively listened to what he had to say.

I stood near Ringo and a few other members of Abel's personnel to stand guard. Dani was seated in the front, next to Ivan. It was a cloudy day and I aimlessly gazed at the stormy sky, lost in thought. I thought about Scarlett and that fateful night. I replayed our argument over and over again. I saw it in my head like a grainy video that kept rewinding. I thought about all the ways I could've ended the argument. All the possible ways I could've prevented her tragic death. All the ways I could've saved her. A heavy ball of guilt weighed at the pit of my stomach. Those feelings came and went as the days dragged on. It would only go away at the end of my vengeance-fueled task when all was said and done.

My head began to throb. I had to stop thinking about her. I found myself forgetting small details about that day. There was details I shouldn't have forgotten. I had a minor form of memory loss. Something I never wanted to acknowledge. My biggest worry was the man that I saw the night my wife was killed. I truly couldn't remember if he was even there that day, or if I had seen him another night. I was confusing myself and running out of time.

I tuned Abel out until the end of his speech.

"You have to stay obsessed and hungry in everything you do. I fought tooth and nail for everything I ever earned. I pioneered and innovated live entertainment when I opened up the *Armoni* nightclub in Rainfall. A dead-end small town? Not on my watch! I revived the party scene in this town. I resurrected tourism in this great place where we live. I am Abel Armoni and everyone in Rainfall knows my name!" Abel shouted.

An inspirational story for anyone who *didn't* know the real Abel Armoni. A quick online search told you that he expanded the Armoni empire to greatness and immeasurable wealth. If you dug in deeper, you saw that he inherited it from his father. All he was doing was riding his coattails and pretending to be someone he wasn't. He used his privilege to conceal the scandalous, allegedly criminal acts he was committing against women. That became clear as time went on. He was a deeply insecure man who didn't take no for an answer. I caught him staring at a few college volleyball players skipping to the outdoor court. He stared at them like they were a buffet. My mind wandered to Scarlett. How often did he look at her like that? I noticed for a flash that Victoria Cole was watching him from a distance away. She was concealing her face. I quietly wondered what was going on with her.

There was scattered applause as Abel slithered off stage. He motioned for Ringo and I to follow him. The other men with us went to get the Phantom. We escorted him to the front gates and waited.

"That was a great speech, boss."

"Those fucking college brats. They didn't understand the value I was delivering for free. I'm never doing this shit again. I tried to instill inspiration. I felt I presented a compelling discussion to the audience. What do I get? A girl in a wheelchair clapping for me in the front. How does that make me feel? Terrible. What is she going to accomplish? She can't even bear children. Fucking worthless. If it were up to me, I'd shove her in a box and float her down a river. Get rid of the weak early and there'll be no problems down the line."

"I understand."

*I can't wait for the day someone shoves you in a box.*

"Do you understand? Ugh. Whatever. Where's the fucking car? How long does it take to bring a car around?" Abel whined.

"Sir, what do you know about a Michael Madden?"

"Hmm? Hurry the fuck up, Brandon! I'm dehydrated and I'm not gonna drink the water they brought out. Cheap shit!" he furiously shouted into his phone.

I took a deep breath and glanced at Ivan. He gave me a blank thumbs up.

"Do you know an employee named Michael Madden?"

Abel fumbled his phone and almost dropped it. I caught it for him and carefully placed it back into his hand. He nervously glanced at me and nodded.

"Sorry, thanks. It's so god damn humid today. Rainfall, right? Never stops raining. So, Michael Marshall?"

"Madden."

"I think he used to work for me as a towel boy or something. When I'd go to the tennis courts to exercise. I don't remember. Maybe Soraya hired him to clean her toilets. I don't know. I have a thousand employees on the payroll."

"Does he still work for you?"

The Phantom came around. Ringo nodded at me and escorted Abel to the car as he took a business call. I turned and searched for Ivan. He was sitting at a picnic table with an umbrella. Dani was with him.

"Hey you," Dani winked. I warmly grinned. Something I hadn't done in a long time.

"I told her about Michael Madden," Ivan mentioned.

"I know him. He used to drop off checks to Scarlett for Abel."

"I knew it. I don't get it. Why is this news to me?"

"She quickly ended it and asked for the money to be transferred online. It was such a mundane thing. I thought you knew about it."

"Maybe Scarlett thought it was a mundane thing too."

"We're just analyzing anything of interest. Everything we didn't know about Scarlett automatically raises questions because…"

"She was brutally murdered," I finished.

"I'll tell you why Scarlett forced Abel to give her the money online. I didn't know this at the time but Michael was a pervert and a creep. He would make sexually inappropriate comments towards her. Abel didn't seem to care but he abided by his stepdaughter's wishes. Awesome guy, right?"

I curled my hands into fists and pressed them onto the table. Scarlett had been sexually harassed her whole life. She felt what Michael had done to her was *mundane*. When something horrible happened to you that often, it became ordinary.

"He also touched her ass and fondled it. He abused her. Who knows what else he did to her?" I wondered aloud.

"You're kidding. I'm so sorry," Dani offered, placing her hand on mine. I stared at her pink, acrylic nails. She was very different from Scarlett. Scarlett had a simpler, subdued sense of style. She exuded beauty through the long, elegant dresses she would wear. She'd wear small diamond earrings and a gold-plated bracelet on our late-night dates.

Dani's style was more vibrant and outspoken. She wore nose piercings, multiple golden rings on her fingers and usually dyed the tips of her hair. She liked red, pink and blonde. Both were quite different on the outside, but looking in, they shared many qualities. Most of all, they were both great women who deserved more.

"They treated my wife like some sort of rag doll or toy. She deserved none of it," I angrily muttered.

"We went to his place, Dani. It looks like he skipped town or he's hiding somewhere. Any ideas?" Ivan asked.

"He could be at *Frank's Motel*. Some junkies go there to smoke crack. Michael was definitely an addict. He's been there a few times. I bailed him out, when I shouldn't have. Abel made me."

"So, Abel does know him well?" Ivan asked.

"He should. He used to clean his boat and I'm pretty sure he supplied him with drugs."

"Do you think Gunner knows him?" Ivan scoffed.

"My ex-boyfriend, Sebastian Gunner? Probably. He's a complete asshole."

"Scarlett dated him too. Don't feel too bad," I briefly squeezed her shoulder.

"Let's hope this guy is still alive," Ivan commented.

"He better be." I slid out my phone and typed in the motel. It wasn't far from the university.

Dani stood up and slung her designer bag over her shoulder.

"Good luck guys. I'm meeting someone for lunch."

"The same loser?"

Dani shook her head at me.

"He's *not* a loser. He's a good guy. I told you this already."

"The guy's name is John Santoro, Ivan."

"That sounds made up. You're dating a pedophile, Dani."

"At least he makes me feel protected. I've been feeling weird these last few weeks. Like someone is watching me or following me. I don't know. I'm probably crazy. I told Damian about it."

"If you ever see anyone, tell me. I'll take care of it," I promised.

"Yeah, we'll rip out their intestines," Ivan chimed in.

"Oh my god. Goodbye, freaks. You're perfect for each other," Dani smirked at us and strode away.

"You think someone's following her?" Ivan asked.

"I don't know. It could be true. I certainly hope not. It's this town, Ivan. That *Rainfall Abductor* psycho has everyone on edge. It's hysteria."

"If you say so."

"I hope that *John Santoro* guy isn't a jackass. Dani deserves someone decent."

"Someone decent huh? You're not moving on *that* quickly, are you?"

"You're insane. She's just a friend. Scarlett can't be replaced," I smacked Ivan's arm.

"I thought so. I still haven't moved on from Lisandra. I don't know if I ever will. Sometimes…I just wanna know that she's dead. Just to know. Am I horrible?"

"There's no handbook for tragedy. You cope with it any way you can. Why else would we get up in the morning? You're not evil for wanting to know."

"Sometimes...sometimes I dream that she might be alive. I don't know. It's silly."

"Nothing's silly about that, Ivan. If she's alive...we'll find her."

---

I parked backwards into an open space in the pot-hole ridden lot of *Frank's Motel*. It had a simple, single-story layout and a row of rooms facing the parking lot. Ivan and I had dressed in our *Pierce Security* uniforms. I had planned to question the motel's manager for any information on Michael Madden. Ivan wanted to stake it out for a few hours first to see if he came out. He had insisted.

"Why don't we talk to the manager first? We don't even know if he's here."

"Sometimes you get lucky. Better if we don't have to talk to a manager. I don't want to draw too much attention. This place has a lot of witnesses. Madden's neighborhood and the old church were empty."

"This is a waste of time," I grumbled.

"This whole thing can be a waste of time. We don't know if we'll find your wife's stalker. Who knows? Maybe the person who stalked your wife and the person who murdered her, are two completely different people."

"I doubt it."

I had considered the possibility in passing, but it didn't make sense. Who else would have the drive and the motivation to kill her? She was also sexually assaulted. I just knew that her demented stalker had been lusting after her for years. He finally got the chance that night...and ruined her life.

From where we were parked, the parking lot was adjacent to many of the motel rooms available for booking. I scanned the motel guests who walked in and out of those rooms. I saw a man who looked familiar. A man I had seen before. He had curly brown hair and dark eyes. He had entered the club on the day someone tried to stab Abel. He scurried past us, out of view, into the abandoned warehouse next to the motel.

*Druggies.*

I then spotted someone I knew too well. I sprang up as my chest tightened with shock. It felt like a volley of ice water had pooled in my stomach. If I blinked I would've missed it. Michael Madden briefly looked out his door then slammed it shut. It was room 104. Someone else had exited his room. Sebastian Gunner. I gripped Ivan's arm and pointed towards him. He looked suspicious and was wearing a black hoodie.

"Shit, that's Gunner."

"He fucking knows Madden."

Without hesitation, I pulled out my revolver from my glove box and stuffed it inside my pants. I flew out of the driver's door as Ivan fiercely whispered *no!*

"I'm tired of waiting," I replied as I shut the door. I wasn't going to let someone else go. I didn't hear if Ivan had also exited the car. Blood was rushing to my ears as I quietly caught up to Sebastian and slowly pulled out my gun. I quickly glanced around and saw that no one was paying attention. A young, goth couple were smoking near the entrance of the swimming pool. A homeless man was digging food out of a trash can. An older gentleman in swim trunks was laughing and talking with a younger woman in a bikini. They both looked high on something. There was nothing to worry about. Everyone was minding their own damn business like I suspected. People often think other people notice them more than they actually do. Ivan's extreme use of caution was unfounded.

I swung my gun underneath my shirt to conceal it. I pressed it against Sebastian's back while I walked beside him. He was startled and stopped moving. He wanted to turn to me but I shoved him forward.

"Don't turn around. Go to the bathroom."

"Who...who are you? What the fuck? What the fuck is this?"

"Go or I'll put a fucking bullet in your spine. Stay close. Move naturally. Don't call for help," I quietly warned.

After a few, nerve-shredding steps we reached the public bathroom that was situated to the side of the motel. As soon as I entered, I locked the door behind me. It was a single-stall bathroom with a cracked mirror and a blackened sink. It reeked of urine and marijuana. I pushed Sebastian forward and pointed the gun squarely at his head. He slowly turned with his hands up.

"Oh, fuck you. Damian? What the fuck? Are you following me?"

"What are you doing here?"

"Fuck off dude. Let me go, I'm busy," Sebastian grumbled.

"If you move an inch, you're in the ground," I threatened.

Sebastian rolled his eyes and stood still.

"I'm conducting business, providing a service...selling drugs. Whatever you wanna call it. As you can hopefully tell, this place is a druggy shithole and it's crawling with my customers."

"I saw you get out of Michael Madden's room. You lied. You know him."

Sebastian shook his head.

"I didn't know him until recently. I asked about him after the church. It turns out that I know some of his friends. They all vouched for him. He was drunk and lost. The last thing he was worried about was Scarlett. He didn't even know her."

"You idiot. He did know her. He worked for Abel Armoni. He used to drop off checks for her. He sexually assaulted her. He knew her well, Sebastian. They either fooled you or you're still stuck on Ivan. Let that go. It was *not* him."

Sebastian's eyes widened as he stared at the floor. He was dumbfounded.

"No way. Prove it to me."

"I don't have to prove anything to you. She was my wife. Do you think I'm playing around? I want you to think for once. Who makes more sense? Ivan or Madden?"

"Look, I know you hate my guts but...we want the same thing. I...I feel guilty about what I did to Scarlett when we were together. I want to make it right. If you're saying Madden had something to do with this...I believe you."

"He was arrested after all, Sebastian. Sometimes the answer you're looking for is the most obvious one."

"What do you want me to do then?"

"We're going to go to his room. You knock and tell him it's you."

"I was just there," Sebastian whined.

"*Let's go,*" I raised the gun and took off the safety. Sebastian swallowed and softly nodded. I unlocked the bathroom door and led Sebastian towards room 104 in the exact same way. I glanced towards Ivan, who was in the car. He got out and gave me a sour look. I mouthed *wait*. He hung back. We reached Madden's room. Sebastian hesitantly knocked. A minute later, Michael opened.

"Yeah? What's up? You forget something?" Michael asked.

"I...do you want more pot?"

"What? Are you okay dude? You already gave me what I needed."

Sebastian suddenly backed into me to throw me off balance and sprinted away. I didn't have the nerve to shoot, especially in a public place like that. Michael saw me and froze. I took the split-second opportunity to bust through the door. I shoved him down and fully expected to hear the door slam behind me. Fear burned in my chest as I swung around with my gun pointing forward. It was Ivan. He had held it. He came inside and quietly shut it. He motioned for me to put it down. I did and redirected my attention towards Michael who was shivering on the floor. He started blubbering and crying. Ivan and I anxiously glanced at each other as his face turned beet red.

The room reeked of rotten food and pot residue. There was a half-opened luggage bag on the floor with clothes, towels and household items spilling out. The bed wasn't made and the white sheets were on the ground. I pulled out a brown chair from a small wooden desk and sat down. I nonchalantly kept my gun on Michael as he fearfully gawked at me.

"That was stupid, Damian," Ivan sighed.

"I wasn't going to let Madden go again. If you didn't lie to me, we wouldn't be here."

"If I told you, he'd be dead."

"He's not dead now, is he?"

"Why haven't you shot him?" Ivan asked.

"I need the truth first. I need to know what happened."

"Gunner's long gone. I didn't want to get near him," Ivan mentioned.

"We don't need him anymore. Did anyone see that commotion outside?"

"I don't know. Anyone could've saw. They saw Gunner running for sure. Let's just say we have a few minutes before the police barge in here."

"Why'd you leave your house, Madden?"

"I...I...I was afraid," Michael sobbed.

"Why would you be afraid if you didn't do anything wrong? Why do you feel guilty?" I questioned.

Michael rubbed his bloodshot eyes with his stained shirt.

"No, no, no, no, no, no. I knew this would happen. The cops arrested me once. Then you guys came around. I didn't do it. I swear I didn't."

"Explain it to us, man. What happened that night? We went through your place. Your old yearbook had Scarlett circled. Other girls, too, like Victoria Cole. Why?" Ivan inquired.

"I...I just found them hot. I swear! I'm sorry. That was all."

It was hard to get a read on Michael. He could've been completely innocent or completely guilty. The incessant crying wasn't helping his case.

"You're crying so hard, you can barely breathe. Tell me what happened that night or I'm going to assume that you're lying to me. You're not going to live much longer if you don't tell me the truth," I warned.

I got up and inched closer to him. I stared down at him with an icy gaze. Ivan remained quiet.

"Someone made me do it!" Michael blurted out.

"Made you do what?" Ivan stepped forward.

"Take the fall for her murder. They said I wouldn't actually be jailed or charged because there was no evidence. I didn't do it. I'm telling you. I'm sorry. I was scared."

"Who scared you?"

"They just wanted the police to think it was me. They...they wanted to take attention away from...from them." Michael was breathing hard.

"Michael, who was it?" I urged.

"I'm really sorry about your wife. I've done terrible things. Really bad things."

I bent over and slammed the side of his head with my revolver. He cried out. I was about to go again but Ivan held me back.

"Stop! Don't do it. You'll kill him. If you keep going, I know you won't stop."

"I should kill him. You touched my wife, you fucking animal! I should crush your head until your brain falls out," I growled.

"I'm sorry, I'm sorry. I'm sorry, Damian," Michael clutched his head while he groaned in pain.

"Your apologies don't mean shit to me," I replied angrily.

Michael blinked rapidly and stared at the ceiling. He looked delirious.

"I shot that girl. All those years ago. The concert. I knew that I knew you. You were there. You chased me. This is my karma. This is my fucking karma," Michael whispered to himself.

"He's clearly on something," Ivan mumbled.

An ice-cold shiver ran down my spine. It was him. All those years ago at the *Skeleton Crew* concert. It had been him.

"It was him, Ivan. At the *Skeleton Crew* concert. He shot that girl. He almost killed me. That son of a bitch. He's the reason I took the job with Armoni. A job I've hated since the day I took it."

"Holy shit." Ivan let go of me and got a closer look at Michael.

"They'll kill me. They already warned me. They'll rip out my insides and lay them on my roof like string cheese. That's what they said," Michael gasped.

"I'll rip out your insides, if you don't tell me who's *they*."

"I...I don't remember," Michael whispered.

The faint sound of police sirens roared outside. It was getting closer and closer.

"Yep, someone saw and called the cops. We need to get the hell out of here. This is considered kidnapping, amongst many other illegal things."

We swiftly brought him up and pushed him forward. I put my gun away to keep him calm and told him to keep moving. We opened the door and turned right. All we needed to do was turn the corner to get out of sight. I needed it to go as smoothly as possible. As soon as we were out of view, Michael fell to the floor. We tried to get him up but he refused.

"Michael, get up! We need to get out of here!" I whispered ferociously.

"No...you all want to kill me. All of you!" Michael hissed.

He chomped down on my hand when I grabbed his arm. I pulled back and cursed to myself. Ivan lost his grip on his leg which allowed Michael to go towards the encroaching police cruisers.

"*Fuck,*" I blurted out.

"They're here, Damian. What the hell do we do?"

Before I could think of our next move, I heard violent shouting and yelling. I tried to make out what was going on but it was all incoherent. I only managed to grasp some orders the police were barking out.

*Show me your hands!*

*Don't come closer!*

*Are you armed?!*

That last one sounded familiar. It had to be Detective Gamble. I scurried towards the corner and peeked out. Sure enough, there were several police officers struggling to contain Michael. They were in front of their police cars, grappling on the street inside the motel's plaza. Michael was yelling like a lunatic and had something in his hand. I focused my vision and saw that he had managed to get a gun.

*A fucking gun.*

It was a scene of complete chaos and imminent danger. My heart raced as I watched on in anticipation. I knew it wasn't going to end well and I didn't know what to do. It all felt longer than it actually was. The whole deadly confrontation lasted less than a minute. All I remembered hearing before the gunshot was *no!* It had been Detective Gamble. The gunshot thundered and tore through the silence of the sky like a razor-sharp knife. It echoed and set off a few car alarms. We all stared at the dark red, lifeless remains of Michael's shattered head as it bled on the blood-splattered street.

He had shot himself or the gun went off at the precise moment where it was aimed at Michael's head. It didn't matter. Michael Madden was dead. Perhaps my shot at getting answers was too. Ivan and I gave each other somber looks. Despite the horrific things Michael had done, his death had been nothing short of gruesome. It still weighed heavy on my heart. Once the police officers snapped out of their collective shock, they started to form a perimeter and called whomever they needed to call. Michael's shirt had been lifted a bit and Gamble took notice.

Several motel guests approached the deadly scene with morbid curiosity. Most of them quickly turned away. Another batch of older ladies screamed and rushed back to the bingo room. The cops made sure to keep everyone else away. I followed Gamble's eyes which were fixated on Michael's chest. Something had been carved into it. It was a darkened scar. I couldn't see what it said.

"*Killer*," Detective Gamble read aloud.

# CHAPTER 10

I told Ivan that it was probably best if he snuck his way to the car. Detective Gamble had spotted me and I approached him. I couldn't leave. It would've been suspicious considering the extreme circumstances. He gave a command to the officers and we met halfway on the sidewalk near the motel rooms.

"What the hell happened here? What are you doing here?" Detective Gamble asked sternly. I could tell he wasn't in the mood for any games. I had to tread carefully. If he took me in, it would take time away from my manhunt.

"Look, I'm only trying to find the truth surrounding my wife. That's all I want. I'm sure that's what you want too."

"You're lucky we're in the same boat, Damian. I know what you're feeling. An overwhelming sense of loss, grief and the burning question...*why me?*"

"That's what I need to know. You know about Lisandra Pierce? Of course you do. Another victim like Jade. Very similar circumstances. Abducted without a trace. Cold cases with no leads."

"I know that," he grumbled.

"No. There is a lead. My wife's murder. It's connected to them. It has to be. They weren't stalked like Scarlett, but how do we know that for sure? We don't. Maybe whoever did this, is getting bolder and more confident. They abducted a detective's wife successfully and without punishment. My best friend's wife was next and then mine. How much longer before another woman is taken?"

Detective Gamble glanced at the bloody scene and sagged his shoulders. He rubbed the dark circles around his eyes. He was tired, beyond exhaustion. He had most likely been chasing the mystery behind the abductions for years. It had taken its toll. Ivan was the same. I took it upon myself to put their burdens on my shoulders. I still had some fresh anger and drive to go deeper.

"I don't know, Damian. I don't know. Right now I have to deal with this situation. Stay out of legal trouble. Don't get yourself killed."

"Look into him, Detective. He was arrested for a reason."

He nodded. He understood. He started to walk away.

"Hey, one more thing."

He turned around, eyebrows raised.

"This is something I noticed. Scarlett, Lisandra and Jade all had dark hair, tan skin and brown eyes. Maybe it's nothing. Maybe it's something."

Gamble's face scrunched up. He seemed to strongly consider the possibility. He rubbed his chin. He opened his mouth, but an officer called out his name. He quickly turned and attended to him. I entered my car. Ivan was lost in thought while he stared at the scene of Michael's suicide.

"How did a crazy drug addict manage to take an officer's gun and...do that to himself?"

"He was a slippery son of a bitch, like Sebastian. A characteristic of drug addicts, I guess."

"*Killer* was carved into his chest. Did you see that? That's some weird shit, man." Ivan finished drinking a warm water bottle and crushed it against his head. The noise made me feel the back of my own head, where my stitches were. I heard the violent crunch when my skull felt like it had been cracked wide open.

"I need to talk to Dani about Michael. I want to know what else he was up to while employed by Abel. Abel may have been involved too. He's her stepfather and I didn't think he'd stoop that low but I don't know anymore. He's a man who doesn't like to be told no."

"It's not that far fetched. Rich people are freaks."

A chime went off. It was my phone, a text message from Abel. He urgently needed me to drive him to a fancy country club. It was *Armoni's Wine Night*.

"Perfect, Abel needs me tonight. Dani will be there. It's a special event at the *Green Meadows Country Club*."

"I'm guessing I'm not invited."

"You wouldn't want to be. It's going to be dreadful. Soraya's gonna be there."

"I'll see if I can track down some other leads in the mean time."

As soon as Abel entered the car, he was pissed off. I made sure to turn down the volume of the radio music, because loud music gave him *hives*. He was shouting into his phone and I chose to remain quiet. I drove at a moderate pace and tried to ignore his unfiltered barbarism.

"This is such bullshit! I don't want to go to that shithole. Marty is the most pretentious idiot I've ever met, but he has money. So, of course I have to go because apparently I need funding. Sometimes I wanna tell my father's financial monkeys to fuck off. They're older than the fucking dinosaurs."

I arrived at the country club and it was as extravagant as I imagined. The grounds were lush and well-maintained. The front entrance welcomed visitors with manicured lawns, immaculate landscaping and a regal clubhouse. Expansive golf courses with rigorously groomed rolling greens and fairways stood out, catching my eye. Rows of tennis courts sat a few yards away from a massive swimming pool. It featured cascading fountains with a rock grotto waterfall. Palm trees were planted around the private cabanas with billowing curtains. Wealthy folks either played volleyball in the pool, basked in the sun or relaxed underneath the shade of oversized umbrellas on sun loungers.

*I hate rich people.*

I escorted Abel inside. We entered a grand banquet hall that was fit for a royal wedding. Tall, ornate doors led into a vast foyer embellished with chandeliers that casted a golden glow. Polished marble floors reflected the shimmering light. As we stepped into the main hall I noticed the high ceilings with elaborate moldings. The decorative tables had fine linens, crystal glassware, and floral arrangements. It was a prestigious display of over-the-top grandeur. It was sickening. I couldn't wait to get the hell out.

I searched the hall for Dani. She wasn't answering her phone, which was strange. In the midst of my search I spotted Soraya Armoni-Santoro, Scarlett's mother. I did a double take and almost jettisoned out of there the instant I laid eyes on her. The last time I saw her was Scarlett's funeral. She caused a lot of strife between Scarlett and I in our relationship. She never thought I was good enough for her and didn't like the fact that I supported her artistic dreams. She thought I had been faking it to get in her pants. She couldn't have been more wrong. She had wanted Scarlett to become a lawyer or a nurse. *Something that actually contributed to society*, she'd say.

I sat down at an empty table near a wall that had an embroidered, floral design. I rolled my eyes. Our views crossed and she gave me a somber grin. I was shocked. I thought she would've ignored me, but no. She glided towards me. She was wearing a long, silver dress and had neatly braided hair that was embellished with a crystal hairpiece. She was her daughter's twin. The only difference was that Soraya's hair was darker and her face had clear signs of age. Soraya still maintained her air of elegance as she always did.

As she came closer, I grew more anxious. A whirlwind of dread stormed in my stomach as she sat down next to me. Soraya's scent was flowery, sweet and intoxicating. She was a woman who made her presence known. It was the main reason why Abel married her. Soraya knew how to charm any man into obedience. Scarlett was similar, but kinder. She was rough around the edges too, like myself. She resented her mother's *pretentiousness.*

"Damian. How are you?" She asked in a slight accent.

Soraya's native language was Spanish, but she had learned English well, just like Scarlett. Life had been an uphill battle for the both of them. If anything, Scarlett had inherited her mother's tenacity.

"I've been fine. You?"

"Horribly depressed, Damian. My daughter was viciously taken from me. I blame you for it. I want you to know that," Soraya intently stared at me, unflinching. It was like her eyes were made of ice. I squirmed in my seat. I had no issue holding a blade to the hulking brute that was Sebastian Gunner. Why did I feel like running away when it came to my former mother-in-law?

"I'm...I'm sorry," I squeaked out.

"I don't care about your apologies. I want you to make this right."

"I'm trying to, Soraya. I swear it to you. I am," I held her solemn gaze.

"I believe you."

Sudden cheering and applause overtook the room. Abel stood up at the front of the hall near a large wine barrel that had been converted into a table with a glass panel. It had several artisanal wine bottles on display. He began talking about them, one by one.

"You like wine, right?"

"Forget about the wine. This whole event is a waste of my time," Soraya whispered.

"I see."

"I need to tell you something very important and you're going to listen to me."

My skin crawled and I felt shivers erupt all over my body. My gut instructed me to pay close attention to what Soraya was about to say. I scooted closer to her. She leaned in.

"I caught my husband looking at pictures of Scarlett in a swimsuit. They were zoomed in. He thought he was alone in the house. I was behind him."

My heart began to pound. I worriedly looked at Soraya then at Abel. I imagined pummeling his head into mush. All I saw was red.

"Did he see you?"

"He didn't think I noticed, but I did. I heard many rumors throughout the years but never any evidence. Now I'm suspecting that his past involves NDAs with these women, whoever they are."

"Let me get this straight, you believe that he has sexually harassed these women?"

"Yes, but even further than that. Damian, I'm an honest woman and I don't mind telling you the truth. I think you've heard the open secret that I married him for his money. I really didn't know he was capable of these things...or maybe I did and I was lying to myself. I chose to put blinders over my eyes until it involved the one person I loved most...my daughter."

Soraya's eyes began to water and I sincerely felt for her. They didn't get along, but Soraya did love Scarlett. A mother's unconditional love for their children transcended everything. I was never lucky enough to experience that.

"I loved her too," I offered her a handkerchief from the table. She took it and patted her eyes.

"My husband knew Jade Gamble as well. She used to come to these types of events with her husband, Albert. The detective."

"Really?"

Things were starting to pile up against Abel. It all seemed to unravel at that event. What he had allegedly done and what he was capable of. The fact that he was ogling his own stepdaughter was enough to make me severely sick to my stomach.

"When she disappeared, Albert stopped coming. Everyone believed that she had been abducted."

"What do you believe?"

"I believe she was taken too."

"Do you know if Gamble ever spoke to Abel?"

"In a general sense, yes. He spoke to all known associates and friends of Jade. There was no evidence of any wrongdoing on Abel's behalf so naturally he was let go."

"Why do you think he was involved?"

"Apparently he used to harass her. These are the rumors that have gone around in my social circles. Abel's *friends*. They know how he really is, but nobody says anything. They're either afraid or they don't want to lose their stream of income. There are many hands in the Armoni family's pot of wealth," Soraya explained.

I couldn't believe what I was hearing. What the hell had Abel been up to?

"This is very alarming information, Soraya. May I ask why you're telling me this now?"

"Well, my daughter's death has made me re-think a lot of things. I look at life a little differently now. I'm sure you can understand. I just want the truth, Damian. That's all I want for my girl."

"I will find it. I promise you."

Soraya gently took my hand and squeezed it.

"After Scarlett died, Albert talked to me. He mentioned you. He told me that he could tell that you were a man who truly loved his wife. I've known Albert for a long time. I'm inclined to believe him."

"Thank you, Soraya. I respect him. We unfortunately have something very tragic in common."

Soraya leaned back and smiled. A mob of young women holding their phones out, suddenly stormed into the hall. A couple of security guards were shouting at them to get back but they had been able to power through. I sprang up along with the other guests as we watched the chaos unfold. I heard a dry laugh beside me. It had come from Soraya. I looked at her and she winked at me.

"My husband is a pervert. This town deserves to know the truth."

"You did this?"

The group of girls began to chant. They were led by Victoria Cole. *Abel harasses women! Abel abuses women! Abel rapes women! Abel rapes women! Abel rapes women! Abel rapes women! Abel rapes women!*

I couldn't believe what I was hearing. It was like being in an alcoholic haze.

"I went to *Deacon V. Snow University* and found a group of incendiary college students who hate the rich. I offered them a lot of money, this address and the opportunity to publicly humiliate someone they absolutely loathed. A woman named Victoria Cole seemed personally invested. She used to work for him in the *Crimson Lounge*."

"Holy shit," I muttered.

Abel nervously laughed and froze. A few country club employees attempted to drive back the angry mob along with the security guards. A violent shoving match ensued with screaming and shouting. One of the girls pushed an employee into the dinner table of a rich couple, shattering it and causing a huge mess. The elderly woman shrieked while her husband fell down. All the guests began making a hasty exit. Abel dashed away, along the wall as the alcoholic bottles he was showcasing were being catapulted towards him, shattering against the wall and spilling onto the floor.

*Tell the truth Abel!*

*How many women have you assaulted?!*

*Where's your assistant?!*

*Where's Dani Shepherd?!*

*She knows the truth!*

*Your wife knows the truth!*

*You can't hide anymore!*

It was a scene of total mayhem and disorder. My head throbbed as my vision began to blur. I saw the man who watched in the corner of the room. The lips on his blurred face curved into a cruel smile.

He looked familiar. I knew I was imagining it, but it was someone I knew. I felt like I was being haunted.

Abel's shell-shocked face appeared in front of me. He gripped both of my arms. I snapped out of it.

"Damian! Damian! Get me the fuck out of here!" Abel shouted, sheer panic in his voice.

"What about Soraya?"

I looked down and saw that she was gone.

"Take me to the car!" Abel commanded.

I instinctively escorted him out of the hall, through a side door. We rushed down a narrow hallway to make it to the exit. We heard stomping behind us. They were following us.

"Fuck, fuck, fuck, fuck, fuck!" Abel whined.

I tackled the door open and made it to the front entrance where the valet service was. A valet driver had brought Abel's car around. I shoved my hand into my pocket, pulled out a twenty and placed it in the valet's hand. Abel threw himself inside the backseat of the car. I slipped into the driver's seat and zoomed away.

As I tried my best to get as far away from the country club as possible, a thought occurred into my head. Where was Dani? Why hadn't she been there? Why wasn't she answering her phone? It started to rain and the raindrops slammed onto the car's windshield like rockfall. I acted fast and turned on the wipers. I swerved through beeping cars and skidded a couple of times. I held onto the steering wheel so tightly, I felt the blood rushing through the palms of my hands.

"You gotta get me the hell out of town, Damian. Fuck! I'm already blowing up on the socials. These bullshit videos are going viral. People are calling me the town rapist. Fucking Victoria Cole. She used to work for me. She has no idea who I am. Can you believe this shit?! No evidence, no witnesses, no testimonies! Just false and incendiary accusations being hurled at me left and right. I'm going to sue all those good-for-nothing whores for defamation of character. If they wanna fuck with me, I'll fuck them right back!" Abel bellowed.

He was beyond enraged. I felt his anger emanating in waves of energy towards me. It looked like his face was on fire from how red it was.

"I'm taking you to the safe house."

"Yes! Good. Great idea. The best idea you've had in your life."

I clenched my teeth. I silently agreed.

"Why were those girls saying those things about you, boss?" I asked.

"What you have to understand about people is that they lie, Damian. They lie through their god damn teeth," Abel snarled.

I understood that perfectly well.

"They're accusing me of touching girls and...raping them?! Have they lost their god damn marbles?! I don't *rape* anyone. I don't rape anyone unless they like it. In that case it's not rape. It's called having good sex. Whatever the fucking case may be...they enjoy it! *All of them!*"

*They were right. Everyone was right. Abel Armoni...you motherfucker.*

"I understand what you're saying, boss. I understand perfectly clear," I muttered.

"I should've brought more security. I didn't know that bullshit was going to happen. It was supposed to be a private event. It was supposed to be closed-off. How did Victoria and those other idiots get inside?!"

"I don't know how that nonsense happened, sir."

"By the way, if my wife calls, don't answer. Don't tell her a god damn word, Damian. I need to get my story straight. I have a lot of people calling me and texting me. I need everyone to leave me the hell alone for a few hours. I'm gonna have a few drinks and relax. I need to think and I need you there to keep watch for anymore gold-digging whores. Fucking women. They're all chicken-brained fucking idiots. *All of them*. Including Scarlett's mother. The apple doesn't fall far from the tree, huh? Good thing you don't have to deal with her shit anymore," Abel scoffed.

*What the fuck did he just say?*

"Are you referring to Scarlett, sir?" The anger was ready to erupt out of my throat.

"I can trust you right? I need people I can trust, Damian." Abel furiously texted away on his phone while his face was still boiling. I swore I saw foam spilling out from the corners of his mouth. It was better that he hadn't heard my question. The car would've been flipped over on his head.

"You can trust me," I lied.

"I know I can. You were Scarlett's husband, after all. You were very desperate, so I knew you were going to do a great job and you have all these years. You don't know too much about me either. You don't ask many questions. You're the perfect employee."

"Thank you."

That was about to change. I took the steep right turn onto the dark, slick road that led to Abel's safe house, a secluded little blue residence that rested near the ocean. There was nothing but rows of trees on my right side while the left was the descending coastline that led to the sea. I slowed down a bit and quietly slipped out my phone. I sent a text to Ivan.

*I need you. Safe house. Hammer. Rope.*

"We're almost there, right? I need a damn drink," Abel whined.

"Yes sir. We'll be there shortly. Will Dani be joining us?"

"No."

There was a pause then a silence. He had nothing else to add.

"May I ask why?"

"She quit and left. She doesn't work for me anymore. How much longer?"

A surge of panic rose in my chest.

"What? What you do mean?"

"She *quit*, Damian. Did you not hear me? How much longer?"

I decided not to press him, but I knew Dani. She'd never quit like that. She'd tell me. She'd talk to me about it. She wouldn't just leave like that. It wasn't like her.

"We're here." The garage opened as I parked inside it. I closed it with the remote control. We had arrived at Abel's safe house. A simplistic, bare-bones house with nothing but canned food, water bottles, alcohol, various tools, flashlights and toilet paper. Abel practically busted the door down while entering. He took one of the few chairs available and sat down. I went to the kitchen and grabbed a wine bottle off the top of the fridge. I uncorked it and handed it to him. He chugged half the bottle and messily wiped his mouth with his sleeve. While his attention was fixed on that, I texted Ivan. He had arrived.

"How are we looking? I'm telling the security team to standby for now."

"Do you want them here?"

That would've been a problem.

"Yes. No! No, no, no. I don't know. Someone leaked...something. Someone's plotting against me. Someone knows. Someone knows what I did," Abel mumbled.

"Sir?"

"Don't do anything yet. I need to see how this plays out. Yeah...I have to be careful. If I'm not...everything...fucking everything...is going to unravel. I'll be ruined, Damian. *Ruined.* My entire career and empire hangs in the balance. I'll put a hit out on that Victoria Cole if I have to."

A door creaked open behind me and shut.

"Who the fuck is that?!" Abel screamed.

"Did you bring it?" I asked.

"I did. You're lucky I still have my bike," Ivan answered.

"Damian?!" Abel bounced up like a frightened squirrel. I lunged forward and grabbed his neck.

"What are you doing? What are you doing, Damian? This is supposed to be a secure safe house!" Abel panicked.

"What I've wanted to do for a very long time." I pulled back my tightly-clenched fist and slugged him right in his jaw. He dropped to the ground and held his face. He spat out blood.

"You...you motherfucker. I thought I could trust you," Abel growled.

Ivan showed up next to me with a black hammer and a pile of rope wrapped around his shoulder. I nodded at him. We grabbed a squirming Abel and pinned him down to the chair. He kicked out his legs like a bratty toddler. Ivan held them down while I tied the rope around him and the chair to keep him in place. He yelled and cursed the entire time.

*You fucking fuckers!*

*Don't fucking touch me! You're not allowed to touch me!*

*I will call the entire U.S. military on you!*

*I will drop bombs on you, you fucking bastards!*

*I'll fucking annihilate you!*

When I was done I took the hammer from Ivan and pretended to hit him. He flinched and stayed quiet.

"I'll rip out your teeth if you keep screaming," I warned.

"Okay. Okay, okay. What...what the fuck do you want? Who's your friend? What the fuck is going on here? Did you set me up? Is that what this is? You planned all of this from the beginning? You're in cahoots with Victoria Cole, aren't you? You slimy, sleazy bag of shit," Abel hissed.

"I'm not, but I seized an opportunity to finally kidnap you. Now I can beat the living shit out of you until you give me what I want," I said coldly.

"That's all good and great, but seriously…what do you want? Are you going to kill me? Oh fuck, you're going to kill me aren't you? Are you holding me for ransom?" Abel quivered in absolute fear. He had no idea what he was in for. I planned to extract every single ounce of information that son of a bitch had. He had done horribly evil things. There wasn't a doubt in my mind about that. Ivan reached into his pocket and took out his phone. I instructed him to unlock it and to disable the GPS.

"What are you doing?" He asked.

"Alrighty, airplane mode on and *Code Green* right?" Ivan asked me.

"*Code Green*. It means that Abel is safe and secure. They are to await further instruction."

"Oh fuck." Abel cursed under his breath.

Ivan continued to search through his phone, to look for anything out of the ordinary.

"I have a lot of questions, Abel. I want the truth from you. If I sense that you're lying, we're gonna have serious issues and you're going to need the dentist."

"He's serious man. He's unhinged. The man lost his wife. What has he got to lose?" Ivan added.

"Okay. I got it. I understand," Abel nervously nodded his head.

"Are you a rapist?"

"Excuse me?" Abel blurted out.

"I won't repeat myself." I slugged him across the face with my fist. Ivan winced. Abel shut his eyes and groaned.

"No. No I'm not."

"Why did those girls call you one then?"

"Mob mentality."

"Why have there been so many rumors, Abel? I've seen you myself. I've seen you feel up Dani. Victoria Cole obviously has something against you. What was going on there?"

"Those...those were mistakes. They were consensual and both situations ended amicably," Abel explained.

"That's complete bullshit," Ivan scoffed.

"Soraya told me that she caught you looking at bikini pictures of Scarlett. Is that true?"

"No! I swear I didn't. I would *never* do that. She was my stepdaughter. I didn't do that, Damian. God dammit, you have to believe me. Why would I do that to my own stepchild?!" Abel pleaded.

I gripped the arms of the chairs and stared into his eyes. He hesitantly met my stony gaze.

"Was it you? Was it you this whole time? Were you the one stalking her?"

"No, Damian. No. I don't steal her underwear and leave boxes at your front doorstep. Are you insane? What possible reason could I have for doing that?"

Fury raged in my chest as I swung the hammer down on his knee. He cried out and clenched his teeth. Ivan gripped my shoulder and pulled me back.

"Hey man. I'm not here to torture the guy. We just need information. That's why we're here."

"He's not going to admit anything unless I beat him within an inch of his life," I snapped.

"We're not going to resort to that. That's barbaric."

"If he did it...he deserves it, Ivan. More than anyone, this motherfucker deserves it. Do you know how many women he's abused? Raped? He's a monster."

"I know, man. You don't think I want him rotting at the bottom of the ocean? Let's just think logically for a second. I didn't find anything weird on his phone. Let me ask the questions. Cool off." Ivan handed me his phone and faced Abel. I placed it down on the kitchen countertop.

He looked up, his face twisted with anguish.

"Please...please don't hurt me. I'll give you whatever you want. I swear."

"We want the truth. What does the name Michael Madden mean to you?"

My mind had been blinded by the rage at what he did to Scarlett that I had almost forgotten about Madden.

"He was just an errand boy. He cleaned my boat. He drove me sometimes. That's all," Abel whimpered.

"He was killed recently. He shot himself in the head. It seemed like whoever scared him really freaked him out. The word *killer* was carved into his chest."

"Jesus fuck...he's dead? Oh god. Oh my god."

"Do you know what he was involved with? Is he Scarlett's murderer?"

"I...I believe so. Yes. He murdered her," Abel whispered.

I stared at him in disgust. He was doing anything he could to slither out of our grasp. I didn't believe him for a second.

"He's lying. He's fucking lying," I stomped towards him.

"I'm not. It was Michael Madden. He raped and murdered Scarlett. That's the truth! I swear, Damian. I swear it!"

"No. It was you."

I clutched his throat as he began to choke. Abel's eyes were bulging out of their sockets. I pressed tighter and tighter. I felt completely justified for what I was doing. I felt...almost serene.

*For you my love. For you Scarlett. I should have done this when you were alive. I will kill him for you. I will get revenge for you, Scarlett. The rest of my entire life is devoted to you now. I live for you...and I'll murder for you.*

Abel's face was turning pink. A rush of warmth flooded my body as I felt Abel's life slipping away.

"Die you *monster*!" I roared. Abel's eyes began flickering. He was beginning to lose consciousness.

"No!" Ivan violently pushed me to the floor. I landed on my back and turned over. I softly moaned. I rubbed the bottom of my spine and sat up.

"I'm sorry man, but we're not doing that shit," Ivan pointed at me. He was breathing heavily and he was stone-cold serious.

I looked at Abel who was coughing profusely. He had tears spilling out of his eyes and the veins in his throat were inflamed. I had lost control. I felt the back of my head, where the stitches had been. Where my head got smashed in. I didn't think it'd have such a lasting effect on me, emotionally and mentally. Day by day I felt like I was becoming more prone to anger and violence. If Ivan hadn't been there, I would've crushed Abel's neck. If he hadn't been there when I was being thrashed, I would've been a dead man. I would've made Scarlett a widow.

I had been a dumb young adult. I wondered if I was still being an idiot and making the same stupid decisions. *No*, I told myself. There was no going back. The decisions had been made. I was committed. Even if I was slowly losing my mind, I needed to move forward. As long as I was alive, I needed to find the truth and exact vengeance. If it wasn't right to anyone else, I knew in my heart that it was right to *me*.

"I'm tired of the lies and I'm tired of not knowing what happened. I don't know how many people we have to go through to find Scarlett's killer. This is getting absurd and I'm losing my shit. I'll yank out every single last one of Abel's teeth if he doesn't start telling the truth."

"I told you, Damian. I won't let you lose yourself. I'm still with you on this but you need to keep a level head."

"Look into John Santoro," Abel wheezed.

"Who?" I slowly got up.

"The man Dani was dating. I was lying about Madden. I...I wanted to save my own skin, but I swear I didn't kill Scarlett. Look into John Santoro and find Dani. She'll tell you that I was home that night. The night Scarlett was murdered."

"Sounds like a very likely story."

"Please, you have to believe me. Find Dani and you'll find the truth," Abel begged.

"I just read some texts between them from that day. She brought him dinner that night. A couple of hours before Scarlett was reportedly murdered," Ivan commented.

"That doesn't mean much."

"Damian, Dani can be in danger. You should find this Santoro guy. It can be the *Rainfall Abductor*." Ivan urged.

"I'll go. I hope she's alright," I sighed.

It was worth investigating. I didn't believe anything Abel was saying but Dani was a close friend who needed help. She wasn't the type of person to go missing out of the blue. I needed to find John Santoro and Dani. Something wasn't right.

"I have his employee records on my phone. Santoro's house address is there," Abel explained.

I slowly approached Abel and held my hand up at Ivan.

"We're not done with you yet. You're not off the hook. If I find out you're lying…you're a dead man. I promise you."

"I'll keep this asshole, company." Ivan pulled up a chair and sat next to Abel.

"I'm not lying," Abel grunted.

"We'll see," I stared him down.

# CHAPTER 11

I called Ringo to confirm John Santoro's employment at the club. He had quit out of the blue. He didn't call and he didn't show up. I didn't know what was going on but something was definitely wrong. I asked Ringo about Santoro's relationship with Dani and he had no idea what I was talking about. She must've kept it low-key. It was a problem. If she never told anyone about it, it was like he didn't even exist. All I knew was a name.

John Santoro's house was located at 132nd and Ruby Lane. Except that there wasn't a house there at all. It was a fake address. All that was there was an abandoned warehouse with no doors. All that was left was a shell of whatever operation had been running there before. Old mining equipment, sawdust, rusted railings, cinderblocks and rusty barrels surrounded a torn-up, two-story building with broken windows and piles of burnt trash. The likely culprits were homeless people who lit it on fire for warmth during the colder months. I parked down the street near *Milton's*.

I crawled underneath a twisted fence that was meant to keep outsiders away. I explored the inner grounds and spotted a couple of beat up *Rolvo* sedans from the early 2000s. One was black with a nasty dent on the driver's door. The other one was grey and had the front bumper missing. Both cars looked like they had been rotting there for years. The whole place was a wasteland. John Santoro was not living there. Nobody was. I scaled an old piece of scaffolding and stood atop of a wooden platform. I peeked ahead over a broken-down cement wall. The warehouse wasn't far from *Frank's Motel*. I didn't know if it meant anything, but drug addicts did frequent that motel. It could mean that some of them came over to that warehouse. A way of getting high while out of sight. Maybe one of them knew the name, John Santoro.

As I pondered that idea, I saw a sleek, black Nissan 350z roaring into the parking lot of the motel. Six police cruisers closely followed in pursuit, their sirens blaring. My heart pounded when I saw Sebastian Gunner jump out of his car with a machete in his hand. The same machete he had back at the old church.

A dozen police officers ran out of their cars with their guns out. They barked at Sebastian, who continued to charge at them. As he approached one of the officers, he attempted to slash them. Gunshots rang out and sliced through the night sky like fireworks. They littered him with bullets and stopped him right in his tracks. The last thing I saw was Sebastian's body violently contorting and twisting as the platform I was on gave way.

I tumbled on the dirt-filled ground and remained still for a second. I wiped off the dust that had accumulated on my clothes and slowly stood up. I couldn't believe what I had just seen. Sebastian Gunner had been shot. That lunatic was wielding a machete at police officers. Was he high? Was he dead? I carefully walked down the street because

I had to see it for myself. It didn't take long for a curious crowd to form as a few officers ordered them to stay back. They formed a perimeter amongst the heated commotion. I stood at the back of the boisterous crowd and caught a glimpse of Sebastian's body. He was dead alright. All I needed to see were two blood-gushing holes in his head. He wasn't coming back from that.

Detective Gamble caught my eye and I returned his frosty stare. I shaped my hand in the form of a phone and held it up to my ear. I pointed at him. He held up a finger and softly nodded. I motioned drinking something with my hand and pointed towards *Milton's*. It was close by. As he began writing something on a notepad, he gave me a thumbs up.

---

I picked out a booth with leather seats and waited for Gamble. I had an ice-cold beer ready for him. In the meantime, I checked in with Ivan and called him.

"*How's Abel?*"

"*He's been sobbing. He wants to be let go.*"

"*I haven't found John Santoro yet. Until then, he's staying put. I don't trust a god damn word that slimy shitball says. Dani's still missing and as far as I can tell, he's somehow responsible.*"

*"What do we do when people start asking questions, Damian? Abel is a rich man in a small town. How much longer before someone finds him?"* The concern was prominent in Ivan's shaky voice.

*"We have time. You'll have to trust me on this."*

*"Alright man. I'll keep you posted and I'll keep myself busy."* Ivan hung up.

He was nervous, but he had every right to be. He was alone with one of the most richest men in town. A town that didn't have many rich men. I knew this. I calculated that we had a week at the most before people started to freak out. I was talking about his club managers, his rich clients, his lawyers, his finance guys...people of that nature. They all figured he was disappearing for a few days until things cooled down. That's what the *Code Green* was for. It was to appease those people for a certain period of time. Thanks to the hysterical mind of Abel Armoni, only I knew about *that* safe house. I had no real vested interest in his finances and he was my father-in-law. I had never asked him for money either.

All those years spent working for him and tolerating his entitled, bad-tempered behavior had seemingly paid off. I had a few days to find the truth. To find out what the hell Abel had been up to. I needed to speak to a man I trusted. Someone who knew Abel well enough. I glanced at my watch. I had waited thirty minutes. Time was running out and I was getting antsy. Thankfully, Detective Gamble trotted in right on time. We made eye contact. He came over and firmly shook my hand. He sat down and blew out a heavy breath. He unbuttoned his jacket and closed his eyes. He looked like he was carrying the full weight of the world on his shoulders. I slowly pushed the ice-cold beer to his side of the booth.

"For you, Detective."

"Oh. Thank you, Damian," Gamble's eyes fluttered open.

He grabbed it and gratefully sipped from it. He set it down and eyed it.

"Lots of long nights?" I asked.

"Yeah. It's been rough. You saw just now. That guy got himself killed. Drug dealers and drug addicts, Damian. What else can I tell you?"

"Sebastian Gunner, right? I knew him. He was actually one of Scarlett's ex-boyfriends. He used to hit her. They didn't last very long."

"Really? Wow. Well, it's a small town. I can't say I'm too surprised."

"He dated Dani Shepherd too. Their relationship was even shorter. She's the girl that's gone missing. Abel Armoni's assistant. My friend."

"Another unit is looking into Dani Shepherd. I was sorry to hear about that," Gamble offered.

"Any information you can tell me? She's a good friend and a great person. She doesn't deserve this shit. Her poor mom must be worried sick."

Detective Gamble sighed and drummed his fingers on the table. He smacked his lips.

"Listen...this'll be public information soon but she was last seen at this very bar. A couple of workers were questioned. She stayed late and then she left. After that...she vanished. There was a man with her but he was wearing a hat and it was dark. No one knows who he was. The department's gonna ask the public for information. It'll be regarding any witnesses who saw a man with Dani Shepherd the night she disappeared," Gamble explained.

*John Santoro. It all leads back to him.*

"Why are they waiting? What's the point? Dani's life is in danger!" I exclaimed, my voice riddled with anger.

"Calm down, Damian. It's bureaucratic. They're trying to mitigate the public's fear. It's this whole *Rainfall Abductor* story that has everyone spooked. Dani's disappearance just adds to the hysteria."

"Yeah, with good reason. That fucker is still out there. He needs to be found."

"We try our best." Gamble seemed miffed.

"If you say so," I muttered.

"I saw that Abel Armoni is missing too apparently. A lot of explosive allegations. Would you happen to know anything about that?"

I stared at the table and thought carefully. He didn't know anything. I was his personal driver so naturally he was suspicious. My hand was slightly shaking underneath. I needed to remain steady. I needed to dodge his little landmines until I had an opening to ask him what I needed to know.

"I don't know anything."

"I find that hard to believe. You're his personal driver and he used to be your father-in-law. You were at that event as well. You were at that country club, *Green Meadows*. I saw the videos online. It was quite the scandal. That Victoria Cole blew the lid wide open. Lots of shady dealings in his *Crimson Lounge*. They called him a *rapist* and an *abuser*."

"I know. I've read the articles. It could be true or it could be false. Innocent until proven guilty right?" I asked.

"You only run if you're guilty."

"He was scared. He's a rich man. He has a lot to lose." I was forced to play devil's advocate. I couldn't have him catching wind that I had kidnapped the bastard myself.

"Where do rich men go when they have a lot to lose?" Gamble leaned over, his hands folded.

"I couldn't tell you. I dropped him off at home. I don't know where he went after that. My guess is that he escaped to some bunker a hundred miles from here with an army of lawyers. They're probably drafting a dozen settlements with NDA clauses as we speak. He's prepared for this kind of thing. He treats this like someone has declared nuclear war on his *empire*."

Gamble took another sip of his beer and scoffed.

"This town is going to hell, huh? Drug dealers getting themselves killed, missing women, an alleged abductor and possible serial murderer...and a rich, abusive monster buying his way out of prison."

"Speaking of drug dealers...why were you chasing Sebastian Gunner?" I asked with strong intent. I needed to change the subject.

"I can't tell you that."

I knew he'd say that, but it was worth a try.

"Is it related to my wife's murder?"

"Alright Damian, what do you want? I'm a busy man. I have the case of your late wife haunting over me every single night. I'm living the same nightmare. The one where my own wife vanished."

"I know. I'm sorry that we both got fucked over. You're not the only one living a nightmare," I replied.

"I had retirement plans, you know? I wanted to move somewhere nice with Jade. I was thinking a Caribbean island or a coastal European city. Maybe Italy or the Bahamas. She had an inheritance from her grandmother coming. That all went to hell when she disappeared. Jade's family doesn't talk to me anymore. When they see me, it reminds them of her. It reminds them of my failure to watch over her. They never want to see me again."

"I have no contact with my own family. Scarlett was all I had."

"I know what that's like. If I didn't have this job…I'd hang myself. I can't have too much time to think about what my future would've looked like with Jade. I'd fling myself off a cliff."

I knew exactly what he meant. The thoughts of what could've been became stormy, overwhelming and consumed you. My purpose was revenge. Beyond that…I didn't know. I didn't want to know.

"I'm sure you know my best friend Ivan…his wife vanished too. Around the same time Jade vanished. Ivan's wife was Lisandra Pierce. He was gonna have a baby with her. She went down to the beach at night to take pictures, like she had done a hundred times before. She never came home. From one day to the next...gone. Just like that. Future ripped from him, just like how it was ripped from us."

Gamble pursed his lips and softly shook his head.

"You plan to spend the rest of your life with someone, but you never think of spending the rest of your life without them."

"I couldn't have said it better myself." That sunk in my chest like a boulder.

"What are you up to these days?"

"I've been catching up on some basketball games and I've been playing some pick-up. I like to get a good sweat in. It beats staying home and drowning myself in my own misery," I lied.

"The things we do to survive," Gamble muttered while he continued to drink.

"Detective...do you know someone named John Santoro?"

Curiosity washed over his face.

"No. I don't know that name. It doesn't ring a bell."

"Are you sure?"

"I am."

Who the hell was John Santoro? If the address he had given was fake, odds were the name was fake too. I cursed under my breath.

"How did Jade vanish? You never told me. What happened that day?"

I wanted to grasp any and all details regarding Jade. I wanted to see if there were any similarities between my wife and his. The investigation was running cold. My only leads were Abel and a man who most likely only existed on paper.

"She disappeared after coming back from the grocery store. She walked back late at night and...vanished. Seemingly out of thin air. Tomatoes and soup cans spilled all over the sidewalk. The shopping had already been done. She was halfway to the house. No one saw anything and nothing was taken. I questioned myself almost every night. *What happened Jade? Where are you Jade?*"

"That must've destroyed you."

Gamble reached into his pocket and took out a polaroid picture he had of her in his wallet. She was a beautiful woman. She had tan skin, dark hair and dark brown eyes. She was tightly embracing Detective Gamble in the photo. I had never seen him smile before that picture.

"It did destroy me, Damian. It ripped out a piece of my heart that will never grow back. That's the cost of loving someone when they're cruelly taken from you."

The strange part was that my wife's body had been left behind. Ivan's wife and Gamble's wife were nowhere to be found. Either something went wrong with my wife's abduction or they weren't connected. I didn't believe that. Especially after I closely studied that photo of Jade Gamble. I had a sudden epiphany, a possible connection that I had made.

I realized that Scarlett, Jade and Lisandra closely resembled each other in appearance. Dani did too. It made me wonder if it was a pattern. It made me wonder if there was a demented reason why all those women had been *chosen*. Was it random...or was there a sinister reason behind their abductions?

"I've come to peace with the fact that she's dead. Whoever took her must've chopped her up into little pieces and burned her. They did whatever they wanted to do to her and got rid of the evidence. Another possibility is that they shipped her off to some foreign country and sold her organs. I've thought of everything. Each possibility is worse than the last. I've given up, Damian. I just wanna move on with my life."

I needed to take a breath and I needed some time to think.

"I just wanna move on too." I got up and shook his hand.

"Don't let the demons win, Damian. Don't give them too much space in your head," he said gravely.

"They won't win."

---

I texted Ivan to meet me at my house. I figured that he wanted to stretch his legs for a while after housesitting Abel. The general area of the safe house was fairly secluded so Ivan didn't have a problem sneaking out while on his motorcycle. It was easier under the cover of the thunderous rain. Ivan and I found ourselves on my couch. We drank beers and caught our breath. It felt like we hadn't stopped for a minute since we had set out to find my wife's murderer. It wouldn't be for long either. Abel was locked up but still needed supervision.

"Wait a minute, Gunner's *dead*?" Ivan was understandably shocked.

"I saw it happen. It was only a matter of time, I guess."

"Shit man. Where the hell is this all leading to? First Michael Madden then Gunner. This is insane."

"I know. I think we're getting close. I can feel it. John Santoro wasn't there but we'll find him. We have to."

There was a prolonged silence. John Santoro had disappeared. Dani Shepherd had disappeared. Two suspects we had spoken to were dead. I knew it was gonna be a hard, bumpy road but I didn't expect so much *death*. But, who was I kidding? I was blazing through town on a path of vengeance. More potential death was in the cards and I needed to accept that.

"Crazy times, huh? Who knew you had the brass balls to kidnap Abel Armoni. Your own boss. That's what the kids call being a *savage*."

"Don't ever say that again," I chuckled.

"No promises." We raised our glasses and nodded. Our own silent salute to our friendship. One that withstood tragedy, travails, lies, death, depression and drunken rants. I had to hand it to Ivan, he didn't have to help me. He could've told me that it was too much. He could've refused to help me lock up Abel in his own safe house, but he didn't. He was fully on board to help me and to keep me in check. That's what friends were for. Real friends.

"Hey Ivan. I don't know if I've said this but…thank you for doing this with me. I know this has been some real tough, crazy shit. You could've said no and I would've loved you all the same. You're my brother. I need you to know that."

"I know that, dumbass. How the hell could I say no to my brother?"

A gut-warming laugh filled my belly. I needed that. I hadn't laughed like that in a while. The last time was before Scarlett had been murdered.

"Do you think Scarlett, Jade and Lisandra are connected? I was talking with Detective Gamble. He was telling me about the disappearance of his wife and showed me a picture of her. Something jumped out at me. All three women have very similar features. I don't know…am I insane? Am I just giving you false hope? Could there be a connection?"

"Honestly man, I don't know. I appreciate you trying to find one though. I guess you never really know. You can find truth in the most unexpected places."

"Unexpected places huh?" I thought aloud.

I excused myself and went into my bedroom. I went towards Scarlett's closet. I hadn't moved or touched a single thing. I examined the painting she had been working on. It was a black figure chasing a deer in a forest. I thought it was ominous. To me, it could've represented the man who had hunted her down to rape and murder her. The murderer was the black figure and she was the innocent deer, running away from him.

I rummaged through her other artistic works as tears began to well up in my eyes. She was so talented. She deserved so much more. It was heartbreaking that she never got to experience true success. I came across one portrait she painted of a simple woman hiding her face with a detailed flower. There was a simple man holding her hand next to her. She told me it reminded her of us. She told me that I was a man who enjoyed who she was as a *human being*. A rarity in her life.

I ran my fingers through the various assortment of ugly sweaters, crop tops, jeans, silky dresses and blazers she had. The closet still smelled like her. A refreshing aroma of sweet vanilla and earthy honey. I found a red cotton long sleeve she used to wear. It had a giant pink heart on it and it said *I love my boyfriend*. She found it cheesy, cringeworthy and absolutely loved it with all her heart. It was the first gift I ever got her for Valentine's Day. We had been dating for several months at that point and I already felt strongly about her. I remembered that day like it was yesterday.

She was downcast because her mother had slut-shamed her for wearing a shirt that showed her belly button. They got into a shouting match and she ran away from home. She asked me to meet her at Darkpond Park. She hadn't wanted to celebrate Valentine's Day because she thought it was silly and that it had no use being a holiday.

*Hey,* she had said.

*Hey baby. I got you something.*

*What? I didn't want you to get me anything.*

*Just open your gift.*

*This...this is so corny.*

*I know, but I thought you'd like it. Sorry.*

*No one has ever gotten me something like this, Damian.*

*Damn...well, I guess I didn't know you as well as I thought I did.*

*Come here you big idiot.*

She had pulled me in for the tightest, warmest hug I had ever gotten from her. She gave me a long, warm kiss on the lips and had locked eyes with me.

*I love you*, she had said with tears in her eyes.

*I love you too, Scarlett.*

I came back to the present and found myself crying over that fond memory. I was holding the red long sleeve like she was wearing it. I dug my face in it and imagined her there with me. Scarlett only lived in my memories after she died. I had to cherish them and remember them.

I had to fight through my head injury and *remember*. I forced myself to. I allowed the heart-shattering grief to pour onto me as it seeped into my skin. I had to *feel*. I wanted to. I began to silently sob. I cried so hard my eyes were shut and my knees were on the ground. I slowly rubbed my head as I laid on the floor. I needed to let it all out.

After the sickening grief began to pass, I felt better. Empty on the inside, but better. I felt like I could continue on with what I had set out to do. I went out through the backyard door to get some fresh air. That's what Scarlett used to do when she tried to find inspiration. I trudged forward and climbed over my wooden fence. I spotted Elsa walking by. She had been staring at my house. When she saw me, her eyes grew wide and she waved. I waved back. She started to approach me. I swiftly wiped my eyes. As she got closer, I saw that she had her hunting gear on which included a camouflage vest, a bucket hat and a Springfield rifle slung around her shoulder.

"Hey Elsa."

"You're a hard man to reach. I need to speak with you," Elsa commented as she gave me a grave stare.

"Sorry, I've been all over," I replied.

"I can see that. I've been watching the local media channels. I heard about that Michael Madden fellow. Shot himself in the head. Drug-fueled lunatic."

"He was one of the suspects but not anymore."

"I have something for you."

"What is it?"

"Another suspect. I found this while hunting in the forest. The police must've missed it. I trust you with it, not them. They can go to hell. They never got justice for my Angela. They're all useless bastards."

She spat on the ground before handing me a damaged ID card with a faded photo. It read **JOHN SANTORO**. It showed a picture of a young man with curly brown hair, a fully grown beard and dark eyes. He reminded me of Bruno McCoy, the art dealer. I couldn't quite pinpoint why. They might've known each other or I might've seen him that same day. The details from that night were still hazy, years later.

"Could this be the man who killed your wife?"

"He looks familiar. He looks like the man who was there that night. The man I've been seeing," I whispered to myself.

"Do you know him?"

"Not personally, but I've been trying to find him. I think he might be responsible for my friend going missing. Dani Shepherd."

"I'm not a woman who believes in fate, but this may be a sign, Damian. You need to find this man and you need to find out what he knows."

"I think you're right, Elsa."

"If you do find him, feel free to call me. I'm here to help. I know how to pull a trigger and I am by no means, squeamish. I can promise you that. Life has hardened me. That's what living with a *Nazi* does to you."

"Thank you, Elsa. I appreciate that."

"I could always use a break from writing my book, *Elsa's Taxidermy Tales*. It's a silly hobby but it helps with the screams."

"What screams?"

"The walls that scream at night, Damian. I am always reminded of what happened and I'll never forget it."

"I know how you feel," I grimly nodded.

Everything seemed to hinge on finding John Santoro. The man with a fake name and a fake address. A man who only seemed to exist on paper. A man from my past. A man who had done a terrible thing to me.

*I will find you.*

# CHAPTER 12
## 2012

The memory was filmy in my mind. The traumatic ones usually were. When I was with my brother Sam at the *Bridge* that night, everything changed. I remembered hearing the low buzzing of insects. It was humid and the sweat on my shirt clung to my skin like glue. There was a cool breeze that was blowing. It soothed the welts that had formed on my legs due to the pesky flies. There wasn't anything inherently wrong about that night. There wasn't any ominous foreboding. There weren't any warnings. That's how life was.

You usually had no warning when something devastating was about to be thrust upon you, violently and tragically, without remorse. Life took whatever victims it wanted and gave nothing in return. It had a name: karma. I believed in it. I had to. If I didn't, nothing would have any meaning. I had to believe that deep down, all the actions you committed in your life and all the consequences you avoided somehow added up. The cruel scythe of death never forgot your face or what you've done. Sooner or later, everyone paid a price.

Sam grabbed a flask out of his pocket and started drinking. He leaned against the railing of the bridge. I joined him. He heavily sighed and gave me a guilty look. I nodded up at him.

"What's up Sam? Something got you down?"

"I have to tell you something bro and you're not gonna like it."

I shifted my body upward and crossed my arms. I eyed him with serious intent.

"You're my brother, dude. You tell me things I don't like all the time. What's different now?"

"I'm in love with Scarlett."

My immediate reaction was laughter. I laughed right in his face, but there was a problem. He wasn't laughing with me. He was a stone wall. I stopped laughing and felt a sudden gut punch to my chest. All the air out of my body seemed to be sucked out of me in one fell swoop. I grew a bit dizzy and leaned too much to one side. Sam caught me and helped me stand upright. All I felt was confusion.

*Why? Why are you telling me this, Sam? Why now?*

*Why now...*

"Quit joking dude. What do you actually wanna tell me?"

There was a long silence. I didn't like that one bit. Sam didn't look at me and took a big sip of his drink.

"Nice night, huh?" Sam commented.

*What?*

"Don't do that bullshit. What the fuck are you talking about, Sam? What do you mean, you're in *love* with Scarlett?"

"I told you...you weren't gonna like it."

"No shit. Listen to what you're telling me. You don't think I'm going to be upset?"

"You told me that you always wanted me to be honest, Damian. That's what I'm doing, I'm being honest."

*Am I about to lose my brother? My only brother?*

I felt that our entire relationship was about to end. I didn't see an out in that situation. It was too much. Sam had said something that should've been kept to himself. Was I selfish for thinking that? I probably was, but I really wished he hadn't said that. It only served to worsen my life.

"I don't get it. I really don't get it. Why are you telling me this now?"

"I've been having dreams about her. Heavy dreams, you know?"

I took a few steps back and gave him an offended look. I didn't know who I was talking to. I didn't understand it. Why was my brother telling me these things?

"*What?*" I angrily blurted out.

"I hate that you're gonna marry her. I hate it. I'm sorry, Damian."

"I fucking asked you if you liked her back then and you said no. *You said no, Sam!*"

"*Because of you!*" Sam boomed. He pointed at me and shrugged me off.

"You…you told me to pursue her because I loved her. I genuinely loved her. I gave you a chance. I told you that neither of us should pursue her because we both seemed to like her but you refused. Fuck, Sam. You *refused*."

"Of course I did. You're my brother. I wanted you to be happy. Is that a crime?"

It wasn't a crime allowing me the freedom to love Scarlett, but shoving it in my face years later was a betrayal. A complete and utter betrayal.

"You shouldn't have said anything. Why are you telling me this now? Jesus, Sam. You're one of the only people in the world who's important to me. You're the only god damn family I have. We promised not to be like dad. That lying, cheating, scheming piece of shit."

"Like father like son, I guess. Right?"

"No. No, Sam. We aren't like him. We aren't. You're not our dad. You're a good person."

I said it but I didn't believe it. My dad had a temper. At a moment's notice, a sudden violent urge would overtake him. An unfortunate, genetic trait that had been seemingly passed down.

Sam finished his flask and threw it aside.

"Scarlet and I kissed. Two weeks before you guys started dating. We never told you for obvious reasons. She...she felt nothing. She wanted nothing with me. I still loved her."

A simmering, insurmountable volley of unrestrained rage charged through all the veins in my body. I shoved him hard against the railing. He cried out in pain and grabbed his lower back. Immediately after I did it, I felt an overwhelming sense of guilt wash over me. I reached out but it was too late. Fire erupted in Sam's eyes.

"*Fuck you!*" He lunged at me and ferociously pushed me to the floor. What I remembered most were his legs. All I saw were his legs as I pushed both hands towards them as hard as I could. Next thing I knew, he was holding on for dear life. He was over the railing, desperately attempting to hang on to a metal pole near the bottom of the bridge. It was a steep fall and there were jagged rocks below, poking out of the river.

I bent myself halfway over the railing and outstretched my hand, trying my absolute hardest to grab him. A paralyzing sense of fear choked my heart as I saw the terror in Sam's eyes.

"Fuck! I fucked up! I'm sorry! I'm so sorry bro! I don't wanna die! Please don't let me die!" Sam begged.

"You're not gonna die. I promise. You're not gonna die, Sam." I reassured him.

"I love you bro. I love you. Fuck me...my hand hurts. My hand hurts, Damian. I...I can't man. Fuck!" Sam yelled.

"Reach out! Reach out for my hand!"

"Okay. I'm gonna..."

It was a sudden, quick fall followed by an unforgiving *thud*. I cautiously looked for his body. It was strewn across the rocks like a bloodied rag doll. I saw one glimpse of his head and fell back onto the platform. It was split open. I saw a wet, gushing river of blood, brain matter and broken skull fragments. I started to hyperventilate as I laid there. I couldn't believe it. One minute, Sam was alive. The next minute...he was dead. My own brother. Someone I had been raised with. Someone I had grown up with. Someone I had bonded with. Someone I had known my entire life. Gone in an instant. I jerked my head to the side and forcibly puked. I wiped my mouth and focused on breathing.

*Sam is dead, Sam is dead, Sam is dead, Sam is dead, Sam is dead.*

I started crying hysterically. I asked myself *why*, over and over again. I hadn't wanted him to die. I was angry with him but I did *not* want him to die. Things had gotten out of hand so fast. I had no idea how it escalated to Sam falling to his death over the bridge. Sam's poor head cracked open by the sharp tip of a deadly rock. I blamed myself. I had murdered him. My own brother. My only brother.

After that it was all a blur. I remembered calling the police and lying straight to their faces. I had been so afraid and I was horribly wracked with guilt. I told him that he had gotten drunk and that he had accidentally fallen over. When they found his flask, they believed me. They didn't even have to test it. It reeked of alcohol. Sam also had a history of drunk incidents in town. He was known to many as "the village drunk."

I was destroyed for a long time after Sam's death. It didn't help that my parents moved away. I wanted nothing to do with my father but my mother had done her best to raise us. It stung when she abandoned me. I was angry with her and at myself. I loathed myself. That's why I loved and needed Scarlett so much. I leaned on her during that time and she let me in like no one else. She comforted me and understood me. Sam's death made me value the people I loved so much more.

That's why I had been obsessed with finding Scarlett's stalker. I knew it wasn't going to end well if I didn't find that demented bastard. I had been right. I failed to find his identity and as a result, Scarlett horribly died. I failed and I paid the price. I promised myself that it wouldn't happen again. I vowed to find the man responsible. He was going to pay the price for what he had done to me.

# CHAPTER 13

After I spoke with Elsa, I returned home. I found Ivan sitting in my swivel chair at my mahogany desk. He was reading a *BREAKING NEWS* article on my laptop. It read:

***SEBASTIAN GUNNER: DRUG DEALER CAUGHT AND KILLED.***

"Anything interesting?" I asked as I stood beside him.

"Well, the police found out that he had dated Dani for a little while so they went to speak with him. Apparently he ran because they found him peddling hard drugs. He became violent and erratic towards them. So they shot him."

"That's what I saw."

"They investigated him further and found no connections to Dani's disappearance," Ivan finished reading.

"Is there anything else?"

"Dani's mother Dawn, is imploring anyone to come forward with information if they have any."

I nodded and rubbed my chin. I had met Dani's mother before. She was a very kind lady who had raised a very sweet-natured young woman. It was a damn shame. Dani didn't deserve to be another statistic. I found John Santoro suspicious from the very beginning and I had been proven right.

"If they were looking into Sebastian that means they have no real leads. They have no fucking idea what happened to Dani."

Ivan closed the browser on my laptop and stood up. He patted my shoulder.

"She'll turn up."

"I spoke with Elsa. She found John Santoro's ID card in the woods," I slid it out of my pocket and handed it to him. He carefully examined it.

"Holy shit. What was it doing there?"

"I don't know, but there's a connection, Ivan. It's fucking there. I just need to find that son of a bitch."

"Does Detective Gamble know about Santoro? Do you think they're looking into him?"

"I asked him about it and he had never heard the name before. He was either lying or he genuinely knew nothing. I don't think he's the type to lie. He'll tell me straight if he can't say anything regarding an ongoing investigation."

"Well, I have to go check on Abel. I'll feed him, hydrate him and make sure he hasn't shit himself."

"I'm gonna go speak with Dani's mother. Maybe she knows something."

Ivan tiredly rubbed his face and went to the front door.

"She must be devastated. That poor woman. Poor Dani. I hope she's alright. I remember when Lisandra disappeared. Can you believe I had let her go by herself?"

"You can't blame yourself."

Ivan's eyes began to water and his lip started quivering. He went to the kitchen and placed his arms on the counter. He stared downward.

"Do you remember when you found me?"

I tried to figure out what he was talking about. I hoped it wasn't what I thought it was. It was an extremely painful memory. One I didn't like to think about. It made my stomach churn and my skin crawl. I slowly went to him but allowed him his space.

"What are you referring to, Ivan?"

"When you found me in my bathroom, gun pressed to my temple...ready to pull the trigger."

I took in a sharp breath. It was a memory that broke my heart, every time I thought of it. I had a key to his house back then. That was two months after Lisandra's disappearance. Ivan's hope had diminished to nothing and he was a shell of himself. One night I walked in to watch a basketball game with him. I found him in his bathroom with his eyes closed. I chopped his arm and kicked the gun away when it clattered onto the floor. He embraced me and sobbed.

We slowly slid down to the floor together. I quietly held him and allowed him to grieve. I waited until all the pain and suffering he had been holding in, spilled out of him like a thunderous, torrential storm. Afterwards, we never spoke about it and he never attempted to do it ever again. That's why he started going to the *Rainfall Rip-It* gun range. He had been ashamed of what he had almost done. He shot that same gun and showed himself that he had control over it. He had the power to move on and to conquer that dark part of himself. The part that had wanted him to die.

"I remember," I whispered.

Ivan got up and looked me in the eye. He smiled.

"Thank you for being there. Thank you for uh...stopping me. I needed to tell you that." Ivan reached out and hugged me. I slowly hugged him back.

"I'm happy you're still breathing, brother." We let go.

"Listen, while I'm watching Armoni, I'm gonna keep looking into this lead I found. It might be nothing, but who knows? I started looking into it when you went to that country club event."

"What is it?"

"It involves your neighbor actually. Ms. Elsa Dietrich." Ivan slipped out his phone and showed me a picture of an old news article titled: **FIRE IN RAINFALL**.

"What happened there?"

"Martin Dietrich and Angela Baron both perished in a barn fire. Foul play suspected, but never proven. Angela's body was never actually recovered. It seemed to vanish as well. Martin's body was the same case. The fire must've been all-consuming."

"That's interesting."

"I don't know if this will lead anywhere, but maybe Elsa's husband was a part of something. Who knows what really happened in that barn? Remember what Elsa said...he looked like a Nazi and acted like one too. Someone from the past might've returned to abduct these women. Someone connected to Angela."

"Someone like John Santoro."

"It's like you said. It's right there. The dots just need to be connected."

"Maybe Santoro knew Madden," I pondered.

"One other thing I noticed. Angela has dark hair, tan skin and brown eyes. Just like our wives."

"Holy Christ," I blurted out.

"It's calculated, Damian. There's a reason why these women were chosen. We just need to find out why."

---

I called Dawn and told her that I needed to urgently speak with her regarding her daughter. Thankfully, she immediately accepted. We had met before and she was fond of me. I treated her daughter with respect and that had resonated with her. She lived in a modest, one-bedroom house in a barren neighborhood. The houses mimicked each other in how poorly maintained they were. They had dried out paint, cracked roofs and splotchy driveways. I was surprised that Dani had allowed her mother to live in such a dump.

There was a 1990's sedan parked in front of Dawn's house and the front yard hadn't been cut in months. I dodged the potholes while crossing the craggy street to get to her front door. I softly knocked on it while I examined the nail-length scratches and chips it had. A small-statured woman with short black hair and dark yet kind eyes opened the door. She stared up at me and smiled. She wore a yellow, floral dress and gave me an unexpected hug. I hugged her back.

"It's so nice to see you, Damian. Please come in!"

"Likewise, Dawn. Thank you for having me."

I walked in and looked around. There was a tattered beige couch in the living room, in front of an old box TV set. A few cardboard boxes were organized against the wall. They had knick-knacks, piles of clothes and electronic equipment stored inside. She had a large, light brown china cabinet in the short hallway that led into the kitchen. I followed her inside and saw a small, rectangular kitchen with limited cabinet space, a tiny stove and a white, mid-sized fridge that took up most of the area. She seemed to be making tea in a small pot.

"Please have a seat on the couch, Damian. I'll be there shortly with some tea and then we can talk," Dawn said sweetly.

"You got it. Thank you, Dawn."

As I slowly stepped back into the living room, I spotted a framed picture of Dani with her mother. They were on vacation on some island, in a small boat that was riding along a coastline. Dani's smile was radiant and her skin was glowing. She got it from her mother. Dani had grown up without a father. Dani had been the result of a one-night stand. The birth father took off upon hearing of the pregnancy news. It instilled a sense of determination in her to live the best life she could. She had always worked hard and her mother did too.

The best job she got was working for Abel, even if he was a massive douchebag. It paid well being his assistant, but the real payment was learning the realm of business under his *tutelage*. It allowed her the opportunity to make numerous business contacts and friends in the financing world. Most of the time, that's what you needed if you ever planned to start your own business. You needed a lot of money and powerful friends.

My stomach twisted into a knot. I didn't know what Dani's fate would entail after Abel was kidnapped by me. I didn't know if she still needed him to ultimately succeed. But that was besides the point, she was still missing and I knew that she needed help. I sat on the couch and patiently waited until Dawn came back with the tea. She sat beside me and handed me a tiny white cup. I cautiously grabbed it and thanked her.

"Pardon the mess. Dani was helping me box things up. We had planned on renovating my house. It needs a lot of work and she had saved some money to help me."

"That sounds like Dani. She's always willing to help." I took a sip and set my cup of tea on a coffee table beside me.

"What can I tell you, Damian? The police told me that they questioned some witnesses who work at that bar, *Milton's*. They saw Dani there the night she presumably vanished. She was with an unidentified man but he left hours before she did. When she did leave, it was very late at night. She wasn't heard from again," Dawn explained.

"I'm so sorry, Dawn. I understand how you feel. I find it very upsetting too. I really hope she's okay, wherever she is," I said grimly.

"I know you understand, Damian. I actually wanted to express my condolences to you, regarding your wife. My Dani has told me about her. She seemed like a very lovely woman."

I fought back the tears welling in my eyes and swallowed down a dry lump in my throat.

"Thank you, Dawn. She was a lovely woman. She was a lover, a fighter and an artist. I couldn't have asked for anything more."

"How is the police investigation going? In regards to her horrific murderer."

I sighed and placed my hands on my thighs. I softly shook my head.

"I don't think they have anyone they're looking at currently. I can't be sure. The lead detective on the case, Albert Gamble, can't share any details."

"I know that man. He spoke with me after Dani disappeared. He's very serious. I see the dark circles around his eyes. I think he's trying his best."

"Yeah. I noticed that too."

"I saw that they arrested that crazy man. I forgot his name."

"Yes, Michael Madden. They arrested him and then they let him go. There wasn't any evidence he had done anything. He just so happened to be in the area."

"Do you believe that?" Dawn scoffed.

"No, not really. He's dead now. I can't do much about that."

Dawn gasped and almost spat out her tea. I raised my hands towards her, trying to calm her down. I didn't know if I would actually calm her down, but it was a basic human instinct I had. I did it towards Scarlett a lot when she was alive. It was a way of reassuring someone that I was there for them and that things would turn out okay. Perhaps I was being silly, but it comforted me. In those days, I needed all the comfort I could get.

"Oh my goodness. He's dead?!" Dawn exclaimed.

"Yes. There was an incident with the police while they were trying to arrest him."

"They were going to arrest him again? For what?"

"It was uh...a public disturbance. Something like that."

I wasn't about to tell Dani's mother that Michael had gruesomely shot himself in the head. She didn't need to hear that from me.

"This town is getting crazier by the second. I can't believe that my girl is gone now...just like those other women who went missing. Lisandra Pierce, Jade Gamble... and my Dani. I've never forgotten their names and I never will," Dawn said solemnly.

"Neither will I. That's what I'm trying to do here, Dawn. I want to see if there's a connection between my wife and all of these women. Your daughter included. Scarlett had a stalker and I believe he's the culprit behind her murder. I don't know if Lisandra and Jade were ever stalked but I think it's possible. Maybe not to the extent of what my wife experienced, but that's the only thing that makes sense to me. Dani herself told me that she felt like she was being followed these last few weeks. Something has to give. My wife's stalker has to be behind all this."

Dawn sipped her tea and furrowed her eyebrows. She stared at the digital clock in the archway of the front door.

"I'm assuming you never found someone who could've been your wife's stalker?"

"There was one man I suspected. Luke Prescott. It was a few years ago. He had started working for Ivan Pierce's security company. Ivan is one of my closest friends. He told me that Luke had asked a lot of questions about Scarlett. He seemed a little too interested in her. We had all known him in high school. He was a freak, to be frank with you. He used to record girls without their permission. To me, he fit the mold. Ivan and I talked to him. I found him suspicious. Before I could do anything else, he was...murdered. It was so bizarre. Luke's clothes were found on the beach in *White Abyss*. They were caked in blood. Luke's wallet was missing credit cards and cash. The license was kept inside and there was no body. It was assumed that it had been washed out to sea. The most likely outcome since his body was never found anywhere else," I explained.

"Oh god. That's horrible."

"What's worse is that after his death, I found a black shoebox at my front door. There were photographs inside. Scarlett's stalker was still out there and had taken pictures of her in public places, without her knowing. He was toying with me, making me feel like a complete fool. I had no idea who it could've been at that point. I had a few wild theories."

Dawn finished her tea and scurried closer to me. She met my eyes with intent and closely listened.

"What were they?"

"I thought someone might've wanted to steal Luke's identity or something. I don't know. Maybe he saw something he shouldn't have. Like, he was a witness to something he should have never seen," I said gravely.

Those were the things that kept me up at night in the past, after Luke's death. I often laid awake at night, staring at the ceiling. I wondered if Luke had seen anything or if it was a plain, brutal robbery. Something in my gut told me there was always more to the story. Something told me that Luke knew something sinister. Similar to Michael Madden, Luke's death wasn't a normal one. It was shrouded in a cloud of doubt and secrecy. Just like the murder of my wife and the mystery of the missing women. I didn't envy Detective Gamble's job one bit. He must've gone insane a long time ago.

"Can I tell you something?" Dawn asked softly.

"Yes, of course."

She inched closer and pursed her lips.

"I never trusted that Abel Armoni. I know you and Dani work for him, but...something's not right with him."

"I agree with you."

"All those rumors about the women he's raped...I believe it. He's rich and powerful. He thinks he's untouchable. He must've touched Dani as well. That sick bastard. He even ran away. Apparently no one knows where he went. He's guilty," Dawn hissed.

"I will find out what he's done. I promise you." I took her hand and squeezed it. She gave me a brief grin.

"I believe you, Damian."

"I need to ask you about Dani's boyfriend, John Santoro. What do you know about him? Did Dani ever tell you anything? He seems to have disappeared as well."

"Oh yes. I saw him twice. They were brief encounters. He seemed...fine. He worked at the club. I'm sure you knew that. I haven't thought much about him. They weren't dating for that long and Dani never gave me the impression that he was a bad guy. I gave the police his phone number. They couldn't find anyone associated with it."

*A phone number,* I thought.

"May I see it?"

"Of course. I have it written down somewhere." Dawn got up and walked to the kitchen. I took out my phone and went to the list of phone numbers I had accumulated. It was all the numbers that had called and texted Scarlett over the years. The numbers that had harassed her with sick messages and creepily silent phone calls. I assumed they were all from burner phones, but you never knew. I wanted to keep them. I was glad that I did, especially after Scarlett's death.

*You can find the truth in the most unexpected places,* Ivan said.

Dawn came back with a post-it note. She handed it to me. It read: *904-417-0226*. I scanned through my list. There were three phone numbers with that same area code:

*904-111-1110*
*904-221-0807*
*904-417-0226*

I did a double take and almost fell out of my seat. It was there. It was the same phone number. John Santoro had either called or texted Scarlett at some point over the last few years. My heart was racing and Dawn gave me a concerned look. I tried to calm myself down as my ears started ringing. I shut my eyes as the back of my head started to throb. I saw bright lights in the darkness. I saw Bruno McCoy's scowl and I saw Scarlett's glowing smile. I saw...the man. John Santoro himself. He had the dark brown eyes, the beard and the curly brown hair. I saw lips that curved into a cruel smile. I opened my eyes and rubbed the back of my head, where my stitches had been.

"Are you okay? Are you okay, Damian? What happened? What happened, Damian?" Dawn's voice sounded muffled, like it was far away. So many thoughts raced around my head, but one was clear. One screaming thought was abundantly clear.

*John Santoro is Scarlett's stalker.*

"Do you...do you remember anything else, Dawn? Sorry, I just...I need to get going. I need to uh...I found something. Something I've been searching for. Do you know anything else about John Santoro? Anything else at all?"

"He had this scar on his leg. It was rather vulgar. He said he got it in a street fight when he was younger. That was one thing I found strange about him. I figured the fight must've been *very* violent."

"Good to know. That's definitely telling. Was that the only strange thing about him?"

Dawn squinted her eyes and stared at the floor. I eagerly awaited her answer.

*I found him. I found that motherfucker. John Santoro is Scarlett's stalker. I'm gonna kill that son of a bitch.*

"Oh, the car. Dani complained about his car a few times. It was old and beat-up. It was a…Rolvo. A Rolvo sedan. It was dark blue or black I believe. I saw it once. It had a nasty dent. He never even used it to go to work. So Dani chose to drive them around because his car was well…a shitbox. That's what Dani told me."

"Holy shit," I whispered.

*132nd and Ruby Lane. The abandoned warehouse. The Rolvo sedan. He's there. That motherfucker…is there.*

"Thank you, Dawn. I gotta go." I raced out the front door, hopped into my car and sped down the street.

"I found you, stalker. I finally found you."

# CHAPTER 14
## 2011

The sky was grey with minimal sunlight peeking out of the clouds. There was a soft breeze and all you could hear were the soft chirping of birds soaring overhead. I was walking back home from the basketball courts. My white shirt was drenched with sweat and my body ached from the pickup games I had played. Dark, wet pools drenched my armpits, which indicated I had been playing for hours. I closed my eyes as I sprayed water from my bottle all over my face, attempting to cool myself off. I heard echoes from Sam and Ivan. I laughed to myself. I loved those guys.

*Pass the ball, you skinny fuck!* Sam had yelled.

*Don't listen to Sam, he's just here for the cardio!* Ivan had replied.

*Let me score, assface!* Sam had argued back.

*If we leave it up to you, we'll lose every game!*

*Your friendship means nothing to me, Ivan!*

*We're not friends, Sam!*

It was always a blast playing sports with my brothers. How I longed for the times when days were simple and when everyone had peace in their hearts. I never knew how good I had it, until one day...it was gone. There weren't any warnings or alerts. No news headlines or notifications on my phone. It happened from one day to the next. When the world became dark and stormy.

When I got home, I found Scarlett in our backyard. She was drawing on a canvas placed on her easel. I snuck up on her and silently admired her as she sketched a round, dark figure who appeared to be holding a double-barrel shotgun. It was pointing towards a bright white cloud that had streaks of lighting in it. The background was a crimson-colored, hellish forest with creepy red eyes peeking out.

"What's that supposed to be?"

"A combination of all the art gallery owners shooting and killing my dreams." Scarlett glanced back at me with glossy eyes.

"Oh come on, honey. Don't say that. Everyone goes through this rejection phase."

"How would you know, Damian?" Scarlett threw her graphite pencil at the canvas and rushed towards me. She glared then softened her expression. She sighed and sagged her shoulders.

"I don't know how it feels to be rejected as an artist, but I was rejected from the high school basketball team. Same idea, right?"

Scarlett wrapped her arms around me and dug her head into my shoulder. I reciprocated and softly kissed the top of her head.

"I'm sorry. I didn't mean that. You don't deserve that from me."

"It's okay. I know you're frustrated."

"I've been rejected so many times. No one wants to showcase my work. I don't know what to do. There's no handbook on this sort of thing." She gazed up at me with pained eyes. I felt a strong tug on my heart. I really felt for her. I didn't like seeing her dispirited.

"Keep going, sweetheart. You're still young. You'll always have my support," I smiled at her.

"What if I'm not good enough? Maybe I just have to accept that. Sometimes you have to listen to what the world tells you. Maybe my mom was right. It was just a pipe dream. I need to get a real job. I need to be realistic."

I powerfully grabbed her arms and bent downward a bit to meet her at eye level.

"Hey! Don't talk like that. You *are* good enough. I promise you, baby. You have talent. I'm not just saying that. I see how hard you work on this. You're a great artist. You won't fail, if you never give up. You got that?" I said sternly.

"Yeah. Yeah, I got that," Scarlett giggled.

"Hey, don't laugh! You're still young! And hot! Really hot!"

Scarlett's cheeks flushed red and she beamed at me. That's how I wanted to see my soulmate. She deserved nothing less. If everyone wanted to count her out, that was fine. I would always be in her corner, fighting for her.

"I really appreciate you, Damian."

"Hey, I appreciate you too. I love you, Scarlett," I softly pulled her in and planted a deep kiss on her lips.

"I love you too."

A couple of days later, I sat on my couch and watched the basketball game on TV. The *Knights* were playing the *Pirates*. I was extremely invested until Scarlett skipped in. She was still in her waitress uniform. It was comprised of a white button-down shirt, a long checkered skirt and brown boots. To top it off, she wore a small cowboy hat. She worked at a restaurant that served southern-style food. She didn't like it very much, but it paid decently. It was also flexible enough to where she'd be able to take days off to work on her art.

She sat on my lap and blocked my view, but I didn't care. I could tell by the look on her face that she wanted to talk. I tried to never ignore her. I always saw how my trash can of a father would ignore my mother. I promised myself I'd never become him. *Never*.

"How was work?" She asked.

"It was good. You can't beat working with Ivan. It's a chill job."

"Until the shit hits the fan." She tilted her face down and raised her eyebrows at me. I playfully ruffled her hair.

"It hasn't happened yet and it never will."

"It better not. I don't want a phone call in the middle of the night. You're not going to die on me."

"Don't even say that, Scarlett. I'm not going anywhere."

She laid down on my chest and I put my arm over her shoulder.

"How was work for you?"

"Same old shit. Drunk husbands catcalling me, sober wives giving me bitchy attitudes and kitchen cooks perving on me."

"My offer still stands. I *will* beat the shit out of those guys. Please let me. Ivan and Sam will help me."

"You're not doing any of that. I don't like seeing you violent. That's not the man I love." She traced her finger around my lips.

"The man you love only wants to protect the woman *he* loves."

"There are other ways to do that. It's not up for debate."

"Fine. You're the boss."

In truth, I only said that to appease her. If push came to shove, I'd murder any man if they touched Scarlett. I meant that.

"But, I have good news! It wasn't just the same old shit today. I met someone. An art dealer who owns a gallery in Rainfall."

"Oh shit, that's awesome. What's his name?"

"Bruno McCoy."

"Oh wow. Sounds like an entitled prick."

"Oh, he definitely is. But this is the way the world works, Damian. These type of guys own these places. What can I do?"

"Find someone better."

"You know I've tried and this is a real chance for me to showcase my work. I need to get my name out there. I showed him pictures of my art, Damian. He really liked it. He was genuine. He offered me a chance to put my portraits in his art gallery."

"Wow baby! That's amazing!" I hugged her tight and kissed her hard. She got up and jumped with excitement.

"I know right?! Right when I wanted to give up, I was given this gift. This is the universe telling me to continue."

"Exactly. This is what I've been telling you. So, when can I meet this guy?"

Scarlett suddenly became silent and stared at the floor. She slowly slid her phone out of her skirt.

"Well...there's just one thing. I don't know if this was a joke or...I don't know. I think it's stupid. It doesn't mean anything. It's happened before."

She handed me her phone. I took it, suspicion growing in my stomach until it felt like an iron hand was strangling my heart. Rage erupted throughout my body in waves of heat as I saw what Bruno had sent her. I wanted to smash her phone against the wall. I wanted to see that phone scattered all over the floor in broken pieces of plastic and glass.

"Why is he sending you nude photos of himself?" I asked angrily.

"I don't know. He just did it. I didn't ask for that shit."

"What the hell is this guy's problem?" I got up and paced around. I was on the brink of losing my shit.

"Baby, I have no idea. I'm a little bit freaked out, but I think it's whatever right? I told him I'm in a relationship. I even showed him a picture of us. He told me we were a beautiful couple."

"He...he's toying with you. He's toying with me."

"What? What do you mean?"

"This is what these rich guys do. They think there's no consequences. They think they can get away with this type of shit," I whispered to myself.

"Baby, what are you saying? What's wrong?"

"I'll handle this."

"How are you going to handle it?" Scarlett rushed towards me and gripped my arm. She gave me an intense look of concern. I did my best to appear relaxed.

"I'm just going to talk to him, man to man. I'm gonna tell him that I find those pictures very disrespectful. There's no consent involved. You didn't ask for that. He stepped out of line. He needs to know this."

"Okay, but please don't make him mad. Don't cause a scene, Damian."

"Don't be naive, Scarlett. I know this is a great opportunity for you, but don't be blinded. If he did it once, he'd do it again. These rich guys are perverts. I've come across plenty of these assholes on security jobs. Ivan and I know the type. We'll handle this."

"Deep down, I know you're right. I...I just hope it gets worked out," Scarlett sighed.

I kissed her on the cheek and warmly embraced her.

"Don't worry baby. I have your back."

*I'm gonna fucking kill this guy.*

---

The memory played back like a blurry video recording in my head. It was late at night and dark out. Ivan had come to assist me. Sam was getting high somewhere. I couldn't count on him that particular day.

*Let's go get that perverted motherfucker,* Ivan had said. We were a bit more rambunctious when we were younger. We didn't think about the consequences. We only knew that we had to stand up for ourselves when life demanded it. No one was coming to save us, we had to save ourselves. If I learned anything from my dumpster of a father, it was just that.

*Sooner or later, you pay the price.* He was right. That meant it was up to me to set things right.

Bruno McCoy's art gallery was down the street from Abel Armoni's nightclub, in the entertainment district. Restaurants, food trucks, vape stores, pothole-ridden parking lots and shady gas stations were lined up and down the smoothly-paved street. That was courtesy of Abel Armoni's father. He did anything he could to give back to the community. So they'd have an easier time going to his nightclub of course.

Bruno's art gallery was a square, beige hole-in-the-wall. It had a large, rectangular glass pane that allowed you a preview of the exhibition room inside. It was an open, white space with strong lighting that displayed various forms of artwork. It included paintings, sculptures, drawings and photographs. It was a simple, minimalist building that commanded attention. I found Bruno outside of it, pretentiously gloating with a few other men who curiously listened.

He was a towering, bald man with a full black beard. He was fit and had bulging muscles that protruded out of his tight, burgundy polo shirt. He had big, meaty thighs that were stretching out his black jeans. By all accounts, he was a *unit* as my friends would say. A man as wide and strong as Sebastian Gunner. I was intimidated but I didn't fear him. I was a young and stupid kid who only wanted to protect the woman he loved. I feared no one.

Ivan and I rushed down the street. He was behind me as I charged ahead with an empty glass bottle wrapped around my fingers. When I arrived within a few feet of him, I stopped and stared him down. He paid no mind to me so I made sure to get his immediate attention.

"Bruno!" I angrily shouted. I threw the glass bottle near him and it shattered on the ground next to him. He immediately stopped talking and stepped forward. He aggressively pointed at me while his entourage gathered around him with scowls on their faces.

"What's up, my friend? What's your problem?" Bruno's face was bright red and his arm was shaking from how angry he was.

"Scarlett del Toro. That's my problem. Why the fuck are you sending her pictures of your *tiny* dick?!" I bellowed.

Bruno's friends awkwardly chuckled and gave him funny looks.

"I don't know who that is and I don't know what you're talking about. Scram guy. Get the hell out of here. Do you know who I am?"

"Obviously. You're Bruno McCoy. The big man with a tiny dick and a tiny set of balls."

Bruno's friends tried their hardest to stifle their laughter while Ivan was quietly cackling behind me. I practically saw steam blowing out of Bruno's ears. He clenched his fists and the veins in his neck were swelling. He leisurely stomped forward with a face of pure viciousness. I felt Bruno's violent intentions. He wanted to beat me to a bloody pulp. He didn't realize that I was about to do the same to him.

"Say that again and you won't be breathing in five minutes," Bruno warned.

"I'd do it in two," I snapped back.

I thought I was being clever. I wasn't. It was a life-altering mistake the minute I rushed Bruno McCoy and tackled him to the ground. While everyone was paralyzed with shock, I got a few solid licks in. I slugged his perfectly punchable douchebag face four times before I was pried off of him by his friends. Ivan had engaged the other two cargo-shorts-wearing art "experts" and was doing a decent job of holding his own. Ivan was always more measured and patient in his approach. He bobbed and weaved. He slapped fists away, he used his legs and had the intelligence to dodge the impulsive, lunging punches those two pretentious idiots were throwing.

I was a wild, untamed bull and I usually allowed my anger to get the best of me. I head butted the guy who was pulling me back and savagely knuckled Bruno in the nose, causing him to stagger back and bleed. He angrily wiped away the blood that was trickling down his chin and hastily pulled something out of his pocket. I was winding up another brutal blow before I was smashed in the back of the head with a rock. I stumbled to the ground and saw Ivan being pinned down by the same two idiots he was fighting.

That's when I realized it was over before it began. Ivan's face was freshly injured. He had a few red blotches where I assumed he had been hit. My face was about to look a lot worse. I gripped the back of my head as it violently throbbed. I didn't remember much about what had happened next, but I did remember seeing Bruno's cruel smile as he slipped on brass knuckles. Ivan was incoherently yelling as Bruno battered my aching face and gruesomely smashed my head in. He busted my lip open, nearly popped my eye out and split open the back of my head like a plump watermelon. At least that's what it felt like.

I felt fresh blood gushing out from behind my head as it drenched my hair. My vision was blurred and my ears were buzzing as I forcibly puked out globs of blood into the ground. It felt like bits of my skin were being ripped off my blood-soaked cheeks as he continued to strike me down with extreme prejudice. I had a hard time keeping my eyes open. I began to lose consciousness due to the barbaric onslaught being inflicted upon me. I managed to make out some things that Ivan was anxiously shouting.

*No! Please, Bruno.*

*Stop this!*

*You're going to kill him!*

*We're sorry!*

*Please let him live!*

Ivan sobbed. All I thought in that moment was how much I wanted to survive and live. I didn't want to leave any of them behind. Scarlett, Ivan and Sam. I wanted to see them again. I knew I had done something incredibly stupid but I hoped I would have the chance to see the sun rise in the morning. That was all I wanted.

"Relax. Fucking idiot kids. I don't kill people. I teach them lessons. Don't fuck with me again, kid. Next time you'll be a mutilated mess of blood, guts, brains and broken bone. If you don't believe me…I want you to try me."

Bruno tightly grabbed my hair then threw me back onto the pavement with great force. I quietly moaned in pain while I held my head, worried that it was somehow about to fall off. That's how much pain I was feeling. Once the adrenaline wore off, I knew I was going to feel like someone was slicing my head open with a buzzsaw.

Next thing I saw was Bruno and his entourage quickly climbing onto a jet-black SUV. I briefly saw a shadowy shape in the driver's seat. A quick glint of light from a lamp post illuminated his face for just a second. I recognized it immediately. It was Luke Prescott. In all the chaos and horror that had occurred I had forgotten about that one nagging detail. It was a memory I didn't recall often. It was a night I never wanted to remember. Ivan had held my hand and was begging me to stay alive on that dark, bloodstained sidewalk. He gently slapped my bruised cheeks and shouted at me to stay awake.

*Stay awake, Damian! Do not fall asleep! Stay with me man. Fucking stay with me!*

I was rushed to the hospital and all I really remembered was Scarlett sobbing on my chest after the medical procedure had been finished. I was in a dim hospital room in a solid, cold bed. There was an IV catheter inserted in my arm and I felt a dull throbbing in the back of my head. I softly ran my sore fingers through what felt like stitches. Scarlett noticed I had woken up and interlocked her warm, shaky hands with mine. I saw that her eyes were puffed up and swollen from all the crying. My throbbing heart immediately shattered in two as I shamefully watched her, drowning in misery...because of me.

She gaped at me with anguished, glistening eyes. She studied my mauled appearance with a mixture of agony and rage drawn on her face. I was apprehensive as to what she was thinking and what she would say to me. My stomach was simmering with a gut-wrenching storm of dread. When she finally spoke, she broke the thick tension that had formed in the eerily quiet room.

"Don't you *ever* do anything like that again, Damian. You selfish asshole. You...you almost *died*. You god damn *idiot*. I swear...I'm not going through life without you. Do you hear me? Do you *fucking* hear me?" she thundered.

I remained deathly quiet and pulled her closer to my face. I slowly nodded. She rested her head near my neck and I placed my free hand on her head as she continued to snivel. It was one of the most harrowing nights of my entire life. Aside from the other agonizing tragedies I had experienced, confronting Bruno McCoy had been one of the absolute worst...only because of how much I had terrified Scarlett. That was the night she thought she became a widow.

# CHAPTER 15

I urgently texted Ivan and told him to meet me at the abandoned warehouse.

*I found him, Ivan. The stalker. It's John Santoro. The stalker is John Santoro. Meet me at 132nd and Ruby Lane. It's a warehouse. Come quietly. Have your gun ready. Park near Milton's.* I sent.

*Holy shit. I'll be right there. We need to talk. I found something.* Ivan replied.

I couldn't wait for him. I needed to find John Santoro before he slipped through my fingers. I needed to get to the truth...once and for all.

I parked near *Milton's* and quietly crawled underneath the twisted fence that was stationed around the warehouse. I crouched behind a pile of cinderblocks. It was dark and quiet. Lightning struck overhead as it began to sprinkle rain. I had an old crowbar in my hand along with a revolver tucked securely behind my pants. I peeked out and swiftly spotted the dented black Rolvo sedan. It was John's car. It had been the exact same car I had seen when I tried to find him the first time. The car that Dani's mom had described. I wondered if he lived in there.

I saw that there wasn't anyone around but I still soundlessly snuck over to the Rolvo. I cautiously peeked through the windows and saw that no one was inside. I saw piles of varying clothes, empty soda bottles and fast food burger wrappers. I went around to the back and used the crowbar to slowly lift the trunk as discreetly as possible. It popped open with a soft creak. Thankfully the car was ancient and falling apart. It made breaking into much easier.

What I noticed first was the abhorrent smell. It smelled like rotten fish mixed in with the stench of wet, filthy socks. The odor was horribly violent and ghastly. It caused me to jerk my head back as I pinched my nose. Salty tears watered my eyes as I continued to inspect the interior.

A pale yellow light illuminated the shocking contents of the trunk. I quickly scanned my surroundings to ensure no one was watching me. I then tentatively sorted through everything. I found women's clothing to start, but not shirts or pants. There were several pairs of women's panties. In addition to that were bras and sets of lingerie. Some of them were moist and stunk of a bleach-like smell. I tossed them away in absolute disgust. I didn't even want to imagine what had been going on in that car.

Strangely enough, I found a few pairs of multi-colored wigs. Suddenly, I was confused.

*Is this the right car? Could this be a prostitute's car? Or maybe a cross-dresser?*

I continued to search and found a tightly wound plastic bag filled with several burner phones. They were definitely burners. I tried turning one on but I soon realized none of them had the battery placed inside. The whole search was becoming more and more puzzling by the minute. I desperately sifted through the rest of the things in the trunk until my heart stopped and my skin ran cold.

I saw the glint of silver flash for a brief second. I peeked closer and found tiny chains that belonged to a silver bracelet. I pinched it with my fingers and held it in my hand. It had an ornament. A cursive, metallic lettering that spelled out *Scarlett*. Before I had a chance to think, I heard the clinking of a fence. I quietly shut the trunk and crouched. I crawled away from the car while stuffing Scarlett's stolen bracelet inside my pocket. I hid behind a rusted barrel that gave a good vantage point to the fence. I hoped it was Ivan. I didn't check my phone out of fear of pressing the wrong button and giving myself away. My hands were clammy and my heart was pounding in my throat after finding Scarlett's stolen bracelet.

The truth was finally clear...Bruno McCoy had sent John Santoro to defile and murder my wife after seven years. I was going to find out why. I slowed and paced my breathing as I saw a shadowy figure walking towards a torn-up wall. It led to a compartmentalized area inside the warehouse. It was John. It had to be. He sat on an old pile of wooden pallets. I saw the glow of a small orange light emanating from his hands. He lit a cigarette. It definitely wasn't Ivan. He didn't smoke.

I became a muted, slowly creeping body as I snuck towards John. I only hoped Ivan wouldn't come at the wrong time. He knew how to follow instructions. He knew how to move silently. I patiently slid out my revolver and cupped it with both of my hands. I took one cautious step after another until I reached a fair distance in the deathly quiet darkness. He seemed to be stuck in his own fantasy land. John's eyes were closed as he smoked and blew out clouds of gray.

He looked more and more familiar as I inspected him. I never had gotten a good look at him. The ID that Elsa gave me was faded and I wasn't even entirely sure if he was the man I had been seeing. The man with curly brown hair and dark eyes.

"Don't move a muscle...John Santoro," I warned. I had the revolver pointed straight at him. I tried to maintain my nerve as I slightly trembled. John dropped the cigarette on the floor and the orange light was extinguished. He slowly turned his head and blankly stared at me. He looked like a deer caught in the headlights. I examined his face and a twinge of familiarity struck my gut like a lighting strike.

He was there with Bruno on that horrible night...the night I almost died. But there was something else. I knew him...from somewhere.

"I'm sorry," John stated.

"For what?"

"Everything."

*Everything. Why did he sound so familiar?*

It dawned on me. I never thought of the possibility. It hit me like a two-ton truck.

"Wait a minute, no. No that doesn't make sense. You're him."

John sprung off the pallets and dashed forward. Adrenaline surged through my pulse-pounding body as I chased him. It was short-lived as he stopped, turned around and shot at me with his own gun. I dodged left at the last second as my shoulder was grazed. I cried out. It was a minor injury. I'd live. I heard another gunshot ring out. It reverberated throughout the night sky and echoed like crackling thunder.

I saw John on the floor, gripping his leg. Someone else had shot him. I inspected my revolver and glanced behind me. I did a double-take as I saw Ivan curled up on the ground with a gun in his hand. He was bleeding and clutching his chest. I raced towards him. I heard his shallow breaths and held onto his arm.

*No, no, no, no. Why is Ivan bleeding?*

I couldn't lose Ivan. I couldn't lose my best friend. It wasn't fair. The cruel scythe of death wanted to rip away everyone I loved, until there was no one left to take.

"Listen, I'm…I'm done. I need…I need you to listen to me," Ivan sputtered out blood from his mouth.

My body became extremely tense and the beads of sweat that rolled down my neck were ice-cold. I refused to believe that I was about to lose my best friend. The man who had been with me through thick and thin. Ivan Pierce, the man who was helping me find the degenerate stalker who had raped and murdered my wife.

"No, no, no, no, no, Ivan. You're okay. You're gonna be okay. Keep your hand to your wound, apply pressure," I ordered him as I helped him. Ivan's blood was spilling all over my hands but I refused to let go. It started raining hard.

"Damian stop. Listen to me," Ivan whispered.

"Just breathe, Ivan. *Fucking breathe*," he softly shook his head and put his hands over mine.

"Damian..." Ivan gasped for breath.

"No, Ivan. Please. This...no. *Fuck!* This can't end like this. It wasn't supposed to end like this," tears flooded my eyes as droplets poured down my cheeks.

"I...I found it."

Ivan's eyes were wide and he had difficulty breathing.

"What? What did you find?"

"Dani's...her...her...look at the files. My office," Ivan grunted. I got closer to him and pressed my ear to his mouth.

"Ivan, what files? What are you talking about? You're not going to die. You are *not* going to die," my voice trembled.

"Look...at...Elsa. Dani...she's there," he mumbled as his eyes grew lifeless. Ivan's hands slipped from my grasp as he became still. I gripped his shirt and tenderly shook him.

"No, Ivan. No, no, no, no, no. What happened? What the fuck just happened? This...this...no, no, no, no. *Fuck!* This is all my fault. Why did I drag you into this? Why the *fuck* did I do this to you, Ivan?"

I gently closed his eyes and sat on the ground. I lost my best friend that day. I had lost my brother, my wife...and my best friend. My heart turned black...into a cold, harsh stone, devoid of any happy emotion. That was gone. All gone. He had been there for me and he was someone who didn't want me gone. Ivan gave me a reason not to slash my own throat and end all of my suffering. I had lived a tragic life and I had wanted it to end. He was the only one left who understood the haunting pain and the suffocating grief that strangled my heart after Scarlett's death.

All that was left within me was a seething, explosive fury. It was ready to be unleashed at the people responsible for taking Scarlett and Ivan away from me. Only one hope remained…Dani. I feared the worst, but she was still missing. There was still a chance. One small chance. The only chance I had at redeeming whatever humanity was left inside me.

I slowly stood up, in a despondent daze. Once I spotted John Santoro limping away, across the warehouse…my stomach became incensed. A ferocious fire had been lit and I found myself impulsively hunting down John. I was going to barrage him with all the volcanic ferocity that was exploding out of me.

# CHAPTER 16

It didn't take long for me to catch up to him. He had been shot in the leg and was barely able to walk, much less run away. He had nowhere to hide and nowhere to go. I planned to end it all right then and there. I hid behind a column as he haphazardly shot a few times in my direction. There was a pause.

I briefly peeked out and saw him limping away. I rushed towards him. He turned, attempting to aim his gun in my face. Before he had a chance to lift his arm, I chopped down on it. He grunted and dropped it. The gun clattered to the floor. It became a mad scramble to the ground as we fought over control of the weapon. I pushed him aside with my body weight and managed to snatch it up. I flipped the safety and stuffed it in the back of my pants. He hurriedly tried to escape, but I grabbed his shirt and yanked him back. He broke free.

I became frustrated and tackled him. I pinned him down. He anxiously faced me and swung his fists. I easily leaned back and dodged his swings. I quickly jabbed him in the chin then punched him across his face. I bashed his head with my reddened, inflamed fists as he tried to fight me off. Every time he tried to kick me off, I slugged him harder.

John's petrified face was getting battered and became severely bruised. He eventually coughed up blood on himself. He begged me with his swollen eyes to stop. I staunchly refused. I was committed to pulverizing him for murdering Ivan in cold blood. I should've ended his pathetic life, but I needed him alive for a few more minutes. He needed to admit to me that he was Scarlett's stalker.

I sprang up, then violently dragged him to a wall by his collar. I stood him up and dug my elbow securely into his neck. He put his slimy hands on my bulging arm and tried to pry me off to no avail. I angrily forced him back and dared him to move. My hostile eyes glared into his terrorized soul. He wasn't going anywhere until I exacted righteous vengeance.

"Who are you? Hmm? Who the *fuck* are you?! Tell me! Tell me who you are!" I commanded.

"Will you let me take it off?" John's voice quivered.

"Take what off?"

He slowly reached his hand up and placed it on his head. I remained laser-focused and was fully prepared to crush his neck with one devastating blow. If he tried *anything*, he'd be half-dead.

"It's a wig," he snatched off the mop of curly brown hair that had been placed on his head. John's short blonde hair was revealed underneath. He tossed aside the wig. It was one of the strangest things I had ever seen in my life. In that moment, I knew that I knew him. I gasped internally. I refused to believe it. It simply wasn't possible. I thought that my mind was playing tricks on me. I thought that my head injury had permanently damaged me and that I no longer had a sane, fully aware mind. The traumatic ordeal I was still processing didn't help either.

"Your real name is not John Santoro. Tell me the truth. Tell me who you are or I'll kill you," I threatened.

"*I want you, red. I need you, red. I'll fuck you in his bed...until he's dead,*" John chimed as he pinched his eyeballs.

"What? What the fuck did you say?" I pressed my elbow tighter against his neck until he started squealing and choking in pain. I relented just enough for him to breathe. He wouldn't be breathing for much longer.

"You don't remember?" John squeezed out small, circular lenses that had been embedded into his eyes. They were contacts. He blinked rapidly as a few tears spilled out of his eyes. John's eyes weren't actually brown they were a soft green.

"I was right. You were my wife's stalker. I remember. You messaged her that, you sick son of a bitch."

My jaw was clenched and I was seriously considering putting my fist through his throat. As I examined him closer...my eyes widened in shock. My body became jolted by shivers that erupted all over my ice cold skin. I struggled to maintain my composure as I shuddered at John's unnerving grin.

"Now you remember me," John proudly declared.

"No, that's not possible. You died. You were murdered. You're supposed to be dead."

"Made it look good, didn't I?"

"You're Luke. Luke Prescott," I whispered.

"I am."

"How? How the hell are you alive? You were killed."

"Lots of blood on my clothes. It left a nasty scar on my leg. That one hurt. Put my wallet and license in the vicinity of my *dead* body. All my money and credit cards *stolen*. Everything right at the edge of the sea. The perfect set up and the perfect murder."

Dawn had told me about that scar. I didn't think much of it. Only that John Santoro was most likely a violent man. As it turned out, John Santoro was Luke Prescott. The motherfucker had been in disguise. I felt sick to my stomach. The man I had seen had been Luke Prescott the entire time. All the wigs, the burner phones and the women's undergarments in the trunk of the Rolvo sedan suddenly made sense. All of it. Everything made sense.

"You're a fucking psychopath, Luke."

"How do you explain my dead body? It washed out to sea and was eaten by sharks or something else. Why were my clothes taken off? It's suspicious but no other evidence to go off of. There was no reason to continue. I knew they'd chalk it up as another tragic murder that would go unsolved. Likely reason? A robbery gone horribly wrong. After all...there are many other cases to follow-up on and no one gives a shit about me. *No one,*" Luke shrugged.

My head was spinning and I had a hard time believing what Luke was telling me. I still couldn't believe that he was *alive*. After all those years, he was alive.

"You're insane. You're absolutely insane. Why? Why would you go that far?"

"I loved Scarlett. I loved Scarlett more than you could possibly know."

"You call *stalking* my wife, love? You call that *love*?! You tormented her for *years*! You made her *suffer*! You took her from me!" I bellowed.

I had turned feral. The man that I had wanted to kill, the man I wanted dead, was finally in front of me. Not only that, he had murdered my best friend too. It took every ounce of will in my being to restrain myself long enough to get the information that I needed.

"I loved her since high school. I was obsessed with her. The beautiful, popular Scarlett Santoro. The talented artist who everyone lusted after."

"That's why you put your last name as Santoro. You really are a sick piece of shit."

"It made me feel like we belonged together. I'm sorry, Damian. I needed her. I needed to see her. I needed to feel her dirty underwear. I needed to smell it. Oh god, it smelled divine. I touched myself to her smell. I imagined plunging myself into her, over and over again. She turned me into a wild animal."

I couldn't believe what I was hearing. It was clear and obvious that Luke was mentally deranged.

"No one does what you did. No one goes that far to steal and smell women's underwear. What the *fuck* is wrong with you?" I glared at him in disgust.

He seemed amused, which pissed me off even more. While my blood was boiling and simmering with utter rage and fury, there he was, grinning like a lunatic.

"What are you talking about, Damian? Do you know how far people go for the people they love? If there's one thing, just one thing in this world that rings true, it's that. People go far beyond what they thought they were capable of, for love," Luke explained.

"You don't know what love is. You don't know what the hell you're talking about," I snapped.

"Damian, everyone has their own definitions of what love is. I have mine and you have yours. Don't believe me? Look at yourself in the mirror. Look at what happened to Ivan. Look how far you've been willing to go to find me to kill me. Your wife's stalker. Look at what you've done to exact revenge on me, Damian."

I remained quiet. He was speaking the truth, but it didn't matter. It didn't take away from the deplorable things he had done. He raped and murdered Scarlett. He deserved to be burned alive.

"You don't know me, Luke."

"You're probably right. What do I know? Look, I'm sorry I shot your little boyfriend. But I'll be honest, I'm glad he's dead. You and Ivan were getting a little too close to the truth. I thought you had figured it out. That's why I faked my death. I felt I would've been better off being a *dead* man anyway. You two would've followed me after that day. I needed peace. I needed to quell my anxieties. I would've never been able to admire my Scarlett ever again. I could *not* have that happen."

"You want me to kill you, don't you? You're the reason she's not here anymore, you fucking psychopath. *You did this*!" I was seething.

"I don't know what you're talking about. All I did was admire your wife from afar. I am devastated that she's dead. I really wanted to *fuck* her. I wanted to *fuck* her nice and slow, until she screamed my name with pleasure. *Harder, Luke. Fuck yes, Luke. I want all of you in me. I want you to cum inside of me, Luke.*"

I had enough. I blew up. I furiously punched him several times in his contorting face as he begged for me to stop. He whiplashed against the concrete wall, streaking it with blood from the back of his wounded head. I shook my hand as it began to ache from how hard I had clobbered him. Luke dryly chuckled as blood spilled out from his busted lip. He let out a throaty cough and drooled out red liquid from his mouth. It was staining his chipped teeth.

"Finally taking your revenge, huh?" Luke whimpered.

"I will. Soon," I warned.

"You can take a beating and dish it out. That's good," Luke groaned.

"What are you talking about?"

"I used to work for Bruno McCoy. The art dealer. You remember him?"

I knew it. I knew he had a connection to Bruno. He was there that day. The day I got my head bashed in. The day I almost died.

"I do. He almost killed me."

"I worked for him when we were younger. I cleaned his cottage, washed his cars and drove for him."

"Where are you going with this? My patience is running thin."

"Those dick pictures that Bruno sent your wife? They belonged to me. He offered his workers a chance to make $1000. He thought it'd be funny. He was that type of guy. He wanted one of us to send pictures of our dick to her with his phone. I jumped at the chance. He didn't know I was obsessed with her."

"You motherfucker. I knew you were there that day. You picked him up right after he beat the living shit out of me."

"I can't believe you remember that, especially with a chunk of your skull missing."

"It took a while," I admitted.

"Full circle moment, huh?" Luke grinned with his bloodied, broken teeth.

I forcefully clasped his jaw with my free hand and squeezed it as he whined in pain.

"I will make your death very painful if you continue to smile at me."

The stupid grin remained on Luke's bruised face as he scoffed at me.

"All I cared about was Scarlett. She's dead now. Do what you want. I have nothing to lose and nothing to live for anymore."

I aggressively clutched his neck with both of my hands and started choking him.

"Do it, do it, I want to die. I have nothing left. Kill me, Damian. Kill me!" Luke begged.

I continued on until it looked like his eyes were about to explode out of their sockets. I let go and pinned him to the wall with an elbow to his chest. He harshly coughed and gagged as he gasped for air.

I couldn't do it. I could't kill him. Not like that. Not in such a savage way. I knew that Ivan wouldn't have been proud of me. I didn't kill him out of respect for my fallen friend. If another time came to take my revenge...I would take it. But I chose not to that night. I was on the brink of insanity. I was seconds away from losing my own humanity and becoming a savage, cold-blooded murderer. The same type of murderer, Luke was.

"No, not yet. I need to know where Dani is. What did you do to her? Where is she?"

"I did nothing to her. I don't care about Dani. She was a plaything. Something to distract me from Scarlett's horrible death."

"You're subhuman. I know you did something to her. Stop fucking lying to me," I growled through gritted teeth.

Suddenly I heard police sirens in the distance. There was a thunderous sound of engines roaring and tires screeching near the warehouse. Time was running out.

"Looks like someone heard the gunshots," Luke muttered.

"Tell me where Dani is before I kill you."

"You won't kill me, not now," Luke sneered.

"Tell me one thing, Luke. Why did you do it? If you truly loved Scarlett in your own sick and twisted way, why did you murder her?"

Luke's eyes broadened and he locked his gaze with mine. A hint of confusion became visible on his face.

"I didn't," Luke proclaimed.

He never broke eye contact and he wasn't smiling anymore. He seemed...genuine. It made no sense to me. I didn't know what to believe anymore. I was at a loss for words. I studied him from top to bottom.

"What? Of course you did. It couldn't have been anyone else. It was you. You *raped* and *murdered* her, you motherfucker. You stalked her for *years* and you patiently waited for your chance. You're gonna rot in the hottest hell. I promise you," I snarled.

"I loved her, why would I kill her?"

"Because you couldn't have her, you sick bastard. That's why."

"You're wrong, Damian. Would I kill you? Yes. Would I kill your friend? I just did. Would I kill Scarlett? You're out of your mind. I *loved* her."

"That doesn't make any sense. *Stop fucking lying to me*," I barked.

"*I want you, red. I need you, red. I'll fuck you in his bed...until he's dead*," Luke whispered.

"Stop with your stupid fucking rhymes, you lunatic."

"What does it tell you?"

Scratchy radio commands, multiple footsteps and miscellaneous pieces of gear were shuffling and clinking towards us. I was out of time.

He didn't look like someone fit to escape anywhere at anytime. I wasn't even sure if he would survive the night. I made an extremely tough decision. A decision that wrenched my heart. I stuffed Scarlett's stolen bracelet deep inside Luke's pocket.

"What are you doing?"

"Something that'll help me find Scarlett's murderer. I don't believe you for a second, but we'll see. We'll see what the truth is."

I chucked him to the floor and made a break for it. I escaped as they crawled under the fence. I tossed Luke's gun in a faraway ditch.

I hoped and pleaded that whatever they found on Luke would be enough. Enough to forget about the inevitability of them knocking on my front door and questioning me. If they asked me why I had brutally assaulted Luke Prescott a.k.a. John Santoro...I didn't have an answer that would exonerate me. I only had what I saw as two justifications. The fact that he had stalked and terrorized my wife for years, which included him breaking into our house and stealing from her. The other justification was that he had shot and murdered Ivan, my best friend. A man I loved and had considered a brother.

# CHAPTER 17

I waited until the police had vacated the area outside *Milton's* to leave. I remained steadfast on my drive home. When I arrived, I immediately went to the bathroom and rigorously washed my hands. I was forced to wash my best friend's blood off of me. I stared at myself in the mirror and silently shook my head. I ferociously gripped the handles of the sink. I pulled on it until I turned red. When it began to hurt, I let go and heavily breathed. I screamed at myself.

*Fuck!*

I dragged myself to the kitchen and took out a couple of beers. I went to go sit on my couch, turned on a college basketball game and drank. I drank and drank until there was nothing left to drink.

I still couldn't believe that Ivan was dead. It hadn't hit me until I sat on my couch and drank away my misery. My best friend. The only man left. I needed Ivan. I had no one to turn to anymore. I felt the world weighing on my shoulders. It was all my fault. I blamed myself entirely. I knew he would've helped me hunt down Scarlett's killer before I even asked. That's the type of man Ivan was. He was as solid, dependable and loyal as they came.

I grabbed the empty beer bottles lying next to me and began launching them at the wall, one by one. They made a loud crash as they broke and shattered into tiny pieces. I stared at the shards that were piled on the floor. That's what my insides felt like. Shards of glass piercing every part of me, bleeding me dry and leaving me breathless.

I thought back to that crushing moment. I should've been shot instead of Ivan. He had been caught in the crossfire. I was Luke's intended target. I should've died, not him. I promised myself that I would find the man or people responsible for abducting Lisandra. I had to. It was the only way to honor his memory. I forced myself to swallow down my constricting feelings of utter torment that were leaving me paralyzed.

I needed to end it. There was a price that I was paying. I needed to make it all mean something. It all started with fulfilling his dying wish. I needed to look into the lead he was investigating, Dani's connection to Elsa Dietrich.

There was a strong knock at the front door. I stumbled over to it and fumbled the lock. I got it to open and pushed the door. Detective Gamble stood in front of me. He scrutinized me with sorrowful eyes.

"I take it that you know Ivan is dead."

"I caught wind," I swallowed.

"I'm very sorry, Damian. I know you two were very close," he patted me on the shoulder.

"Thank you, Detective," my eyes were glassy and I tried my best not to break down in front of him.

"I warned you. I warned you to be careful."

"That doesn't help much now, does it?" I scoffed.

"I saw you there, Damian. You were driving away in your car."

*He knows.*

"Do you have proof?"

"My memory serves as proof."

"What are you gonna do then? Arrest me? You can't prove that I was there," I stated firmly.

I couldn't implicate myself. I couldn't go to jail. Not with so much on the line. My only hope was Luke keeping his mouth shut, but why would he? He had every reason to name me and ruin what was left of my life.

"Listen, I'm just trying to piece together what happened. The shooter's name is John Santoro. He told us that Ivan beat him and then waved a gun at him. Ivan ran away and that's when John shot and killed him."

"Charge him with Ivan's murder then."

"There are some irregularities with the story he told us. There's no marks on Ivan's hands, but John said he did use a weapon. Apparently he used a brick. A brick that should have John's blood on it, yet it's nowhere to be found. A very strange occurrence. Would you care to elaborate?"

"No I wouldn't, because I know nothing."

*I can't trust you right now, Detective.*

"If I remember correctly, you mentioned the name John Santoro to me at *Milton's*."

"You are mistaken," I quickly replied.

Detective Gamble softly nodded.

"Okay, fair enough. I'm sure the truth will come out soon. Any word on your boss, Abel Armoni?"

"We can assume he has quietly left town for an extended period of time."

"Always hard to find powerful men on the run...even harder to prosecute them. One headache at a time." Gamble glanced at my hand and I winced. I hid it behind my leg. It was still reddened from beating Luke half-to-death.

"Is John Santoro the man who murdered my wife? It's him, isn't it?" I asked.

"I know you won't tell me anything, but I thank you for the *anonymous* tip. We searched the beat-up Rolvo sedan and found a lot of incriminating evidence on Santoro."

"Yeah, Ivan must've found out. He confronted him without me. I wish I could take it back, but I can't. I have to live with him gone." I wiped falling tears off my face and rubbed my eyes.

"I understand. I'm sorry to hear that. Why would Ivan confront John without telling you?"

"I don't know, Detective. I wish I did. Maybe time was of the essence. Maybe he was desperate to find anything he could on Lisandra."

Gamble peeked inside and saw the shards of the broken beer bottles strewn about.

"You're lucky. This is a very delicate, complicated criminal case. We will be speaking again," Detective Gamble promised.

*What I set out to accomplish will already be done.*

"When will I know John's the killer?"

"Wait a few days for the media. It'll explain everything. Give it some time, Damian. Don't do anything hasty."

I shook Gamble's hand and shut the door. I felt exposed and vulnerable. Detective Gamble knew that something was up. A shootout in Rainfall with someone dead in a random warehouse was not something that happened everyday. I had close ties to Ivan and once Luke ratted me out to the cops, I'd be in trouble. They'd drag me down to the police station and grill me alive. I needed to avoid that at all costs. Once Detective Gamble left, I grabbed my car keys and went for a drive.

### *LOCAL MAN FAKES SHOCKING DEATH.*

*A developing news article by the Rainfall Page told the story of Luke Prescott a.k.a. John Santoro. It had been an alias. Luke Prescott had strategically faked his own murder in the White Abyss. When he was asked why he did this, all he said was that he did it for a woman named Scarlett del Toro and that it was out of love. Police believe it is somehow connected to how he would reportedly stalk and terrorize the murder victim for years. In the past, police have files on record indicating that they had been called numerous times in relation to an unidentified individual stalking and harassing her in many forms. Luke would send sexually explicit, anonymous text messages to her in the hopes of winning her over.*

*He was believed to be living inside of an old Rolvo sedan parked near an abandoned warehouse on 132nd and Ruby Lane. The police found a mountain of incriminating evidence inside. Multi-colored wigs, fake IDs, color contact lenses, several burner phones and several sets of women's undergarments and lingerie. Most of the women's undergarments allegedly belonged to Scarlett del Toro. The most incriminating piece of evidence was a bracelet with an ornament attached. It had a cursive, metallic lettering that spelled out Scarlett. It was found in Luke's pocket. That proved to the authorities that Luke Prescott had broken into Scarlett del Toro's home and had robbed her of her possessions.*

*The police also found several photographs of Scarlett stuffed inside a manila folder. Luke had taken pictures of her while she was grocery shopping, at art galleries, painting in her backyard, even through her window, while she undressed in her bedroom.*

It made me livid, but I was relieved that he was in the hands of the police. There was nowhere for him to go with all the evidence mounted against him.

He would be tried and convicted for the rape and murder of my wife...or so I thought. I continued on with the article and couldn't believe what I was reading. The police had evidence that Luke Prescott was *not* in town the night Scarlett was raped and murdered.

He was clocked into work one hour away at a factory called *Gaumont Scientific.*

There was video footage to confirm it and his supervisor maintained that he was at work that night. It was the nail in the coffin. He couldn't have been the perpetrator if he wasn't there. It was sickening. My head pounded with rage and confusion. Stomach bile rose in my throat and I violently spewed it out.

There also wasn't any concrete evidence that he had anything to do with Dani Shepherd's disappearance. It was confirmed that he was the man who was with her at *Milton's* the same night she vanished. But he had left hours before her. The employees confirmed that. He could've done something to her after she had left but there simply wasn't any evidence. It was all speculative.

She could've been alive somewhere but there wasn't any way of knowing for sure. She was abducted in the same manner as Lisandra Pierce and Jade Gamble. It was another mysterious case involving the *Rainfall Abductor.* The police didn't believe that Luke Prescott was behind the kidnappings. He was a sick, twisted individual, but he wasn't a kidnapper. Dani had told me that she felt like she was being followed while she was *with* Luke. There was a real possibility Luke wasn't responsible, but it didn't make any sense to me.

Nothing was making sense to me. The rest of the article detailed how the police were formally charging Luke with Ivan Pierce's murder. They had found a gun in a nearby ditch with Ivan's blood smeared all over it. A gun they pinned on Luke. I wasn't interested in reading about the other details.

I locked my phone and slipped it back inside my pocket. I was beyond frustrated. Michael Madden and Sebastian Gunner were dead. They weren't behind Scarlett's murder. I thought I had finally found the culprit, Luke Prescott a.k.a. John Santoro. He was her stalker, after all. Ivan and I had been right all those years ago in that room with him. Luke Prescott was my wife's stalker.

He wasn't her rapist or her murderer though. The police had confirmed this and I had no logical reason to believe that they were lying. Luke had solemnly stared me in the eyes and told me he didn't murder Scarlett. Part of me had believed him then. For a man as vile, pathetic and twisted as he was…Luke had been in love with Scarlett. It was a deranged, abnormal obsession…but he called it love.

Why would he murder the woman he loved?

All who was left was the man directly in front of me. The man who knew the dark truth. The man I was about to erase from the world. Abel Armoni.

# CHAPTER 18

I knew revenge would lead to destruction and not peace. All the things that had happened in the pursuit of my wife's killer had been telling. However, I felt that I owed it to Scarlett and Ivan to see things through. I needed to end what I had started. If I didn't...it would've all been for nothing. I couldn't have that. If I ended up dying, so be it. If I lived...I promised to be better. I'd sell the house and move away. I'd move far away from Rainfall. I'd move to a place that didn't remind me of Scarlett, Ivan and Sam. A place where I'd be able to start anew and begin the slow process of forgiving myself for everything I had done.

I was at the safe house. Abel Armoni was squirming in the chair he was tied up in. I had duct tape on his mouth as I finished reading the news article. Detective Gamble had called me numerous times in the two days leading up to the article, after he visited me. I answered him once and I asked him if it was about my wife or the missing women. I hung up when he had said no.

He texted me numerous times that we urgently needed to talk. I wasn't planning on talking to him anymore. I ignored every message he sent me. I didn't know what he wanted and I didn't need to know.

I couldn't trust him. If he had information regarding my wife, he would've said so.

I got up and ripped the duct tape off Abel's mouth.

"*Ow! Fuck!*" Abel screamed.

"Calm down," I stood in front of him and glared at him. He fearfully looked up at me and shut his mouth.

"News is finally out. The wait is over. John Santoro isn't responsible for Scarlett's rape and murder. If it was Michael Madden...he's already dead. He sexually harassed her. There's nothing tragic about him being gone. If it was Sebastian Gunner, he's dead too. He used to hit her and he abused her. Nothing to cry about there either. The world is a better place with them buried in the ground. I imagine it would be even safer if you took your last breath...here." I got closer to him and bent over. My vicious, bloodshot eyes at his level.

"What?" Abel squeaked out.

"Do you understand what I'm saying?"

"No, no, no, no. You're making a huge mistake. A *big fucking mistake*. Damian...Damian please listen to me. I need you to listen," Abel pleaded.

I rose and took a step back.

"You're the only one left. The only suspect I have left to cross off my list. You're a rapist and an abuser of women. Odds are, you raped and murdered my wife. Wouldn't you agree?"

Abel's eyes popped out as his lip began to tremble. He began sobbing as multiple streams of tears poured down his flushed cheeks.

"It wasn't me Damian. It was not me! I swear to fucking god!" Abel screeched.

"Where the fuck is Dani then? Where is she, Abel?"

"I don't know. I don't fucking know. I swear to you. I have no...no fucking idea. She ghosted me. She cut me off! I swear! I did nothing to her! Please don't do anything to me! Please!" Abel begged.

I felt the handle of my revolver behind me and pulled it out. I took off the safety. I squarely pointed it at Abel's head.

"Okay, okay, okay, okay. Wait a second! Wait a goddamn second! I'm rich! I have money! I have so much *fucking money*! I will give whatever you want. What do you want, Damian?! *What do you want*?!"

"The only thing I want...are the people that I love to be alive. You can't give me that." I placed my finger around the trigger.

"Wait! Wait, wait, wait, wait. Okay, okay, okay, okay. I...I did it. I did it, Damian."

"Did what?"

"I...I raped those women. It's all true. I raped Dani Shepherd, Victoria Cole, Soraya Santoro and many other women. I'm...I'm a monster. I admit to it. That's the truth. But I didn't rape Scarlett or murder her. I also don't know what happened to Dani. I...I was inappropriate with Scarlett but I never *ever* raped her. Michael Madden murdered her and raped her. That had been the truth. He was the only one there that night. It was him," Abel confessed.

I plunged back into my chair and sank. My eyes watered and I quickly rubbed away the tears. I felt a deep sadness choking my heart. It had been Michael Madden after all. Abel had confessed to it all.

"You don't know how badly I want to kill you."

"I...I know." Abel squealed.

"You're not done yet. You're going to repeat everything you said on video and I'm going to release it. Your empire, your image, your wealth...that's all gone."

Abel gaped at me with shocked eyes.

"If you don't do it, you're dead Abel. You are *dead*," I promised.

He gave a slight nod.

---

I left Abel tied up in the chair. I set up his phone on a tripod he had in the storage closet. He had used it to film *travel vlogs*. I bet he wished he was back in that time, recording himself surfing and drinking mojitos at clubs in Cancun. That time was over. Abel Armoni's life was over. I tapped open the *Camera* app and zoomed in on his face. Once I pointed at him, he knew he had to spill. He had to confess to everything.

"No," Abel said defiantly.

"*What?*"

"This will ruin me. This will destroy me forever. It will wipe out all the hard work I've done. No...no, no, no. Those whores...those god damn *fucking whores* wanted it! They wanted it! All of them! Dani, Victoria, Carly, Emily, Joanna, Soraya...they all wanted me to do it. They went into my *Crimson Lounge*. They knew what they were in for. A few drinks here and there. Everyone's drunk. Who even remembers what happened? Liars...*fucking liars*!" Abel screamed.

It looked like Abel was losing his sanity. I turned off the phone in disgust. I was done. My stomach churned and became volcanic with rage. I smashed his phone to the floor. It left behind a cracked screen but was still in tact.

"What the fuck is wrong with you? Why would you say that?"

"It's...it's...the truth. The whole truth. I am *not* guilty. I am *not a* bad man. Do you see what I've done for this shithole of a town? I've brought jobs and opportunity. I've brought all of my fucking wealth," Abel pleaded.

I had enough. I rushed to the kitchen and took out a big, glass bowl. I placed it under the sink and filled it with water. I carefully treaded back and placed it on the floor next to Abel who was looking at me like I was insane.

"What? What are you doing? What the hell is going on? I'll give you anything you want. Anything you want at all! You need to free me! I'm an important man! They'll be looking for me! Don't be fucking stupid!" Abel shouted.

"You're not in charge here, Abel. You'll never be in charge again." I went back to the kitchen and pulled out a sharp knife from the drawer. I grabbed Abel's hair while I cut him free. He groaned in pain as I finished. I threw him to the floor. He tried to escape but I pulled him back by his legs.

"No! Let me go! Let me go, you psycho!"

"You're the psycho, Abel. You *fucking rapist.*"

I seized his head and shoved it into the glass bowl of water. He struggled to go free as I kept him submerged. Panicked, muffled screams rippled out of him as water splashed all over. I used my full weight to pin him down. He slowly stopped and gave up as I drowned him until he stopped breathing. I waited a couple of minutes to ensure he was dead. I pulled him out. He was dead. I tossed him aside and took a deep breath.

"Sorry boss. That's revenge for all the women you wronged. I hope it was a painful death for you. You traumatized those women for a lifetime. You'll never do it again," I said breathlessly.

Before I rose, I tucked his phone into his pocket. I took one last look at his cold, lifeless eyes and left him there to rot.

---

Before I released Abel's location and revealed everything he had done, I needed to complete one last task. I needed to fulfill Ivan's dying wish. I needed to go to his office in his security warehouse, to see what he had been looking at. I continued to avoid Detective Gamble's calls while I arrived at Ivan's small office. I quickly got to work and searched through several manila folders in his desk drawers. I didn't see anything of particular interest as I popped down in his swivel chair. I turned around and decided to check his laptop.

I opened up a minimized browser and saw that he had been looking at an old news article. The title was: **FIRE IN RAINFALL**. Ivan had showed me the article right before I went to talk to Dani's mother, Dawn.

It detailed the tragic barn fire that took the lives of Martin Dietrich and Angela Baron. In the article, Elsa stated that she didn't believe it was an accident and something terrible had happened inside that barn. She speculated that Martin was doing something he wasn't supposed to and he didn't want anyone to know the truth. That shocked me. I had never heard about that. It was such a long time ago. I figured Elsa didn't want anyone to know about what her husband might've done.

I examined the grainy photograph they had of Angela. She wasn't Martin's daughter. She was Elsa's daughter from a previous marriage. That's why her last name was Baron instead of Dietrich. She also had dark hair, tan skin and brown eyes. Something Ivan had pointed out. She looked similar to Scarlett and to the other missing women. Angela's body had also vanished but it was suspected to have been incinerated in the barn fire. Martin's body wasn't recovered either.

It was very strange. The fire must've been incredibly intense. I analyzed the pictures of the barn in the aftermath. It had been burnt to a crisp. All that was left was a grey pile of ashes. I wondered what could've caused such an accident. Well, *alleged* accident. Jade

Gamble, Lisandra Pierce, Dani Shepherd...Angela Baron. What was the connection? Where was Dani?

I searched through everything on top of Ivan's desk. That's when I found it. It was hiding in plain sight in between the desk lamp, notepads, staplers, desk trays and other miscellaneous files. It was on top of the household potted plant. Dani's necklace was there. It had the silver '*D*' amulet. I found the sticky notes posted next to it. It had Ivan's handwriting on them.

*Found necklace in Elsa's front yard.*
*Dani went to Elsa's house? Why?*
*Did she find something out?*
*Maybe something about her daughter, Angela?*

These are the questions Ivan had asked himself. Questions I never got to discuss with him. I had no choice. I had to go to Elsa's house for answers.

---

I didn't want to be seen by Detective Gamble, so I took a quick taxi to Elsa's house. I left my car parked inside Ivan's security warehouse. I took a small backpack that had a few emergency supplies. My flashlight, a water flask, my revolver, a hammer and a multi-use knife. I planned to trek back to my house through the Darkpond Woods. I didn't want to speak to Gamble or any other police officers until I was finished with what I needed to do.

When I was dropped off, I spotted her outside. She was speed walking to her front door. She seemed to be in a hurry. She was wearing a camouflaged hunting jacket with black cargo shorts. She had a bucket hat with her Springfield rifle slung over her shoulder. Nevertheless, I approached her and called out her name. She glanced in my direction and was startled.

"Oh, hello Damian. What are you doing at my home?"

"Sorry to bother you, Elsa. I just wanted to ask you if Ivan had come by? He mentioned it to me."

"Oh...oh yes. He did come by. He seemed...spooked about something. He asked me some questions regarding Dani Shepherd's disappearance. I told him I knew nothing. That was the end of it and he left."

Elsa's eyes were darting in multiple directions. She refused to look me in the eye. She was acting even weirder than usual. I didn't know what to make of it. She seemed nervous about something. Like someone was after her.

"Well, I don't know if you heard. You probably didn't. He's dead. Ivan...is dead."

Elsa is taken aback and stared at me in complete shock. She took off her hat and wiped the sweat off her forehead with a brush of her free hand.

"Oh my god. I'm so sorry to hear that. That is very sad."

"Yeah. It is."

Elsa briefly nodded and fumbled the house keys in her hand. She dropped them to the ground and cursed at herself. She hurriedly bent down to swoop them up. I got a closer look at her. She had specks of red on her hands. It was blood. There was also blood on her shirt. She glanced at me and awkwardly grinned. I reciprocated.

*What the hell is going on with this lady?*

"Sorry to bother you again. Looks like you're in a rush. Were you hunting?"

"Ah, you saw the blood. Yes, I shot a deer. It was long distance," Elsa answered robotically.

"You got it inside already?"

"No. I have to go get it now. I have a process. It's a taxidermy job. Work never stops," Elsa chortled.

"Right...yeah. I know how that feels."

"Goodbye Damian. Have a nice week," Elsa opened and slammed her front door shut.

"Well that was fucking odd," I muttered.

I began the march back home and thought about what Elsa had said. She had shot the deer from long distance and hadn't brought it to her home yet. I found it strange that she had gotten blood on herself. Maybe it was from some other game she had hunted, but I wasn't sure. I definitely felt like something was amiss.

*How well do I really know Elsa Dietrich?*

*Why was Dani there?*

*What was Ivan on to?*

*How did Elsa factor into all of this?*

I decided to veer off path and crossed the vacant street. I climbed up a hill that was near Darkpond Park. It had a great line-of-sight on

Elsa's house. I hid beneath some shrubbery and grass. I felt like an idiot, but I needed to wait for her to leave. An hour later, I finally spotted her trudging out with a drag strap and a hunting backpack. I couldn't believe she dragged those dead animals by herself, but she was a tough, burly woman. I estimated that she wouldn't be back for another thirty minutes to an hour.

Once she was out of sight, I rushed down and snuck all the way across the street. I reached the back of Elsa's house and climbed a wooden fence that led to her backyard. My eyes shot towards a rectangular side window that showed a view of her living room. I put my face against the glass and cupped my eyes. It looked exactly like the last time I had visited. Except for one thing. There was a stray shoe on the floor. It stuck out like a sore thumb because it obviously didn't belong. It was a black satin pump. The same type of heels Dani always wore. I felt my stomach drop.

I immediately knew that something was very wrong. A crippling sense of utter dread and terror infected my body. I took a few deep breaths and attempted to think logically. I needed to listen to my instincts. I needed to pay attention to the signs I had been given. After all the tragedy and heartbreak I had been through...it was about time.

I had to follow the loose threads of the sinister mystery that cloaked the Dietrich residence. The whole, terrible truth was finally in my grasp. I felt it in every fiber of my being. I dropped my backpack to the ground and took out my essentials. I inserted my flashlight, my revolver, a hammer and a multi-use knife in the various pockets of my pants. I calculated that Elsa was still a lengthy distance away. It was grueling work dragging a dead animal without any help. I went ahead with my plan of action.

I gently tapped my hammer against the window until it cracked. I carefully pushed away the broken shards and inserted my arm inside the house. I clicked a lock and slid the window open. I vaulted over and crouched down. I scanned my immediate surroundings as I landed in the living room. Everything looked the same. I spotted the brown, antique chairs she had near a front window. The interior of her entire house was still wrapped in catriona wallpaper. She had her taxidermy mounts of deer on top of her rustic fireplace laid with mahogany bricks.

Above the front door was a glass encasement that was empty. It usually housed a hunting rifle. She had obviously taken it. Porcelain figurines, framed pictures, and vases were placed inside an integrated wooden cabinet near heavy silk curtains. The hardwood floor was polished but it wasn't squeaky clean. I closely inspected it. It had streaks of blood that traveled somewhere. It was a trail. I followed it.

The suspicious floor creaked as I slowly snuck across it. The brass chandelier attached to the ceiling gently shook and chimed. My teeth slightly chattered as I grew more and more apprehensive. I lost balance and palmed the adjacent wall. I scolded myself and regained my footing. I continued forward. The trail ended at a white door that had a thick, draft door stopper thoroughly tucked underneath. It didn't have a typical doorknob. It had a metal latch with a dense padlock.

I used my hammer and smashed it barbarically until it gave way. It took several, heart-pounding minutes. I felt like vomiting but I kept my nerve. After the lock crashed to the floor, I sprinted to the front of the house and carefully peeked out the window. Elsa was nowhere to be seen. I sprinted back and undid the latch. I paused for a brief moment.

"Well...fuck it," I shuddered.

I dragged the door open and was fiercely smacked in the face with a putrid, pungent odor that stung my eyes and caused tears to sprinkle out. I immediately pinched my nose and gagged. I stumbled around in the room and saw nothing but dark shapes. I ran my fingers along the wall and felt a switch. I flicked it up. A single white light buzzed to life. It illuminated the room from above.

The concrete floor was cold and hard. To my left I saw a long, wooden table with a butcher's axe pierced into it. It was marked with stains of blood and red. A thick, metal baton was neatly placed next to it. Taxidermy mounts of deer and other small animals decorated the walls. There was a framed photo of a scribbled stick figure drawing with red eyes as well. To my right were four animal carcasses covered in extra large, black trash bags.

In the center of the room was a wooden desk with several empty taxidermy plaques. I stepped towards it and investigated it.

"Nothing here but a stench that smells worse than shit...and dead, stuffed animals," I grimaced at the idea.

As I got closer to the desk, a guttural shriek exploded out of me.

"*No! Fuck! What the fuck?! Oh my fucking god...*"

I saw Scarlett's shocked, carved out face…nailed to a plaque.

# CHAPTER 19

I broke down and began gasping for breath. Elsa...Elsa had been the killer all along. From the look of things, she had murdered Scarlett. But why? I was hopelessly confused in a raging whirlwind of my own renewed grief and anguish. I remained paralyzed due to the sheer shock of my discovery. A minute later my eyes darted to the black trash bags. I catapulted myself towards them. I yanked them out. I had been wrong. They weren't dead animals. They were the dead, stuffed bodies of Jade Gamble, Lisandra Pierce, Dani Shepherd...and what I assumed was Angela Baron.

I shivered as I studied Dani. The color was drained from her terrifyingly emaciated face. The inside of her mouth showed a purplish discoloration as it hung open. The texture on her hair looked coarse and brittle. I quietly sobbed to myself. I had failed her. I had failed Dani. Another person I loved...was dead.

Jade and Lisandra had been preserved, to a degree but they had gaunt, ghastly appearances. Angela was barely recognizable. She was a melting skeleton with loose skin, rotting teeth, blackened eyeballs and a full set of dark, shiny hair that had to be a well-maintained wig.

I was beyond horrified. I couldn't believe what I was seeing. Why did Elsa have those dead women in a locked room?

She had to be the murderer. She had to be the *Rainfall Abductor*. There wasn't a single doubt in my mind about that. I still had vital, urgent questions that remained. One was more important than the rest. Why did she do it? What could've possibly driven her to abduct those women and murder them? Why did she turn them into taxidermy? Why did she slice off my wife's face and make a depraved ornament out of it?

The frenzied thoughts storming my head were interrupted by a faint beeping sound. I frantically surveyed the room. I found a small alarm box embedded to the base of a wall near the door. It had a red light that had been set off.

*Fuck me.*

I bolted out of the room and towards what was left of the window I had broken into. I prepared to jump out but immediately ducked at the last possible second when I saw the glint of a rifle's barrel. It was pointed straight at me.

*Boom!*

The deafening crack of the gunshot shattered the stillness of the air. It echoed throughout the house like a thunderous clap. Sheer adrenaline surged through my veins like electricity as I desperately crawled away from the window. I sprang up and cautiously approached the front door while I was crouched. I hastily pulled out my revolver with shaky hands and gripped it tightly. I took off the safety and made sure it had bullets. My aim trembled as I pointed it at the door.

*Boom! Boom! Boom!*

Three bullets pierced the front door and whizzed by the living room. The door was continuously fired upon until it burst open. I held my breath. Everything seemed to stop. All motion was paused and time was standing still. A rifle's barrel poked through the bullet-riddled door and pushed it open. It was soon directed at me. I panicked and dropped to the floor. I wildly shot three times in the direction of the front door. I hit the wall twice and broke a lamp. I quietly cursed at myself.

Elsa charged through the door and ferociously shrieked when she spotted me. I hurriedly crawled away as she shot the floor I was lying on. I got up and stumbled into the kitchen. I hid in front of the fridge by the doorless, arched entryway. My breathing was ragged and it felt like my heart was tightening my throat. An icy shiver crawled down my spine. I kept both hands on the revolver and aimed it down. I waited until I heard Elsa moving.

From the creeping noise the floorboards were making, it sounded like she was slowly but surely coming towards me at a steady pace. I wrapped my finger around the trigger and prepared myself for what I needed to do.

"You found my toys. Very good, Damian. Very, very good."

I kept quiet and remained focused on shooting Elsa. I briefly thought about Abel. It hadn't been him and that...that made my stomach churn. I heard his frantic screams through the water as his head sloshed around in the bowl. I sensed the pure desperation oozing out of his skin as he tried his best to survive.

I shook my head. There was nothing to feel guilty about. Abel was a serial rapist. Elsa was an abductor and a serial killer. I had done things no one else had been willing to do. I unveiled dark truths and exposed the most sadistic, sinister beings humanity had to offer. I exacted revenge for those who couldn't. For those who were no longer amongst the living.

"Nothing to say? Hmm? I don't like male toys. Maybe I'll put your face next to Scarlett. You two would look great together," Elsa mocked.

"You're a *sick* bitch! You were the one who murdered Scarlett. You murdered all of them!"

"I had been watching her for a very long time. As I do with all of my victims. I'm a patient person," Elsa answered.

"God, lady. All this time....all this *fucking* time! You lied to me! You're a fucking psychopath. You need a fucking lobotomy!" I shouted. I peeked around the corner for half a second. There wasn't anyone there. She hadn't reached me yet.

"I have reasons for the things I do, Damian. People always have their reasons. You shouldn't judge me. Look at yourself. Look at the things you've been willing to do, to get revenge for your wife. Look at what you've become."

"You don't know anything about me," I snapped.

"I know you well enough," Elsa replied.

"Why did you kill them all? Why?! Jade, Lisandra, Dani...my wife...what the hell did they ever do to you?!" I angrily questioned.

"This world was very cruel to me. In response...I am cruel to it. This is my lifelong revenge."

I stayed silent. I didn't hear the floorboards creaking anymore. I peeked around the corner with my revolver out. Elsa wasn't there. My palpitating heart raced as I crept forward. The beating deafened my ears as I made it to the middle of the hall. The front door was in my line-of-sight. She wasn't there either.

I silently panicked as I heard it. A faint ruffling. It sounded like blades of grass being crunched. I urgently backtracked and crouched under the broken window. The one I had vaulted through. I heard shuffling footsteps and leaves being trampled.

*Found you.*

I popped up and shoved my revolver out the window. I saw Elsa crouched on the ground. She was reloading her rifle. I aimed below her stomach and shot.

*Crack!*

I hit her knee. She instantly dropped her rifle and began writhing on the ground. The pain must've been excruciating. She clutched her knee and growled at me as I jumped through the window. I cautiously approached her and kicked away her weapon. I kept my revolver on her as she scowled at me with furious eyes and bared teeth.

"You...you worthless *son of a bitch*," Elsa snarled.

"I finally caught you. You're the *Rainfall Abductor*, aren't you?"

"Someone finally noticed," Elsa cackled.

"You're batshit insane."

"I was made this way," Elsa kept pressure on her wounded knee as blood spilled all over her hands.

"You're gonna tell me what you did to Scarlett and you're gonna tell me now."

"Or else?" Elsa asked.

"I'll kill you."

"Why not get it over with?"

"I want to know the truth. I want to know what happened."

Elsa nodded. She smiled like a witch.

"I haven't been able to tell anyone this at all. I've always wanted to tell my story. But no one wants to listen to someone kidnapping and butchering young women. Do you know how frustrating that is for me? I've only written it in my book...*Elsa's Taxidermy Tales,*" Elsa explained.

I felt a sudden vibration in my pocket. I reached in and clicked the lock button.

"I'm listening, Elsa. *Talk.*"

I knew that I didn't have much time but I had a few minutes, possibly more. Multiple gunshots were heard near Elsa's house, but people knew that Elsa Dietrich was a hunter with guns. They had no reason to believe something out of the ordinary was happening.

"I had been hunting in the woods that night. The night she came. She was alone and upset. Scarlett's guard was down. It was my chance. My opportunity had finally arrived. I smashed her head and dragged her further into the forest. I raped her, like the others. I have a metallic baton I use to violate them the way they should be violated. The way they deserve it."

I was breathless. She sounded like Abel.

"What? What the hell is wrong with you? Why would you do something like that? You're inhuman!"

"I preserve dead bodies that remind me of her. The only way to get the dead bodies I want is by killing them. It's the same with animals. I personally hunt down my victims."

A hunter who hunted animals and people. A truly deranged human being.

"Remind you of who?"

"A little lady who loved Martin, my husband. That slut...Angela Baron. May she suffer in the hell she belongs in," Elsa spat on the ground.

"Angela Baron? She's your daughter."

"She was from a previous marriage. Martin is not her father. My husband and my own daughter betrayed me. I caught them having *sex* in that barn house. The one that burned down. There was a terrible argument. Next thing I knew...the barn house caught on fire."

Angela had sex with her own stepfather? It was one of the most twisted things I had ever heard. I also didn't believe it. Elsa said Martin had behaved like a *Nazi*. I thought it was entirely possible that Martin was a monster and raped Angela.

"Who set the barn house on fire?"

"Martin did…or maybe it was Angela. It was a long time ago. All I know is that they knew their lives were over. They happily perished in the fire."

"I searched your house. You have Angela's body in that room. How?"

"I saved it when she died from burning. No one asked any questions. I had lost my family in the most horrific way imaginable after all."

"That still doesn't explain why you kidnapped and murdered those women," I angrily stated.

"My life has been nothing but a horrible tragedy. I decided to kidnap, kill, rape and preserve all women who looked like Angela. I do it as a reminder of what she was. A horribly ill young woman who destroyed my marriage and my life," Elsa said coldly.

*Dark hair, brown eyes, tan skin.*

"Your *Nazi* husband should've been the one to blame. He sounded like a predator."

"No! You're wrong! Those were just rumors. Silly, stupid rumors! He was a good man at heart. He was good!" Elsa screeched.

I couldn't believe how sick and twisted Elsa was. I thought about the horribly tragic circumstances she had experienced. Elsa's own daughter slept with her husband. In the most likely event, he sexually assaulted her and Elsa refused to believe that. Afterwards, they both burned to death. That must've caused some serious and permanent psychological trauma. It wasn't a mystery as to why Elsa became an insane serial killer.

"Why did you act like you were helping me? Why did you give me John Santoro's license?"

"I wanted to misdirect you. I saw how hellbent you were on finding the truth. If I became a suspect in any way, there would've been major issues. If my house got searched, I would've been done for."

"You're done for anyway."

"I know," Elsa frowned.

"Why didn't you take Scarlett's body?"

"The whole thing became a mess when that drunk idiot Michael Madden stumbled upon me killing Scarlett. I forced him to lie and to take the fall for the murder. I scared him to death. He never even knew my name. I made him show me his license and warned him that I would rip out his insides if he said a word of me to the police. When he was released, I knew I had to quickly find him and make sure he hadn't said anything. He was at his garbage dump of a house. I carved *killer* into his chest as a warning. It was good handiwork."

I violently shook my head and got closer to her.

"Why are you talking about it like it's a respectable profession? You're a fucking murderer! You killed and raped Jade, Lisandra, Dani and Scarlett. They were all good women. Lisandra was my best friend's wife. Dani was a great friend. Scarlett was an amazing wife and a talented artist. Jade was Detective Gamble's wife. You ruined him forever. You destroyed...all of us forever. You obliterated so many lives. Do you have any idea what kind of absolute *monster* you are?! You deserve *death*!" I bellowed.

" I was ruined forever. A monster made me what I am. Angela Baron. If you want to blame someone...blame her."

I couldn't stand to look at her anymore. I was responsible for my brother's tragic death. Elsa was responsible for the deaths of Ivan, Dani and Scarlett. If she hadn't done what she did...they'd still be alive. Jade and Lisandra would still be alive. Gamble and I wouldn't be broken men.

"The only good thing about all this...is that you're bleeding on the ground and you're going to die in front of your little house of horror. You'll *never* take anyone's life ever again. Your madness has ended. You're done Elsa. *Forever.*"

Elsa heavily sighed and looked off, into the distance.

"I'll miss the birds chirping in the morning...and the walls screaming at night."

"I won't."

"Are you going to kill me?" she asked softly.

"I am."

"Go ahead then. My work is done, Damian."

I fired the rest of the revolver's bullets straight into Elsa's chest, killing her once and for all. She jerked and twitched for a brief moment before shutting her eyes. She silently died. I slowly approached her dead body and inspected it. I reached inside my pocket and clicked the unlock button again.

"Your killer is dead, Scarlett. She's finally dead," I said aloud.

I had exacted revenge for Scarlett. I finished what I had set out to do. I found and unmasked the whole, sinister truth. It had come at a grave cost. It took every single ounce of being I had within me and as a result, Ivan had been killed. I promised never to forget him or any of Elsa's victims.

Despite attaining vengeance, I felt hollow. In the end, I knew that revenge wasn't the answer, but I had some comfort in knowing that the evil incarnate known as Elsa Dietrich had been purged from the world. I thought of Scarlett, as I often did. I missed her very much. I wasn't sure when I'd recover. I wasn't sure when the torturous, heart-wrenching memory of Scarlett would fade away, or if it ever would. Only one thing was for certain. I had been forever changed.

# EPILOGUE

After Damian shot Elsa, he paused to gather himself. He was about to stand up, when he was suddenly pulled in by her outstretched arm. A razor-sharp hunting knife was savagely plunged into Damian's heart. Elsa twisted it in deeper as Damian coughed out blood. Elsa shoved him aside with the knife still inside Damian's heart.

Damian's eyes flickered as he began to lose consciousness. He convulsed and choked on his own blood until he abruptly died. The final thing he saw was Scarlett's face, twisting into a warm smile.

Elsa took off her hunting gear and revealed a bulletproof vest underneath.

"Your brother is dead, your best friend is dead, your wife is dead...and now you're dead," Elsa viciously whispered.

She clutched her injured leg and cursed under her breath. She wouldn't make it much longer without serious medical attention. She tried to devise a plan as she suddenly heard police sirens blaring. She froze as she heard rushing footsteps echoing inside her home. An inquisitive head poked out of the broken window. It was Detective Albert Gamble. Deep concern was etched on his face. He took in the bloody, chaotic scene he was presented with. He saw Elsa on the ground, holding her bloodied knee. Damian was right next to her. He glanced at his dead body and grimaced. He clenched his jaw.

*God dammit, Damian. God fucking dammit.* Detective Gamble thought.

He had come to care for Damian's safety. He considered him one of the only people who understood him and what he had been through. Ivan Pierce was the other man. He was also dead. Detective Gamble was the only one left. He barked an order at the other officers, telling them to secure the house. He slowly vaulted over the broken window.

"Oh my god, you're a policeman. Thank you so much for coming. I need medical attention. This man tried to kill me. He went on a rampage. He shot me!" Elsa cried.

"Is there anyone else in the house?" Detective Gamble asked.

"No...no one else."

Detective Gamble slowly took out his firearm and aimed it towards the ground.

"What's the stench in there?"

"It's uh...it's the animals. I'm a taxidermist. Please sir, I need an ambulance! It's an emergency! I will bleed out!" Elsa shrieked.

"They're on their way," he replied calmly.

"Thank you. Thank you, Detective. I need help. I need immediate help," Elsa smiled and nodded. She had her hand around her back. She was concealing something.

"Why did Damian try to kill you? Aren't you neighbors?"

"I have no idea. He went insane. He had a psychotic break. Remember...his wife was raped and murdered," Elsa pointed out.

*Holy shit! What the fuck?!* An officer cried out. Detective Gamble briefly turned his head as panic crept through his veins. Out of the corner of his eye, he saw the glint of a silver object in Elsa's hand. He lurched his head away from the twirling knife that had been flung to his face.

He immediately turned back to Elsa who had shocked eyes and a rage-fueled scowl on her face.

"Fuck," Elsa mouthed.

Detective Gamble raised his gun and shot Elsa six times. Blood, brain matter and bits of her broken skull exploded off her head as she tumbled to the ground. Detective Gamble bent over and grabbed his knees. He retched. When he was finished, he quietly sauntered over to Damian's dead body and crouched down.

"Fucking Christ. Elsa Dietrich, huh? Thanks for finally answering my call. I managed to track it. I didn't catch most of the conversation between you two. I'm sorry we were too late. At least you can rest now," he gently patted his body.

One of the officers appeared in the broken window.

"What happened?! Are you okay?!"

"I am now."

"Well, it looks like we are in quite the shit show, Detective. You have to come look in this room. We got...we got dead bodies."

"I know," Detective Gamble whispered.

*In the end you wanted revenge, Damian. You achieved just that...but you paid the ultimate price.*

---

The Detective and the other Rainfall police officers thoroughly searched Elsa's home. They quickly realized she was the *Rainfall Abductor* once they discovered her locked room. Gamble immediately deduced that she had been a hidden, deranged murderer for many years. She was fully responsible for the abductions and murders of Jade Gamble, Lisandra Pierce, Dani Shepherd and Scarlett del Toro. They weren't sure what to make of Angela's skeletal remains.

Gamble had mixed feelings about the whole ordeal. He had accepted the fact that his wife had most likely been murdered after her kidnapping. He didn't count on her being brutally mutilated and raped by Elsa Dietrich as well. Regardless of that, he felt a somber, bittersweet relief when he actually recovered her body. He knew the truth, even if it was horribly evil.

A few possessions belonging to Jade, Lisandra, Dani and Scarlett were found hidden in the house. They had been found in a locked chest in Elsa's bedroom closet. There were also grisly photographs of the victims in various states of torture and sexual abuse at the hands of that psychotic monster, Elsa. Gamble didn't study them too closely.

A tattered, hand-written journal was also found in the chest. It was titled *Elsa's Taxidermy Tales*. Most of it was ramblings of madness and lunacy. A few, decently legible sentences alluded to Martin Dietrich sexually abusing Angela Baron. It gave insight into what may have really happened the day the Dietrich barn house was burned down. It gave credence to a few possible theories regarding Martin and Angela's tragic deaths. It potentially explained why they perished in that fire that day. That's all it was, however. They were theories. Everyone involved in that terrible incident was dead and it was a long time ago. The whole, real truth was open to interpretation.

Abel's dead body was eventually found in his safe house by someone named Ringo and other members of his security team, much to their horror. Due to the nature of the situation he was in, regarding the multiple sexual abuse accusations hurled against him, his death was ruled a suicide. The death of Abel Armoni cemented his ruined legacy. Thanks in large part to one of his victims, Victoria Cole. She had worked in the *Crimson Lounge* which was inside the *Armoni* nightclub. She revealed all and ensured the truth about who he really was would come out.

He was posthumously branded a serial rapist and abuser of women. It was a grand fall from grace. The Armoni family name was tarnished for decades. The empire that Abel had been building in Rainfall crumbled to the ground. It was destroyed for good.

## *18 MONTHS LATER.*

Detective Gamble was investigating the old, dilapidated church that had been known as St. Michael's. He was following a lead regarding a missing persons case. It involved Patricia Cain and Isabel Forrester, a pair of young women who had vanished after they had made plans to hang out at a popular shopping mall. A high school acquaintance had stepped forward with new information. She told Detective Gamble that they regularly frequented the St. Michael's church to pay their respects.

Cold, unrelenting rain poured down Gamble's windbreaker as he investigated the ruins of the church. He cautiously inspected the broken stone fragments and walls that covered the dark, wet landscape. He stepped over a black puddle and heard a slight *crunch* as his foot met the muddy ground. He pulled it up and saw a silver object in the moist grass. He crouched down and picked it up. It was a necklace with an engraving that spelled out *Patricia*.

Gamble's phone vibrated. He stuffed the necklace in his pocket and answered the phone.

"*Detective, we ID'd the guy in the mall,*" A police officer stated.

He was referencing security camera footage that Detective Gamble had managed to find and request from the shopping mall owner. There was limited footage consisting of Patricia and Isabel traveling from store to store. There was one man present in all of them. He seemed to be following them.

*"The name is Nathaniel Griffin. He's somehow out on parole and has a history. There's a gnarly domestic violence case you're gonna want to take a look at. You know the drill."*

*"Let's go then. We have a job to do. Let's find those girls."* Detective Gamble replied firmly.

He hung up the phone and hurried back to his police cruiser. He turned the key into the ignition and raced down the slick, shadowy road.

He remembered Damian and what he had accomplished. He vowed to find the *Rainfall Abductor's* copycat. He was prepared to do anything and everything necessary to find the culprit responsible. He had a renewed sense of justice and duty after Elsa's depraved murders were unveiled. He wanted to make them proud. He wanted to remember the victims by being willing to pay the price. He didn't want anyone to go through what he had gone through.

He knew that monsters like Elsa Dietrich and Abel Armoni would always exist in the world. He reckoned it was a good thing there would always be people hellbent on stopping them. People like Damian del Toro and Ivan Pierce. He recalled a quote he had read online once. It was from a true crime article that originated from the town of *St. Devil*. It had been written by a *V. Duarte*.

*"Monsters never win."*

Detective Gamble set out to prove her right.

# THE END.

# THANK YOU READER!

Thank you so much for reading *MY WIFE'S STALKER*. If you loved this book, be sure to stay subscribed to my newsletter for free books, updates about future books and more!

Sign up at spencerguerreroauthor.com!

# PLEASE REVIEW!

Please do not forget to leave a review on Amazon, Goodreads, and other social media platforms! Your reviews are always read by me and greatly appreciated!

You can follow me on Instagram, Facebook, Goodreads and Amazon!

Instagram: @spencergauthor

Facebook: @Spencer Guerrero – Author

# MORE BOOKS AVAILABLE!

I have FIVE other standalone psychological mystery-thriller novels OUT NOW!

*MY SON IS A MURDERER, MY FATHER IS A SERIAL KILLER, A MURDER IN THE NEIGHBORHOOD, MY MOTHER-IN-LAW MUST DIE,* and *THE NIGHT THEY TOOK MY SON!*

They're available in paperback/digital formats on Amazon and on Kindle Unlimited!

# ACKNOWLEDGEMENTS

I want to give a huge shout out and thanks to my family for supporting me and encouraging me throughout my long journey of wanting to be a writer and an author. Mom, Dad, Sebastian, and Sophia. There has been a lot of ups and downs. There were even times where I wanted to give up and was frustrated beyond understanding. You could've easily shot down my dreams and tell me that I would never make it. That has never been the case and I'm very lucky for that. I love you guys and I appreciate you!

There are a lot of other people who have given me words of encouragement and support in other ways. Please know that I appreciate you all! Whether you recommend my books to your friends, or you spread the word in general — thank you so much for your support!

To my new and loyal readers, you are the lifeline. You are the reason I write books. You are the reason why I'm so passionate to get these stories out there. I'm very lucky to have you all. I read and appreciate every single review beyond measure. I love writing books and I love being able to share mine with you all!

Thank you to all of my ARC readers on my ARC team for reading and reviewing! I owe much of my success to all of you!

A BIG thank you to all Facebook Book Groups for your support! "Psychological Thriller Readers", 2x "Psychological Thrillers Book Club", "Sarah's Book Club", "In My Kindle Girl Era", "Bookmark Baddies", "Tattered Page Book Club", and "Linda and Friends Book Club."

# ABOUT THE AUTHOR

My name is Spencer Guerrero. I was born and raised in Florida, and I am of Nicaraguan descent. I am a self-published author of psychological thrillers.

I used to be a freelance screenwriter and was hired to write a religious sci-fi/fantasy book adaptation, an animated Christmas film script, three short films and other work that included writing and outlining stories for licensed animated characters.

I decided to switch avenues so I could focus on the type of stories I wanted to write. Self-publishing looked like the best route and I haven't looked back since.

My favorite genres are YA fiction, mystery-thriller, fantasy, and literary fiction. Other than that, I like funny cat memes, dark comedies and I play basketball!

Printed in Dunstable, United Kingdom